Kate Hill
R. Casteel
Elizabeth Stewart

Forever
Midnight

ELLORA'S CAVE
ROMANTICA PUBLISHING

An Ellora's Cave Romantica Publication

www.ellorascave.com

Forever Midnight

ISBN # 1419952161
ALL RIGHTS RESERVED.
Silver Cuffs Copyright © 2004 Kate Hill
Shadow-Time Lover Copyright © 2004 R. Casteel
A Matter of Duty Copyright © 2004 Elizabeth Jewell
Edited by: Briana St. James and Martha Punches
Cover art by: Syneca

Electronic book Publication: September, 2004
Trade paperback Publication: June, 2005

Warning:

The following material contains graphic sexual content meant for mature readers. *Forever Midnight* has been rated *E-rotic* by a minimum of three independent reviewers.

Ellora's Cave Publishing offers three levels of Romantica™ reading entertainment: S (S-ensuous), E (E-rotic), and X (X-treme).

S-*ensuous* love scenes are explicit and leave nothing to the imagination.

E-*rotic* love scenes are explicit, leave nothing to the imagination, and are high in volume per the overall word count. In addition, some E-rated titles might contain fantasy material that some readers find objectionable, such as bondage, submission, same sex encounters, forced seductions, etc. E-rated titles are the most graphic titles we carry; it is common, for instance, for an author to use words such as "fucking", "cock", "pussy", etc., within their work of literature.

X-*treme* titles differ from E-rated titles only in plot premise and storyline execution. Unlike E-rated titles, stories designated with the letter X tend to contain controversial subject matter not for the faint of heart.

Contents

Silver Cuffs

Kate Hill

Prologue
New Hampshire
January, 1785

The wolf growled, his eyes blazing and his teeth gnashing the cold night air. Ice and snow flew beneath his paws. His heart throbbed with the insatiable need for vengeance.

Another more foreign emotion pulsed through him. Fear.

A shot exploded. The wolf shrieked as pain ripped through his shoulder. With a mighty lunge, he pounced on the cloaked, musket-toting man fleeing in the distance.

The wolf dragged the man onto his back and placed his paws on the heaving chest. Savage eyes stared into his captive's terrified blue ones. Unable to speak in words, the beast's look demanded its desire. *Where is she?*

"I don't have her, you evil bastard. Look for Stratford. He's the one you want," the man bellowed.

The scents of other people filled the air. Hoofbeats thudded across the snow-packed countryside.

Then he caught it. *Her* scent. Turning in the direction of the woods, he saw her.

The wolf left his captive panting in the snow and raced for the dark-haired, brown-eyed woman. As she ran for him, a storm of bullets pierced the night. The wolf's high-pitched cries of agony stunned his attackers. Those shrieks were far too human.

Gunfire ceased. The white snow beneath the gasping wolf turned red with blood and his vision blackened.

"No, no, no," she cried, her hands caressing his face.

Opening his eyes halfway, the wolf saw through the dimness and blur of impending death that her clothes were stained red.

He tried to speak, but the words would not come. Still, his emotions shone in his eyes. *I love you.*

"I love you," she cried and buried her face in his thickly furred neck. "I love you."

Chapter One
New Hampshire
2004

Pierce Durant's eyes narrowed as he glanced at the paperwork on his desk.

"It's all finally yours, Pierce." Lee Smith grinned. "It took some doing."

"Everything can be bought," Pierce said, leaning back in his chair and glancing out the window of his office. Surrounded by buildings, it was nothing like the quiet, pleasant New Hampshire towns he'd visited as a child. His mother had left when he was six. Once in his father's care, Pierce's old life had been brushed aside like a fading dream. The finest schools, the best material things, and years of performing in the corporate circus had taken the place of his middle-class environment. For the past twenty-seven years, Pierce had learned the value of the almighty dollar. No matter how he'd worked and studied to please his father, it had never been enough. Only in death had the old man revealed faith in his son by leaving him in charge of the business he'd spent his life building. That was five years ago.

Since then, Pierce had tripled the company's profits. He'd done more than the old man had ever dreamed of doing. If his father had been considered a tyrant, then Pierce was a demon and proud of it.

If there was something he wanted, he'd stop at nothing to get it. Early in the year, he'd spotted acres of property that would be perfect for condominiums. Real estate was how he made most of his profits. With land as inexpensive as those acres, he could almost smell the cash return. The only problem had been some stupid pre-revolutionary war mansion stood right in the middle of the land. The local historical society protected the place like it was built of gold.

Though it took longer than Pierce would have liked, he'd pulled some strings, cut through the red tape, and was now staring at the deed to the house.

"We can bulldoze the hovel and get on with the condos," Pierce said. "It's about time."

The intercom buzzed and Pierce's secretary said, "Mr. Durant, Tabatha Lane from the Philmore Historical Society is here to see you."

"I told you what to do with her," Pierce growled. The last thing he wanted was to talk with some lumpy, old, sock-and-sandal-clad yuppie bitch whose only purpose in life was to preserve useless, broken-down buildings.

"She won't leave this time, Mr. Durant. Shall I call security?"

"Tell her to call the police," Lee said. "We should press charges for trespassing."

Pierce shook his head in his lawyer's direction, his brow furrowed with annoyance. "I'll talk to her, Ms. James, and see that this time she leaves for good."

Standing so abruptly he almost knocked over his chair, Pierce strode to the door. He flung it open, glaring, his voice just short of a growl. "Where the hell is she?"

"Mr. Durant, I'm so glad to finally meet you." Tabatha stepped forward, her hand extended.

Pierce experienced an unaccustomed jolt of surprise. This had to be a mistake. The stunning black woman who'd approached him wearing a pleasant smile on her lovely face was not the dog-show champion he'd expected. Her dark brown hair was arranged in a loose French braid, her smooth, rounded face lightly touched with makeup. He guessed she was somewhere in her late twenties to early thirties. Her wide-set, dark brown eyes were so beautiful he could have stared into them all day without getting bored. Though plump, her body was well proportioned with full breasts, flaring hips, and a stomach that looked like a soft, smooth place to nestle against. The scent of her floral perfume hovered around him like angelic mist.

His cock leapt in his pants. It wasn't like Pierce to go for a woman who so obviously reeked of middle-class, but what the hell? There was something refreshing about her flowing, pink and yellow flowered dress and multi-strapped high-heeled sandals on the prettiest feet he'd ever seen.

"No, *I'm* pleased to meet *you*." He smiled easily and accepted her handshake. Her grip was firm, her hand soft and warm. He continued holding it as he gazed into her eyes. "I've been quite busy lately."

"Yes, I know. Busy buying Whittle House."

"Yes. You should get a good look at it this week, because next week it'll be bulldozed."

"That's what I wanted to talk to you about." Her smile faded and she tugged her hand from his. "I don't think you understand the full value of that house."

"Perhaps you'd care to tell me over dinner?"

Her eyes widened a bit. "Yes. I'd like that very much. Where and what time should we meet?"

Pierce's smile broadened. He didn't give a damn what she had to say about the house, but he definitely wanted a date with her. Some people might consider his tactics dishonest and seedy, but dishonesty could go a long way in the world.

"I can pick you up at six, if you like?"

"All right."

"We'll go to the Royal Hill Room. Just leave your address with my secretary."

A pleased expression brightened her face. "I've never eaten there before. I hear it's excellent."

"It's the finest, like my dinner guest."

She laughed. "Mr. Durant, you flatter me."

"Flattery can be a very pleasant thing, Ms. Lane."

With a fading smile, she turned from him to his secretary who supplied a pen and paper for her to write her address as Pierce stepped back into his office.

Lee asked, "Did you get rid of her?"

"I made a date with her."

"A date?"

"I haven't seen a woman that cute since... Come to think of it, I've never seen a woman that cute. More beautiful yes, but definitely not as cute."

"Oh, shit, Pierce." Lee wrinkled his nose. "We spend all this time and money securing that property and now you're going to leave the house standing where our condos should be?"

"The house is going to be, as they say, history. Have you ever known me to be influenced by anybody?"

"No, but there's a first time for everything and that's what scares me."

"Do I look like an idiot?" Pierce dropped into his chair, his legs stretched out in front of him. "I don't care what kind of bleeding heart story she gives about the historical value of that dump. All I want to see is if I can get that hot little piece of ass between the sheets. Trust me, she'll be a lot easier than bartering for that property was."

Chapter Two

"I don't believe it," Tabatha said as she walked into the Philmore Historical Society's little one-room office. The meeting with Pierce Durant had her tingling from head to toe. She told herself it was because she'd finally breached the man's corporate defenses, but deep inside their encounter thrilled her on a more intimate level. Though she wasn't usually attracted to white men, especially obnoxious, greedy ones, something about him seemed to latch onto an unexplored region of her soul. The sensation was creepy yet compelling at the same time. "I never imagined he'd actually talk to me about the house."

"Over dinner at the Royal Hill Room?" Sean Owens, another Philmore volunteer and Tabatha's good friend raised an eyebrow in her direction. During a conversation on their cell phones, she had told Sean the details of her confrontation with Pierce. "Good grief, sweetie. The man obviously doesn't care about the house. He just wants to get you on a date."

"Me? What for when he has his pick of rich, eligible women? Wasn't he voted Bachelor of the Year last year or something?"

"No. The Country's Richest Bachelor. He has offices from coast to coast and more money than a god. Sweetie," Sean stood and placed a delicate hand on her shoulder. "Don't let this SOB screw you, not even over the Whittle House. It ain't worth it. Trust me. I've had my heart broken enough to not want the same happening to you."

"He's not going to break my heart, Sean." Tabatha smiled, shaking her head. "I can see right through him. I know he only wants one thing. He thought I'd be impressed by having him give me a second look and offering to take me to the best restaurant in the state. I'm going to use this opportunity to try to save Whittle House. Nothing more."

"You have a good head on your shoulders, that's for sure, but from what I remember about the bachelor article, he's damn good-looking."

She shrugged. "He's all right."

Sean raised an eyebrow again. Tabatha couldn't even lie well about Pierce's handsome appearance. No one should have brains, money, and looks, but Pierce Durant had all three. The man was very tall and lean, his neck powerful and his shoulders incredibly broad. She doubted she'd ever seen legs quite that long. Thick, wavy brown hair topped his head and dusted his firm jawline with five o'clock shadow. His smile had been pleasant, though it hadn't reached those shrewd, beautiful, blue eyes.

"All right, he's gorgeous, but he's nasty, Sean. I can see it in his eyes."

"If he's nasty, then why waste your time trying to convince him to leave the house alone?"

"Because I have to. No one from Philmore has gotten an opportunity to so much as talk to him. Now I'll have an entire dinner date to let him know how much this house means to the town and to American history itself."

"Well." Sean sighed. "Good luck, sweetie. You want me to go along to chaperone?"

"No." She laughed. "I'll be fine."

No matter how attractive she found Mr. Durant, she intended to keep this dinner strictly business. The man might stir her, but she hadn't exaggerated about his mean streak. No one got as far as he had without stepping on anyone who got in his way, including innocent historical society volunteers.

* * * * *

Tabatha took a sip from her water glass. Her heart pounded and her mouth felt dry.

Pierce sat across the intimate table for two in the softly lit Royal Hill Room. His dark blue gaze fixed on hers in a most unsettling manner. Aside from blatant lust, she could read nothing of his emotions. Those eyes, though physically beautiful, were hard and cold. How could she possibly hope to convince such a man to spare Whittle House?

In spite of her dislike of him, he aroused her. He possessed sexual appeal such as she'd never seen before. His expressions and the way he moved his tall, big-boned body with masculine grace made her belly clench with desire. Beneath her silky slip and simple black dress, her nipples tightened as she watched his large, long-fingered hands butter his bread. What would those hands feel like on her flesh, stroking, teasing, rubbing...

"You look beautiful tonight, Ms. Lane."

"Please, call me Tabatha."

"All right, Tabatha." He spoke slowly, his deep voice caressing the words in a way that made her pulse race out of control.

"As you know, I've come to talk about Whittle House."

"Why don't we just enjoy the evening, at least for a while?"

"I won't enjoy the evening until I discuss the house."

"All right." He placed his bread on his plate and leaned back in the chair, his intent gaze fixed on her. "Talk to me."

"I assume you're familiar with the Whittle family who owned the house?"

"No."

"Not at all?"

He shrugged. "I thought you planned on telling me."

"Well, if you don't know the house's history then how can you possibly place any value on it? Let me explain. Allen Whittle came to America in the mid 1700s. He was a wealthy merchant, one of the richest men in early America. When the war broke out between Britain and the States, his loyalty remained with King George. Of course he believed his only son, Samuel, would also be on the side of the crown. Unbeknownst to the Whittle family, Samuel's circle of friends included many patriots. It was rumored that he was part of the Boston Tea Party. He joined the army in 1776 and fought until freedom was won. Only once did he return home. He'd been badly wounded and came back to New Hampshire to recover. His father was dying, but even then he would not make peace with his son. He cursed Samuel for his choices. Wounded both physically and emotionally, the patriot decided to return to battle right away. There was a heavy winter storm that year. As Samuel made his way through the snowdrifts, he was attacked by a wolf. Somehow he survived. He rejoined his patriot brothers and became part of Knowlton's Rangers."

"Who were they?"

"Goodness, Mr. Durant, don't you know anything about American history?"

"What's the point of knowing history? It can't do anything for me now. And call me Pierce."

She sighed, exasperated. "History is more important than you realize."

"About the rangers?"

"Knowlton's Rangers were an intelligence group used by Washington to perform dangerous missions. Samuel Whittle was one of them."

"I see. So because he lived in the house, I shouldn't knock it down, is that it?"

"According to legend, it wasn't a normal wolf that bit Samuel, but a werewolf. It was said that when the moon shone, he turned into a savage beast, though not one completely unintelligent. Supposedly he attacked the redcoats in the dead of night. He was what some called Washington's secret weapon—though of course most people think it's just a story."

A smile played around his finely drawn lips. "And you don't?"

"Do I look like a fool, Pierce?" His attitude irritated her so much she forgot how gorgeous he was. "Of course I don't believe in werewolves, but I believe in preserving history. Samuel Whittle was not only a war hero, but a local legend. Haven't you ever heard the poem?"

"I'm sure you're going to tell me."

She recited —

"His father was loyal
to the British crown
Rebellion, said he,
it must be put down

Our comforts come
from across the sea
Any Whittle son
must be a Tory

Samuel denied
his father's will
For freedom
his blood would spill

He joined the ranks,
to follow Washington
The rift was dug
between father and son

Wounded in battle
Samuel returned
Still was by
his family spurned

His father cursed
A demon heard
Samuel left
without a word

In the snow
the young soldier fell
his shoulder ripped
by a beast from hell

Some things are not
what they appear
Samuel's curse
redcoats did fear

Moonlit battles
a dreaded wolf won
the Patriot's weapon
when faded the sun

The Whittle Curse
now you know
A man turned wolf
long ago

He searched for justice
and found it there
Among savage teeth
and beastly hair

When the moon rises

over Whittle House

When beasts cry in the dark

Beware, my friends

Don't walk too late

The werewolf makes his mark"

When she finished, Pierce laughed aloud. "That's just bad poetry."

"Whether it's good or bad doesn't matter. It's the legend that counts. I don't believe you could have walked through that house without feeling anything."

"I've never walked through it."

"Then do it. Step into that old mansion and tell me you believe it should be destroyed."

"Tabatha, you're a lovely woman. Don't you have anything better to do than nose around old houses? I think you need some fun in your life."

He reached for her hand, but she tugged it away, not willing to admit that his warm touch alone sent her desire off the scale. Never a woman to be lured by a handsome face, she required substance in a lover. Pierce Durant was all show and no soul and she was smart enough to know it.

"You haven't paid attention to a word I said, have you?" she asked.

"Of course I have. Washington. Whittle. Norman's Raiders."

"That's Knowlton's Rangers."

"Yes. Whatever. The fact is, Ms. Lane, in six days Whittle House will be dust and the foundation for a slew of condos will be where it stood."

"How would you like it if two hundred years from now someone knocked down the buildings *you've* built?"

"In two hundred years, I'll be dead, so it won't matter much to me one way or the other. I want to be satisfied now, while I'm alive to enjoy it, not when I'm rotting in some graveyard like your Samuel Whittle has been for the past two hundred years."

"One hundred sixty-three."

The waiter approached wearing a pleasant smile. "May I take your order, ma'am?"

"No." Tabatha stood, grasping her purse and glaring at Pierce. Anger burned inside her. Never in her life had she met such an ignorant, arrogant man. "I'm leaving."

Pierce also stood. "I'll take you home."

"Don't bother." She curled her lip at him and stormed away from the table.

* * * * *

Pierce blinked sweat from his eyes as he raised the barbell above his head. He lowered the heavy weights and ran a hand through his hair as he left his home gym to start his daily run. Every morning he awoke early to get in a couple of hours of exercise before heading for the office. Unlike his father, he wasn't content to let his body deteriorate because of a sedentary career. Sure, he worked long hours, but that was no excuse to ruin his health. Pierce liked feeling strong. He also liked sex and the better his physical condition, the more fun he had in bed.

If only he'd managed to get that pretty bitch Tabatha between the sheets. When he closed his eyes, he could still smell her sweet, floral perfume and see the curve of her face. How he'd love to take that voluptuous body of hers in his arms and bury his cock deep inside her hot, wet pussy.

Too bad she was frigid. After last night he was certain the woman didn't have a lusty bone in her body. All those good looks and she had the sex appeal of a rotten egg. Her problem was she had her head buried in the past. All that reading and history research had her so smitten with legends that she couldn't see the opportunities for pleasure right in front of her.

"Look at Whittle House, she says." Pierce shook his head, then shrugged. Why not? His house was only five miles from it. He ran about ten every day, anyway.

As he stepped into the brisk morning and stretched, he gazed at the woods and grass around him and a pang of old memories stabbed him. Though he lived in a rural area, he scarcely noticed it. Usually when he jogged or drove to the city to work, his thoughts spun with business deals. After work, it was too dark to really look at any scenery, even if he was so inclined.

This was the first time in years he'd taken a good, long look around. Why the sudden change? Maybe that bitch had gotten to him more than he wanted to admit.

No. Impossible. One thing was certain, no one ever reached the heart of Pierce Durant.

The pounding of his sneakers on pavement and the huffing of his breath echoed in the still morning as he jogged toward Whittle House. As he neared it, a strange, anxious feeling settled in his chest. He paused running, his eyes wide. Heart attack? No. He was thirty-three years old and in great shape.

"Paranoid bastard." He continued jogging toward the house. It loomed in the distance, dark and enormous. Though he'd never set foot inside, he knew the gray, Georgian-style mansion had twenty-five rooms, all of which retained the original furnishings from the time Samuel Whittle lived there. The furnishings were to be auctioned off in three days.

Maybe he'd give some of them to the Philmore Historical Society as a tax-deductible donation or something.

What are you crazy, Pierce? Fuck the historical society and that crazy bitch Tabatha Lane. All she's done is make you think about things that don't really matter.

He'd nearly reached the long, cobbled walk when his beeper went off. Shit. He didn't have time to stroll around

Whittle House. He needed to jog home, wash up, and get to work.

As he turned back to the road, an odd cry—almost like a howl—pierced the stillness. Glancing back at the house, he noticed snowflakes drifting around it.

"Shit. It's not that cold." Pierce narrowed his eyes and held up his hand to catch some of the icy crystals. Nothing. There was no snow. His gaze flew to Whittle House. It stood, bathed in morning sunlight, not a snowflake to be seen.

"You're losing it, Pierce," he muttered, picking up his pace and heading for home. "Tabatha Lane and her stupid Revolutionary War werewolf."

Chapter Three
Two Days Later

Tabatha's pulse raced as she stepped into Pierce's office. She'd phoned the day before and asked for another meeting with him. He'd obliged. Though she didn't believe she'd convince him to save the house, she had to at least try to rescue some of the items inside.

"Ms. Lane, how good of you to come," he said with false pleasantness. Sitting behind his desk, he signed paperwork, not bothering to look up at her. How he infuriated her. The man dipped beyond rude and sank to downright inhuman.

"Mr. Durant, I've come to ask you once again to hold off on auctioning the furnishings at Whittle House. Give Philmore the chance to raise the money to buy them from you."

He laughed. "Those are antiques. People will pay a fortune for each piece. Philmore couldn't possibly hope to raise enough money to interest me—at least not in a reasonable amount of time."

"Don't you have a shred of decency in you?"

His grin seemed permanently attached to his face as he tossed the pen aside and leaned back in his chair, his discerning gaze fixed on her. It was late, long past dark. The office was empty except for one or two eager beavers and Pierce who appeared to spend his entire life there. The top buttons of his blue dress shirt were opened, revealing the hollow of his throat and part of his chiseled, hair-dusted chest. Tabatha tried not to focus on those hard-looking pecs just calling for a woman's touch. He would have been far better off with less good looks and more decency.

"None whatsoever, but I love a good bargain. Maybe you have something I'd take in exchange for the Whittle House antiques."

"What?"

His leering sapphire gaze swept her from head to foot then settled on her full breasts straining against her tie-dyed T-shirt tucked into faded jeans.

"I don't believe you," she snapped, repulsed by his vulgar implication.

"You might enjoy it."

She flung him her most withering look. "Never."

"Then we have nothing left to talk about. Goodnight, Ms. Lane."

"But the house—"

"Listen to me." He pushed his chair away from the desk and gestured toward the enormous bulge in his pants. "Either you get that arousing ass of yours over here and onto my lap, or get the hell out and don't bother coming back."

Any attraction she had once felt for him disappeared completely. "You are a sad, pathetic excuse for a man. It's obvious you've never cared about anyone or anything in your entire life, so how can I possibly hope to appeal to your sense of humanity. You have none."

He grasped his crotch, his brow furrowed and a nasty grin on his lips. "Is that a no?"

Turning on her heel, she left, slamming the door behind her.

* * * * *

Alone in his office, Pierce sighed, his smile fading. Tabatha was right, he didn't care much about anything. When he'd been a boy, before his mother took off with some biker she'd met during one of their weekend trips, he'd imagined himself growing up to be a forest ranger or a fireman. He'd liked the idea of helping people, being a hero, even if it meant not making a whole lot of money.

Living with his father had changed all that. Money, not blood, was the driving force of life. Build an empire. Crush anyone who stands in the way. That's how it's done, son. Ivy League schools didn't train fireman. You didn't go to impressive colleges to major in forestry.

What about family? Marry a rich woman from a prestigious family. If you see another class of woman you like, sleep with her. No emotional involvement allowed. That's what he'd done with Pierce's mother. If cancer hadn't stolen his ability to create any more children, he might not have admitted to fathering Pierce, either, but half a blueblood was better than none.

Pierce had been cleansed of his naïve and simple dreams. He had power. He had money. What more could he possibly require?

I need nothing more. Not a thing.

Pierce stood and headed for the door.

At home, he showered and ate dinner then took a walk down to his wine cellar. He usually wasn't one for drinking, but tonight he was in the mood for a special vintage.

Making his selection, he brought both bottles to his car and drove to Whittle House. Taking a stroll through the place was in order, if just to prove to himself that none of Tabatha's words meant a thing to him at all.

He drove onto the lawn and he parked so close to the house he could see in the parlor window. By the light of the full moon, he discerned the outlines of chairs, tables, and a hutch. A fireplace took up most of one wall. Several paintings hung over the mantel. It looked ordinary enough. Nothing to warrant all the fuss Tabatha and her damned historical society were making.

"What the hell?" Grasping both wine bottles in one hand, he walked to the house. He unlocked the front door and stepped inside.

Drawing a deep breath, he paused in the foyer, his heart thrumming. Another odd feeling encompassed him, similar to the one he'd experienced on the morning he'd jogged over.

Shaking his head, he placed the bottles on a tiny wooden table by the door and reached into his pocket for his flashlight and a corkscrew. He opened one of the bottles and took a long swallow, his gaze darting around the foyer and sliding up the long, narrow stairwell to his right.

The lights didn't work. He'd cut off electricity once he'd bought the house. With the flashlight in one hand and the wine bottle in the other, Pierce ascended the steps. They creaked with each footfall.

Upstairs, the hallway stretched in both directions. Choosing a door to his left, he entered a bedroom furnished with rope rugs, a dark wooden bed draped with a blue and white quilt, and a fireplace.

The furniture and accents were attractive and appeared in excellent condition. The next three bedrooms he searched looked similar. Landscapes and paintings of sailing ships hung on the walls. The polished wooden floor beneath his feet was strewn with carpets. Unlike most old houses, Whittle House didn't smell musty, but fresh, as if the wood, furnishings, and varnish were fairly new.

It was cold, though. Autumn nights in New Hampshire were usually on the chilly side. Pierce walked downstairs and into the parlor. Logs were piled by the fireplace, so within moments he had a fire blazing in the hearth. Squatting in front of it, he warmed his hands, then took another swallow from the bottle, rolling the wine in his mouth and savoring the flavor.

Suddenly he imagined sharing the bottle with Tabatha. How good it would feel to have her wrapped naked in his arms, snug in a quilt by this very hearth.

Moron.

Standing, he gazed around the room. The house really was quite nice. Brighten it up a bit, and it would be a decent place to live.

He walked around, studying the fine craftsmanship of the variety of silver cups, ornaments, dishes, and trinket boxes throughout the room. A finely carved wooden clock rested on the mantel. He gazed at the portraits covering one entire wall. He guessed they were Whittle family ancestors. Several wore white wigs. They seemed to stare down their long noses at him with looks of contempt.

One painting in particular caught his interest. It was of a young, attractive man. His dark brown hair curled around his collar. Rather than a high-neck fancy suit, he wore a billowy white shirt. Though his expression was arrogant, it was also steadfast, yet there was something else deep in his eyes. Something wild. Something desperate. This man had secrets, of that Pierce was sure.

A creak from the foyer caused him to start. Narrowing his eyes, his breath quickening, he strode out of the room. The foyer was empty, just as he'd left it, but that meant nothing. There were twenty-five rooms in the mansion.

Pierce slipped his gun from its holster. Shooting was a hobby of his, though lately he'd been too busy to spend as much time as he'd like at the range.

Placing the bottle aside, he systematically made his way through each and every room. Relaxed by the wine, he wasn't too disturbed by the thought of finding an intruder.

Moonlight shone in through the windows, so bright at times that he didn't even need the flashlight. The rooms were surprisingly clean. The Philmore Historical Society had taken damn good care of the place. Maybe Tabatha was right after all. It seemed like a shame to bulldoze such a nice house.

Shaking his head, he closed the closet in the last room and jogged down the stairs. Insanity. The condominiums would be just as nice. Nicer. He'd make plenty of profit off them.

The wine bottle was almost empty. He finished it in a swallow and opened the second bottle. As he walked back to the fireplace, he wondered why he was drinking so much tonight. It was work. All the stress. Crazy hours. Never even a weekend off. He needed to unwind. Then what the hell was he doing in an empty mansion that had once belonged to a werewolf?

"Werewolf." He laughed and dropped to the floor by the fire. By the time he'd finished half of the second bottle, he was nearly asleep. The warmth of the fire, the stillness of the night, and the effects of the alcohol had him ready for bed. There was no way he could drive home like this. Not now.

A thick, old-fashioned quilt was draped over the couch. He tugged it off along with one of the rather hard pillows and stretched out on the floor. Moments later, he was asleep.

* * * * *

Pierce awoke screaming, his entire body aflame. Something was ripping him apart from the inside out.

"God," he bellowed, writhing on the floor. "What is it?"

Through blurred eyes he noticed the fire still burning. Whittle House.

Another scream and his thoughts faded into something else. Primitive emotions. Rage and agonizing hunger. The ripping, burning pain faded, replaced by so much power he nearly burst from it.

Low growls filled the room. His chest heaved as if he'd sprinted ten miles, yet he was filled with boundless energy. The room was suddenly too small and cooped up. He sprang over the couch and directly through the picture window. Glass shattered and he raced across the snow-covered ground.

Chapter Four

As dawn broke, Pierce's thoughts cleared. Overcome by exhaustion, each step was a duty in itself. His breath came in shallow gasps. His racing heartbeat skipped as he staggered toward Whittle House looming too far in the distance.

Shivering from severe cold, he wrapped his arms around himself and glanced down in shock. Where the hell were his clothes? Sure, he'd been drinking the night before, but not *that* much. No wonder he was so cold. His bare feet, bluish in color, nearly sank in the snow.

"Mr. Whittle," A feminine voice shouted followed by the echo of—could it be hoofbeats?

Pierce turned, tripping over a tree branch buried in the snow, and landed on his knees as a wagon approached. The young woman wrapped in a dark wool cloak reined in the horse and leapt to the ground.

"Thank the Lord," she murmured, tearing off her cloak and draping it over his shoulders. "I never thought we'd find you."

"Who are you?" His words were scarcely discernable through his chattering teeth.

"It'll be all right, sir." Her brown eyes, lovely and kind, searched his face. She slipped an arm around him and used her smaller frame to support his as they walked to the wagon.

Climbing inside, he tried pulling the cloak more tightly around him, but he hadn't the strength. Completely exhausted, he lost consciousness.

* * * * *

Pierce awoke to a gentle hand stroking his forehead. His eyes flickered, blinking away blurriness, before focusing on...who the hell was she?

Chocolate brown eyes gazed at him. A tender smile tugged the corners of her full lips. "Mr. Whittle, how are you feeling, sir?"

His brow furrowed. Pierce sat up on the large four-poster bed. Glancing at the clock on the mantel across the room, he saw it was seven—in the morning, by the look at the sunlight pouring in through the open window. Horrible for a hangover. His head was about to explode.

"Sir?"

"Good. I'm good. How did you get in here?"

"I work here, sir. It's Maggie."

"Maggie?"

"Yes, sir."

"This is Whittle House?"

She smiled, appearing relieved. The covers had fallen down to his waist, and she pulled them up, but not before her gaze swept his torso. A glance downward and he nearly leapt off the bed. That wasn't the body he remembered. It wasn't bad—a little short for his taste, but well-muscled.

The door opened and a round-faced man wearing a smile and a shrewd though likeable expression approached. He wore a white shirt, vest, and—what the hell kind of pants were those?

"He's having another of his spells." Maggie turned to the man with a concerned expression. "He doesn't recognize me again."

"Again?" Pierce's gaze switched from Maggie to the newcomer who dragged a chair near the bedside. Panic threatened, but he held it at bay. Though everything seemed strange, there was also something familiar about his two companions.

The man sat on the chair, his gaze holding Pierce's. "Samuel, do you know me?"

When Pierce didn't reply, his visitor and Maggie exchanged concerned looks.

"It's Paul. You escaped last night. I've already started working on stronger cuffs. Don't worry, you won't get out again."

"Get out? My name's Pierce."

Maggie gasped, her eyes wide, and clamped a hand over her mouth.

Paul grinned. "Don't be alarmed, Maggie. He hasn't lost his mind completely. Back in the early days, a bunch of us called him that because he was sure to pierce whatever he aimed his rifle at. He was one of the best marksmen we had. Want to go by that old nickname again? Fine. I'll play along. I'll tell you, Samuel Whittle, you sure know how to stir up old memories."

Samuel Whittle. That was just a story. A werewolf story told by...who had told him? The dream seemed so far off. Nightmare was more like it. There had been tall buildings—ugly and gray—and metal arcs rolling down black streets. It made him shiver just thinking about it.

"Samuel?" Paul rested a firm hand on his shoulder. "Are you all right?"

"How can he be all right?" Maggie sighed. "He's just spent the entire night running around the countryside. He's lucky he didn't catch his death being caught in that snowstorm without so much as a stitch of clothes after the fur faded."

"Fur? Oh, God." Samuel—Pierce—whoever the hell he was, clutched his head in his hands. "It's true. The werewolf..."

"Didn't harm anyone," Paul told him. "A few sheep were killed at a farm last night, but that was all."

"I can't believe this is real."

"I know. You always have memory lapses after the beast comes." Maggie opened a chest of drawers and brought him a clean shirt, breeches, and a waistcoat. "It's amazing you're able to retain any semblance of humanity at all."

"It's getting harder, though, isn't it?" Paul asked.

"Y...yes." Samuel reached for the clothes. An important memory filled his mind. *Washington's secret weapon.* "What year is it? Is the war over?"

Again Paul and Maggie glanced at one another, sympathy in their expressions.

"Yes, it's over." Paul told him. "We're free."

Nodding, Samuel pulled on the shirt.

"You remember the battles, then?" Paul inquired.

"Yes. A bit."

"You were a great help, once you managed to harness that power of yours."

"I don't think I *can* harness it."

"That's why I've fashioned the cuffs. I'll be back in a moment."

Paul stood and left the room. Reaching for his breeches, Samuel's gaze fixed on Maggie who stared at him with those deep brown eyes. Something in her expression reached out and clasped his soul in a manner both comforting and unsettling. A sheepish smile touched the corners of his mouth. "If you would give me some privacy?"

"Of course, sir." She moistened her lips and dropped into a quick curtsy. When she reached the door, she glanced over her shoulder and said, "I'm so glad you're safe."

"Maggie, before you go, what year is it?"

Her expression softened even more. "It's 1785, sir."

She left, closing the door behind her. The woman made his blood catch fire. His pulse quickened just from the look in her eyes and the curves of her breasts and hips beneath the plain servant's gown she wore.

He pulled on the breeches. Using the basin of water on the table by the bed, he cleaned his teeth and face, then stepped into the hall.

Sounds from downstairs caught his attention and he followed them. Paul sat on a chair by the fire, examining a pair of sterling silver manacles. As Samuel approached, he glanced at the familiar ancestral portraits on the wall across the room.

"Here they are." Paul held out the cuffs. "Far stronger than the last pair. And the silver is of the finest quality, guaranteed to subdue the beast better than anything else."

Samuel took the cuffs and ran his hands over them. "These are worth a fortune."

"Priceless to you." Paul grinned. Standing, he clapped a hand on his taller friend's shoulder. Though Samuel couldn't fully remember who Paul was, by the way the man spoke and acted, he guessed they had known each other for quite awhile and even served together during the war. Paul's offering of the handcuffs revealed that he must be a silversmith, too. "I need to get back to Boston. It's been a fine week visiting, but I can't stay here forever. Will you be all right? It can't be easy running this entire household alone."

"He has me." Maggie stepped into the parlor, a tea tray in her hands.

"Dear Maggie." Paul shook his head. "The only one brave enough to stay in the cursed Whittle House."

"The only one?" Samuel held her gaze.

"You won't get rid of me, sir," she said in a hushed voice that held implications he didn't miss. "That's for certain."

Samuel nodded, the lingering look he shared with his maid disturbed by Paul clearing his throat loudly.

"Are you sure you won't stay for tea, sir?" Maggie asked their guest who had donned his cloak.

"No. I really must not waste the day. Luck to you, my friend." Paul winked and clasped Samuel's hand. "*Pierce.*"

Samuel smiled and watched as Paul left the house. Moments later, hoofbeats thudded on the snowy ground as the silversmith rode away.

Maggie rested the tea tray on the table by the fire. "Would you like eggs, sir?"

"I'd like you to sit down and join me."

She drew a sharp breath. "Join you, sir? Isn't that inappropriate?"

"Seeing how you're the only person willing to live with me, I don't believe it is."

"Well, if you put it that way, sir."

"Stop calling me sir. I'm Samuel."

"Samuel, yes. Earlier, when you called yourself Pierce, I had the strangest feeling."

"Why?" His interest piqued. In spite of his attachment to the nickname, he couldn't remember the circumstances that inspired it that Paul had found so amusing.

"I don't know. It's like something out of a dream, a memory."

"Maybe it's from the old days with Paul?"

"No, sir. I've only worked here for the past three years. If it hadn't been for you, I'd have been on the streets."

"You have no family?" Why the hell couldn't he remember all the details he should know?

"No, sir. After my husband was killed at Yorktown, I lost our farm. You saved my life when you hired me."

"And how many times since have you saved mine?"

She smiled, casting her gaze down. "A man with your powers doesn't need saving."

"Except, perhaps, my soul?"

Her gaze met his and he could almost sense her desire to touch him. He felt the same. Still, it would be out of place, wouldn't it? To take advantage of a servant?

"If anything had happened to you, sir—"

"Samuel." He cupped her face in his hand.

"I can't." She stood and drew a deep breath. Beneath the fitted top of her brown dress, her breasts swelled. Desire stirred Samuel's belly. He reached for her, but she slipped from his touch and hurried to the kitchen, calling, "I'll have your eggs ready soon."

For several moments he wandered around the room, collecting himself. Now that he'd been awake for awhile, everything finally made sense—at least as much sense as his twisted life *could* make. He remembered that night so long ago when, alone and barely recovered from his battle-injury, he'd struggled down the snowy road away from his father's house— this house.

Samuel believed in the cause. Still, he'd badly wanted to make peace with his father. The old man would have no part of it. He'd despised Samuel and his decisions until his dying breath.

"Ungrateful whelp," his father had rasped upon Samuel's arrival at his bedside. "You're not just disloyal to the King, but to me. I must die soon but I hope you live a long life and every moment of it be in misery."

The wolf had attacked him that night and left him bleeding in the snow. As he lost consciousness, Samuel thought he would die as well, but had awakened healed and stronger than ever before. At first he thought it was a miracle, proof from God that his father's hatred didn't extend unto heaven. Several nights later, he learned the horrible truth. When the moon rose full in the sky, Samuel was stricken with agony such as he'd never known. Pain soon faded into power and a savage, insatiable hunger that sent him chasing after any creature that pumped blood. He'd killed men that night. Hessian soldiers. However, they might have been his own. The lust for flesh and blood was so strong that for many months it overshadowed reason. Eventually he was able to retain some memories of his life as a man. With the help of a few trusted friends, he learned to focus his violence. Few knew the part he played in the Revolution's battles. Some whispered rumors surfaced about a wolfish creature that cleaned its teeth and claws on anyone who opposed the rebellion. Most considered it a story to frighten the enemy.

If only that were true.

Samuel drew a deep breath and released it.

After the war, he'd retired to his father's house, now empty but for the servants. The war was over, but the curse lingered. Servants began talking of a wild beast roaming the woods outside the mansion. Dead animals and a maid and stable hand terrified in the midst of a midnight romp sent the servants into a panic. By the third full moon after Samuel's return, he'd lost his entire staff, except for Maggie. He thought for certain she would go as well, especially when talk started in the town about the young widow being the sole servant in the household of a wealthy and—according to the villagers—handsome man.

Samuel had to admit to some truth in what they said. For months he'd done his best to ignore her soul-searching eyes and voluptuous curves. He tried not to relish the beauty of her smooth brown skin and full lips just made for kissing. There was no denying the way she looked at him, as well. Just that morning hadn't she stared far too long at his bare chest?

Perhaps it was the desperation of two lonely people, the natural urge for sexual gratification when neither had the opportunity to sate it, but keeping his hands off her suddenly seemed impossible.

He strode to the kitchen where Maggie had cracked eggs into a frying pan heating on the big black stove.

Upon seeing him, she appeared startled. "The eggs will be a few more minutes, sir."

"To hell with the eggs, Maggie." He stood so close that he saw the ultra-fine lines on her lovely lips. Her gaze met his. The rise and fall of her breasts was enough to harden his cock and quicken his pulse. "I want to ask you something."

She nodded, swallowing visibly. Perhaps some part of the wolf still lingered, for he caught the enticing scent of her arousal. An image of their faces close, their mouths nearly brushing, filled his mind.

"I've almost kissed you recently, haven't I?"

"Sir, please." She turned back to the pan, but he took her face in his hands and forced her to look at him. "Yes. You have—almost."

"What stopped us?"

"Besides the fact that it's not permitted? I'm your servant."

"You're my friend."

"But—"

"Why have you stayed here, Maggie?"

"Because I've nowhere else to go, especially now."

"Especially since you've been loyal to me?"

"Yes, sir. No one in the village so much as speaks to me, let alone considers allowing me in their household."

"But you could have gone with the others."

"And who would take care of you?"

He laughed. "Am I a child?"

"No, sir, but—"

"Why have you stayed, Maggie? Please. I must know." Expelling a long, slow breath, he tilted her face to his. "Forgive me. It's just that I have so many pieces in my mind and I'm trying to make them fit."

"It'll come back, sir. It always does—at least for a while. Then the closer you get to the full moon—"

"The more my thoughts drift from reality."

"It's not your fault. It's the beast in you. Sometimes, really close to the full moon, you frighten me, but..."

He turned his gaze to her, waiting, his entire body tense. The scent of her excitement was almost a tangible thing. "But what?"

"It thrills me too." Her words were hushed and speedy, but he heard them and a strange feeling warmed him from the inside out. All his memories might not be clear, but one thing he knew without doubt. He loved this woman.

"Maggie..." His hands slid down her back and grasped her waist as he tugged her closer.

Her eyes half-closed as she leaned forward the slightest bit. Their lips met. At first it was a warm brushing of flesh. Then his arms tightened around her and he applied more pressure.

She moaned softly and slid her hands up his back, her small, strong fingers gripping the taut muscles. She felt and tasted so good.

Her lips parted beneath his tongue. Hers darted out to meet it. They caressed one another with warm, wet strokes. His rock-hard cock was trapped between their bodies. How he longed to raise her skirt and bury himself to the hilt in her pussy. He knew by her scent that it was slick and damp, well-prepared with the evidence of her lust.

Maggie stood on tiptoe to better reach him. She freed his thick, dark hair from the ribbon at his nape. It flowed through her fingers. Samuel's eyes closed tightly and he lost himself in sensation. She tasted sweet and hot. Her splendid curves crushed against his body's hard planes stirred his lust like nothing he remembered.

The thud of hoofbeats on snow roused them from their desirous stupor.

"I should see who it is," she said, gazing up at him with those enormous brown eyes still hazy with passion.

"I'll see." He rubbed her arms, warming them with his hands, before heading to the door on which someone relentlessly pounded.

Outside, Paul looked frantic.

"I thought you were returning to Boston?" Samuel asked.

"I was, but I came upon the townsfolk. They're on their way here and are furious about the ravaged sheep. Hide the cuffs and collect yourself. Deny everything, as always."

Samuel turned to the parlor where he'd left the cuffs on the table, but Maggie already had them in her hands. She hurried to the fireplace, removed a loose brick, and hid the cuffs behind it.

The sound of more galloping horses filled the snowy morning and a small group of men, armed with muskets, came into view.

"Good thing I made it here in time," Paul whispered.

"Yes, by the look of them." Samuel stared at the approaching party.

"Where were you last night?" demanded the man in the lead. He was tall, silver-haired with a hawkish nose and a stern expression in his close-set eyes.

"Here. Where do you think I was?"

"I think you were roaming across the countryside. Covered in hair like a beast from hell, you devoured two sheep from Solomon Smith's farm."

"That accusation again?" Samuel feigned boredom.

"Everyone knows the stories, Whittle. During the battles, wherever you were stationed, the beast appeared."

"He was always stationed with General Washington," Paul interjected, "yet I see no one accusing *him* of being a beast."

"Except for the men who served under him," grumbled a man from the back of the crowd. "But Washington is an honest man without curses heaped upon him by members of his own family."

"Think about what you're saying. Does he look like a demon to you?"

"You don't need to defend me, Paul." Samuel held each of his accusers' gazes in turn. "I know what I am and what I am not."

"I say we kill him now," continued the leader. "Save us any more loss of livestock, or more important, our own lives."

Everyone's gazes turned to yet another man approaching on horseback. Beneath his cloak, the newcomer wore the collar of the clergy.

"Please talk to them," Maggie begged the reverend. "They want to kill Mr. Whittle."

"I told you men that violence begets violence," the reverend snapped. "Without proof, you cannot accuse this man."

"I'll give you the proof." The leader glared. "Lock him in the jailhouse during the next full moon and watch him turn into the devil's hound. If we don't, more than sheep might be lost next time."

"Edgar." The reverend pointed at the leader. "If you would stop and listen for once in your life instead of inciting trouble, you might learn something. The killer was found. It was a lynx that had wandered in from the woods. Thomas Williamson shot it this morning. All of you go home and leave this man in peace."

"We'll leave him," Edgar snarled, "but not in peace. Everyone knows what he is, reverend. Even you. The only way he'll find peace is in death."

The reverend stood with Samuel as the group galloped off. Glancing at Maggie, Samuel noted fear in her eyes. Her hand trembled at her side and he took it in his, squeezing it tenderly.

"Thank you," Samuel told the reverend.

"Don't thank me too soon, boy. I know someone who may help you, though I've probably damned my soul by asking for such heathen advice."

"Who is it?" Maggie asked.

"His name is John Longmeadow."

"I've never heard of him," Samuel said.

"No reason why you should. I don't believe he's ever set foot in any town for years. As soon as I arrange for a meeting with him, I'll let you know."

"Would you join us for something to eat?" Samuel offered, hoping to elicit more information over a meal.

"No. I must get back to the church." The reverend's gaze turned harsh as he stared at Samuel and Maggie's entwined fingers. "You should come with me, my dear. As I said before, maybe I can convince someone in town to take you into service."

"No," Maggie stated. "I'm happy where I am, thank you."

"Umm." The reverend lifted his chin. "Not too happy, I hope. For both your sakes."

Turning his horse away from the house, the reverend disappeared around the bend.

"Maybe I should think about leaving New Hampshire entirely." Samuel ran a hand through his hair and shook his head. "Sometimes I think it was easier in the army. I was told where to go and what to do. The skills I had, no matter how unconventional, were put to good use."

"Times are still difficult," Paul said. "People have already forgotten those who fought with heart and courage, who gave their entire being for these past years. It's not fair, when you think about it. Your curse—or gift, as it was in battle—was necessary but feared. Men of extremes, such as you and Sam Adams, are good to win a war but bad to run a country."

Samuel smiled sadly. "I'd say my extremity is a bit worse than his."

"I suppose it depends on who you talk to." Paul winked. "Now I really must go."

Together, Samuel and Maggie returned to the house.

"So you might find employment elsewhere?" Samuel said.

"I'd rather not. Unless you want me to."

Gazing deeply into her eyes, he tugged her close, one hand gently clasping her nape, his other arm wrapping around her waist. "God, Maggie, I should send you away for your own good, but I'm weak. I could bear loneliness, if not for you."

"Sir—"

"Samuel. I told you to call me Samuel. If you tell me you don't feel the same, I will never touch you again." He held her gaze. "Tell me."

"I...I can't. Oh, Samuel." She clung to his neck, her body pressed so close to his it felt as if their hearts beat in unison. Love for her squeezed his heart. A woman like this deserved better than him. Still, he could not resist her. "I want you so, so badly."

"I'm taking you, Maggie." He slipped off her white cap. Thick, dark curls, fragrant with the scent of lemon, tumbled down her shoulders and back. He buried his hands in the soft tresses and spoke against her lips. "I'm going to pleasure you in ways you never dreamed of."

Her lips parted as her breath came in lustful pants. Her hands roamed over his shoulders and back, then slipped up the back of his neck. The burning beauty of her eyes seemed to pierce his soul. His cock, nearly bursting with need, strained against his breeches. Sweeping her into his arms, he headed for the stairs.

"If you don't want this, Maggie, tell me now. When we get upstairs, the man will become a beast again. He'll need the taste of flesh, but not in a manner that brings death or pain. He'll devour your breasts in savage hunger. He'll lap the soft flesh between your legs until you scream in ecstasy. I'm telling you now because once we begin, the beast will not be stopped; do you understand me, my rare, dark-eyed beauty?"

"Yes," she breathed, clinging to his neck with one arm while her free hand stroked his face and traced the shape of his lips. "This will ruin us, Samuel. One way or the other it will ruin us, but I don't care anymore. I need you so much I feel I'll burst if I am denied your touch a moment longer."

"You will burst, Maggie. I swear that no cannon fire shall ever rock the earth as you and I will shatter each other tonight." Before she could speak, he claimed her mouth in a kiss filled with lust and power but also with tenderness. He wanted her so badly that, if he was so inclined, with a couple of wild thrusts he'd explode inside her. What a terrible waste that would be. This was a woman to be savored, enjoyed, and loved. Giving her pleasure would be as exquisite as receiving pleasure himself. And today they would exchange oh-so-much pleasure. It seemed like forever since he'd bared himself to anyone. Inside he was so tightly coiled from secrecy and rejection that her gentle touches and soft, willing body was like freedom to a man long chained.

He was starving, just like the wolf starved for blood, and he intended to eat of her until they both were sated.

Chapter Five

Maggie's heart pounded so hard she thought it might leap through her chest. Her breath quickened as she gazed deeply into Samuel's intense blue eyes. From the moment she'd first seen him over three years ago, an incredible pull dragged her towards this strange, courageous man.

She was a servant and had no right to him, but somehow she knew they belonged together. Something in his soul called to her. That was why, when everyone else abandoned him, she needed to stay.

At first she hadn't believed the rumors about him — the idea that he was cursed. Until the night she'd been faced by the wolf himself. It had been in the midst of a thunderstorm. Wind had blown open the barn door — at least she thought it had been wind. She'd entered the barn to find Samuel in the midst of the change. Halfway between man and beast, his facial features, though covered with hair, were still discernable. Silver cuffs bound his wrists so tightly the dark hair matted with blood. Upon seeing her, he'd flown into such a hideous rage of gnashing teeth and flashing eyes that she'd nearly panicked. Instead she'd run to the house and packed her few belongings. For some reason, she'd hadn't gone. Something in the creature's eyes had touched her heart. Those eyes held sorrow beyond words. Beneath their wildness, Samuel's soul lurked, struggling to repress the beast.

She'd spent a sleepless night locked in her room. At dawn, she'd taken Samuel's rifle and, trembling, headed for the barn.

Samuel, appearing as a normal man, lay naked and shivering in the straw. As she approached and prodded him with the weapon, he'd turned to her with such an expression of shame and sadness that she knew she could never abandon him to his curse. She vowed to do everything in her power to help him.

Samuel had revealed all that led to his horrible state of half-man, half-demon. His friend and fellow patriot, Paul, a silversmith in Massachusetts, had been helping him with his situation for years. He'd designed the cuffs that restrained the beast, as silver seemed to do the creature the most damage.

Maggie knew she was a fool to stand by him, yet she'd tried choosing the safe route all her life and where had it gotten her? She'd married a man who appeared decent and stable. He'd turned out to be a vile-tempered, sullen companion who had abandoned her to take up arms. Their marriage was so unhappy that she'd been glad to see him go. After his death, she actually preferred poverty to the thought of spending the rest of her life with him, had he survived.

The first man she'd ever really trusted was Samuel.

Samuel who now held her in his arms and whose mouth plundered hers with kisses that weakened her knees and strengthened her passion.

Running her fingers through his thick, wavy hair, she met the tender strokes of his tongue with hers. How many times had she admired his powerful body and longed to run her hands over his broad, hair-matted chest? Now it was about to happen and she could scarcely contain her excitement.

Sometimes she believed Samuel's wolf-madness infected her as well. Just a few nights ago, after waking from a dream in which she'd been with a tall, blue-eyed, strangely dressed man, she felt as if she was someone else. The dream had been so real. In it she'd gazed into a mirror. Though her own eyes stared back at her, the rest of the face and form belonged to someone else. That was how Samuel sometimes described feeling as the wolf. It was him, yet someone else.

She'd awakened from the dream murmuring the name Pierce. Pierce. The man in the dream. It had taken her off-guard to hear the name spoken by Samuel and then to discover he'd once been called the same. It was as if there was a madness in the house itself, seeping into their souls. After all, the curse had been initiated in the house, perhaps there was some power in it?

"Maggie," Samuel whispered against her lips, his chest rising and falling with passion as he stepped into his room and placed her on his bed. Staring at him, she tore off her apron and began removing her dress. He gently nudged her hands aside and said, "Let me."

Her breath came in shallow pants and she tingled from head to toe as his large, deft hands unfastened the ties. He slid the dress down her shoulders and gazed at her breasts pressed against the thin shift beneath. Cupping the warm, round globes, he rolled his thumbs over her dark nipples.

Maggie's belly tightened and she resisted the urge to groan from the pleasure. Her husband had never bothered touching her in such a way. His idea of lovemaking was to raise her skirts, rut her while she was still too dry for comfort, and roll over once he'd spilled his useless seed.

This was altogether different. Samuel's gaze fixed on her nipples as he toyed with them. Sliding off her shift, he bared her breasts completely to his touch. Running his index finger over the areola, he raised little bumps of pleasure. Bending, he caught one of her spiked nipples between his teeth and rolled his tongue over it.

It was almost too much for Maggie. She uttered a groan of pure desire and buried her hands in his hair, pressing his head closer as he lapped and sucked her nipple. Her pussy was so hot and moist. Her clit throbbed and ached. To increase the sensation, he slid one of his hands between her legs and cupped her soft mound.

"Oh, Samuel," she moaned, wiggling closer to his rubbing hand. Her hips thrust against him. One of his fingers slid inside her. It came away slick with moisture that he used to circle her clit. The touch of his wet, gentle finger rubbing where she was so, so needy sent her pulse racing. She collapsed onto her back, panting and moaning while he continued sucking both of her nipples, stroking her clit and slipping his fingers deep inside her.

"I want you, Maggie. Feel how much I want you."

Taking her hand, he guided it to his crotch. His cock felt like steel threatening to tear through his breeches. How she wanted to feel his warm, velvet flesh. Within moments he'd discarded them. Wearing only his billowy white shirt, he grasped her beneath the arms and hauled her higher on the bed.

"Let me keep touching you." She unfastened the buttons on his waistcoat and pulled off his shirt, thrilled by the sight of his naked torso He knelt above her, one of his hard thighs on either side of her waist, his well-muscled arms braced on either side of her head. His closeness stirred her like nothing she had ever experienced before. With the shirt gone, the broad, warm expanse of his chest was bared to her touch. She ran her hands over the powerful muscles, relishing the sensation of the curling mat of hair against her palms.

"You're so beautiful, Maggie, so kind." He bent, kissing her brow and her lips.

"As are you." She stared, her pulse racing with desire, as he sat back on his knees and stroked her belly. His cock, so thick and ruddy, stood out like a velvet-skinned pike. The balls beneath dangled, heavy as those of a prized stud. Unable to resist, she clasped the rod in both hands.

"Yes, Maggie, yes." A grin touched his lips. His eyes gleamed with desire. Placing his hands over hers, he showed her how to pump the staff to provide the greatest pleasure.

She stared at his marvelous cock as she stroked, removing one hand to clutch his balls and roll them in her palm. Every part of him reflected pure, masculine beauty from his intense eyes to the thick, perfectly formed cock snug in her hand. His breathing increased and his dark blue eyes closed halfway.

"I want to feel you inside me."

"Maggie…" He covered her body with his. Supporting most of his weight on one forearm, he stroked her face with his free hand. His touch was so tender and affectionate that love for him overwhelmed her. It seemed like forever that she'd dreamed of lying with him like this, of feeling his body so close to hers.

The sensation of his naked flesh against hers, the softness of his breath against her face, and the fresh, manly scent of him thrilled her like nothing she'd ever felt before.

One of his large, warm hands, callused from years of carrying weapons and training for battle, parted her thighs. He stroked them while devouring her mouth with a kiss that nearly stole her breath. With a smooth shifting of hips, his cockhead brushed her outer lips. He circled her slit gently before sliding inside, inch by delectable inch.

Maggie gripped his shoulders. Her fingers pressed against solid muscle as she drew a long breath, not releasing it until he was buried to the hilt.

Opening her eyes, she met his passionate gaze.

"It feels so good." He brushed his lips across her temple and down her cheek. "Deep inside you, Maggie, my love."

"Your love." A slight smile touched her lips and inside she warmed with joy.

"I don't know what I'd have done without you, these past years."

"I haven't done much, sir."

"Sir?" He chuckled. "You still call me sir even when naked in my arms and filled with my cock? From now on I'm Samuel."

"But the townsfolk—"

"Mean nothing to me. They want me dead. Why should I care what they think?" His expression softened and he traced her lips with his fingertips. "It's you I'm concerned about. By staying with me, you're putting yourself in danger in so many ways. If they find out we're lovers—"

"They suspect it anyway. Truth be told, Samuel, I don't care about them, either." She tightened her arms around him and lifted her hips. "Lord, Samuel, I could stay like this forever."

"I wish I could, but I'm afraid my body has limits where my spirit does not." Nibbling her ear and circling it with his tongue, he began thrusting into her. The long, rhythmic sliding of his thick, hard cock drove her up a summit she'd reached too few times in her life, and only by her own hand.

"Oh, Samuel," she cried as the pleasure built and his thrusts quickened. "Yes, yes, oh, yes."

"Maggie." His voice grew ragged. He kissed her, his tongue lashing hers. Capturing it, he sucked it in time with his thrusting hips, not allowing her to pull away even as orgasm overcame her.

Trembling, her body hot with passion, she gasped into his mouth and clung to him until her arms and legs ached.

The pulsations slowed. If not for his continued motions, she might have relaxed, but apparently he wasn't ready to give her up so quickly. His deep kisses plundered her mouth as his steely cock drove into her with increasing speed. Again she neared the summit. Just as she shattered, he stiffened and lunged hard. Tearing his mouth from hers, he cried out, a magnificent sound of pure masculine pleasure. It sent ripples of desire up her spine as much as his cock sent throbs of lust through her pussy.

Rolling onto his back, he tugged her to his heaving chest and stroked her shoulders and arm in slow, soothing motions.

"I'll always care for you, Maggie," he said. "You'll never want for anything again so long as you have me."

She must have been a complete fool, for she believed every word he spoke.

Chapter Six

Maggie awoke with a smile the following morning. She reached across the bed, expecting to feel Samuel's warmth beside her. He wasn't there.

Jumping up, she glanced around the room. Her dress, which had been tossed on the floor the previous night, was spread across the bed. A pitcher of water and a basin awaited her on the night table.

Standing, she shivered as the cold floor touched her bare feet and the crisp morning air fanned her naked body. After pinning up her hair and washing, she stepped closer to the fire blazing in the hearth across the room. Squatting, she rubbed her arms as she stared at the leaping flames.

The door opened and her gaze flew to Samuel. Dressed in dark breeches and a long, white shirt untied at the throat, he smiled at her.

"Pleasant morning." He approached and wrapped his arms around her.

Maggie buried her face in his chest, rubbing her cheek against its warmth. Sliding her hand inside his shirt, she caressed his ribs and ran her fingers through the curling mat of chest hair. Raising his shirt, she kissed one of his nipples.

"What am I to do, Maggie?" he sighed, resting his chin against the top of her head. "If it was just myself, I wouldn't care what happened, but I have you to consider. You can't spend the rest of your days with a half-beast. This relationship is dangerous in so many ways—at least if we stay here."

"What are you saying?" A sick feeling weighted her belly. She should have known. Like all men, after the rutting was over, so was his semblance of caring.

"I'm saying maybe we should leave New Hampshire, like I suggested."

"We?"

"Unless you've decided you don't want me after all?"

"Oh, I do." She drew a deep breath and gazed at him.

"Good." He tightened his arms around her and kissed her mouth. "Because I don't know if I could go on living without you, Maggie. You don't know how many times I've considered ending it, having Paul fire that silver bullet he made right through my heart—"

"What silver bullet?" Her pulse raced. The thought of Samuel dying was too much to bear, not when they'd only just begun exploring their love for each other.

"The one I had him make long, long ago, while the battles were still being fought. It was agreed by myself and those who knew my secret, that if I ever lost complete control of the beast, I should be destroyed. If I ever turned on my own men, then it would have to end."

"There must be a way to end this curse, Samuel." She pushed away from him and paced the room, her fists clenched.

"I've searched." He ran a hand through his hair. "There are some legends among the Indians about animal spirits, but none have told of a way to expel one from the body of a man."

"The reverend claims to have found someone who can help." Maggie clung to that hope. Quite by chance the reverend had learned of Samuel's curse. He'd told them how, late one night, he had had been visiting parishioners far on the outskirts of town. So close to the forest, it wasn't unusual for wild animals to wander the dirt path leading to their cabin. The reverend had crossed a black bear and would have been mauled had it not been for the gigantic wolf who sprang from the trees and killed the other predator. The reverend ran, terrified for his life. The wolf followed. As dawn neared, the wolf's cries sounded strangely human. Stumbling, the reverend fell into the dirt. As he pushed himself to his feet, terrified that the wolf would kill him, too, he saw that the creature's hair had receded. Its eyes lost their enraged glow. Moments later, Samuel lay it at his feet.

The reverend admitted his first reaction was to call upon his parishioners to destroy this man obviously touched by the devil. Then he remembered the bear and the desperate look in Samuel's eyes before he lapsed into the unconsciousness that always followed the change. Being a man of God, the reverend believed that there had to be a way for good to combat such evil.

He made it his duty to help Samuel find a way to exorcise his demon. Now he claimed to have found someone who might know of a cure. Maggie prayed it was true.

"Perhaps…" Samuel's voice trailed off. His concerned expression faded for the most part as he offered her a smile. "The wolf won't appear until the next full moon, so we must not waste what time we have. Would you like to go for a ride in the snow?"

"Very much. After we eat. I'm starving."

Chuckling, he dragged her close and kissed her. "Lovemaking works up an appetite."

"It certainly seems to." She grinned, her palms straying to his buttocks which she squeezed. "Now release me so I can go cook and perform my duties as a servant should."

"I find, Maggie, our roles have reversed." One of his hands pressed the small of her back so her body fitted snugly against his. He buried his hand in her hair and gazed into her eyes. "I am your humble servant, my sweet, dark beauty."

His words made her tingle yet she nearly laughed aloud. "I hardly think so."

"If not for this curse, I would take you as my wife in a heartbeat."

"Wife," she breathed, trying to pull away, but he wouldn't let her. "Samuel, you know that's impossible. We would never be accepted anywhere. We would—"

"My father was a man who lived by tradition. He tried to ensure that I would be the same, but it's not inside me, Maggie. I truly believe that no man should bow down to another, that we all deserve freedom and happiness. I fought for that belief and I will uphold it until my dying breath. I love you and nothing or no one will tell me I cannot have you. Not laws, not gossipmongers. No one. Tell me you feel the same."

"I feel it." She held his gaze as she slipped her arms around his neck. "But it's not that easy. Just because you say we belong together will not simply make it possible."

"When has life ever been simple?"

Maggie couldn't argue with that. As far back as she could remember life had been all too difficult. Perhaps it could work between them, two people from completely different worlds.

"Will you try, Maggie?"

"Yes. I'll try."

"Whatever happens to me, I'll see to it you'll never want for anything again."

She embraced him tightly. No one had ever been as kind to her as Samuel. No one had ever inspired her love and respect as much as this man. One thing was for certain, he would have her love and loyalty forever.

* * * * *

While Maggie washed the breakfast dishes, Samuel left to brush and saddle his horse. When she stepped outside, wrapped in a heavy cloak, he and the gray stallion stood in front of the house. Puffs of cold air floated from Samuel's mouth and the horse's nostrils. Both looked magnificent, two tall, well-muscled studs waiting to carry her off into the snowy morning.

Maggie smiled as he helped her onto the horse then mounted behind her. Drawing a deep breath, she tried to still her giddy stomach. His chest, so warm and hard, pressed against her back and his arms wrapped around her as he held the reins. Desire stabbed her as she glanced at his steely thighs so close to her.

Upon Samuel's command, the horse cantered across the white fields. A thrill of excitement coursed through her as the stallion soared over a frozen brook and landed without missing a beat.

When the house had disappeared from view and only fields and forest surrounded them, Samuel slowed the horse to a walk. Tugging down her hood, he brushed aside her hair and kissed her nape. A ripple of desire raced through her.

"Oh, Samuel," she sighed, leaning against him as he slid his hand inside her cloak and traced the shape of her breasts. In spite of the heavy dress and shift separating her flesh from his fingers, her nipples tightened beneath his caresses. Her clit throbbed and ached as he continued stroking her breasts and kissing her neck. He ran his tongue along the side of it, tracing a pounding artery before taking her earlobe between his teeth and nipping it gently.

Maggie tried to steady her breathing, but it was next to impossible. She gasped as one of his hands dipped between her legs. His palm and fingers rubbed her clit through her dress. Growing wet and hot, she thrust against his hand and closed her eyes as she rested her full weight against him. If he hadn't steadied her, she probably would have fallen off the horse.

Her neck and ear tingled from his lips, tongue, and teeth. Her nipples felt so wonderfully tight. If he continued rubbing her, she was going to come right then and there.

"Samuel, stop," she panted, her entire body tingling with desire. Her nipples turned to red-hot beads beneath his touch. She wanted him to fuck her so badly.

"Why?"

"We're outside."

"No one can see us."

That much was true. They were completely alone and as free as two people could be. There were no walls and no rules.

So true. Why should she refuse this kind of pleasure?

He tugged up her skirt so a cool breeze brushed her flesh. The stroking of his palm over her thigh warmed her quickly. Maggie's eyes closed halfway and she leaned against him, completely surrendering to the lust coursing through her.

Wriggling a bit in the saddle, she tried pressing closer to him. He stroked through the hair between her legs. One fingertip brushed over her clit. Leaning back a bit more to accommodate him, Maggie's pulse leapt. Their wild behavior thrilled her, and she wanted so much more.

As if sensing her needs, Samuel slid two of his fingers lower, gathering moisture from her pussy. His wet fingers slid over her clit and along the side of it. The pulsing bud of flesh throbbed. Shifting her hips, she tried to rub against his fingers.

"Impatient, my beauty?" he purred close to her ear, yet he accommodated her by stroking faster, circling her clit and sliding his finger up and down its sensitive side. To Maggie, the day was no longer chilly at all. Her entire body burned with the need for release. Her belly clenched and unclenched mercilessly and her heartbeat seemed to keep time with his rubbing fingers.

Suddenly his stroking slowed. Maggie whimpered when his touch left her clit. Once again his hand settled on her thigh, soothing and caressing. His lips teased the side of her neck, sending little ripples of pleasure coursing though her. Using the tip of his tongue, he drew random patterns on her flesh, then pressed gentle kisses down the back of her neck.

These sensations thrilled Maggie, but also touched her heart. She could scarcely believe that she and Samuel had denied their love for so long. Moaning softy, she leaned her head against his shoulder. His cheek rested against her hair and his hand returned to her clit. This time he used his palm to caress her soft mound.

"I love how hot and wet you are, Magge. You're so beautiful."

"Oh, Samuel, I can hardly believe this is happening."

Once again his deft fingers returned to her clit. His stiff cock pressed against her, evidence of his lust. Still, he made no attempt to satisfy himself, either by dismounting and taking her standing up or by asking her to turn in the saddle. His desire to please her excited her as much as his marvelous caresses.

"My Maggie," he whispered against her cheek, his fingertips rubbing in fast yet gentle circles over her clit.

Maggie panted, completely lost in sensation. Her eyes closed tightly and she squirmed in the saddle, allowing him to hold her steady. Using one finger, he slid the entire long length of it up and down the side of her clit. That slow, steady caress pushed Maggie over the edge.

"Ah. Samuel," she cried, bursting with pleasure. Her hips jerked and her heart pounded. Orgasm pulsed through her as she rubbed herself against his stroking hand.

"I love you, Maggie," he said close to her ear, his deep, husky voice enticing her almost as much as his caresses.

"I love you, too." She turned, holding his gaze. "Samuel, tell me you'll have Paul destroy that bullet. Promise me you won't ever give up on finding a way to lift the curse."

"I can't do that, Maggie. I don't want to die, but if I become a danger to others, especially those I care about, the only possible way is for me to end it."

"I don't want to lose you."

"You never can. We're in each other's hearts. Nothing can separate that kind of love. Not curses, not the will of others, not even death, Maggie."

"That sounds wonderful, but you know as well as I do that loving a memory is not the same as sharing physical warmth with a person. If you're dead, you can't take me in your arms."

"Close your eyes."

"Why?"

"Just close them."

She did as he asked. The horse stopped and all three stood in complete silence. She was intensely aware of his arms around her, of the rise and fall of his chest against her back. Even more were the sensations she felt deep inside. This was a memory she would treasure forever.

"If you're ever alone, think of this moment," he said. "As will I, should I ever be lonely and need to feel your presence. Pretend, if just for a brief time, that we're together in this field with the cool wind and the warm sun. Know how much I love you and always will."

She opened her eyes and folded her hands over his. Silently, thoughtfully, they headed for home.

* * * * *

Samuel and the reverend stopped their horses along a narrow, twisted path that disappeared in the trees. The animals snorted, pawing the cold, snow-dusted ground.

Samuel's face brushed the back of Maggie's hooded head and his thighs pressed harder against her. He was glad she'd accompanied him on the ride. His pulse raced as he realized that maybe this was the first step in ending his curse.

"I can't go any further," the reverend said. Both Samuel and Maggie glanced at him and he continued, "I've always met with Longmeadow along this path or at the edge of the woods. He said you were to go to his home."

Samuel's brow furrowed. "How am I supposed to find it?"

"He said if you are what you say you are, you'll find him."

Maggie turned slightly in the saddle and looked at Samuel with concern in her lovely brown eyes. "I'll go with you."

"No. Wait here. It will be safer."

"But—"

"Do as I say, Maggie," he stated without room for discussion.

Samuel dismounted. Pausing, he drew a deep breath. What did Longmeadow expect from him? True, the wolf was always with him, yet after the full moon he reverted to almost complete human form for at least a week. Then, gradually, the beast took over. Little by little his disposition would change as his senses heightened and primal emotions struggled against more civilized ones.

Stepping into the trees, he felt hopeless. Chances were he'd get lost in the woods instead of finding Longmeadow. The day was frigid. By the look of the sky—what he could see of it through the tree branches—a storm was coming. If they didn't get home before it started, they all might be caught in it. He should never have allowed Maggie to accompany him. Wait. The reverend would leave if the storm started, and he'd see that Maggie… Impossible. If Maggie got it in her head to remain, no one would change her mind.

Samuel drew a deep breath and released it slowly, closing his eyes for a moment. If he was to find Longmeadow, he would need the utmost concentration.

He tried remembering how it felt to be the wolf.

Wind whistled through the trees' naked branches and blew bits of ice onto Samuel's face. As he concentrated on the forest, he became of aware of the scurry of tiny animals' feet and the echo of birds' pounding wings. The scent of each forest creature wafted on the cold air.

Opening his eyes, he gazed through the trees, his vision keener than before. A movement ahead caught his attention and he walked toward it. The flash of fur and amber eyes of a timber wolf lured him, quickening his pulse along with his feet. He raced through the trees, ignoring the lashing branches and unhindered by the rugged ground. A new scent had caught his attention. Human.

The scent grew stronger and stronger. The wolf was in sight now. Moments later, he'd cornered it against the side of a cabin. It growled yet cowered, apparently sensing Samuel's beast in spite of his human form.

At the sound of footsteps, Samuel turned slightly, his gaze fixed on a tall, gaunt man with long gray hair and a beard that brushed his chest. He wore animal skins and knee-high boots. As the wolf darted into the trees, Samuel glanced at it then returned his attention to the man watching him with pale blue eyes more chilly than the winter wind.

"John Longmeadow?" Samuel asked.

The man nodded, his grim lips turning up in the faintest smile. "Come inside. We'll talk."

Samuel studied the man carefully as he followed him to the front of the cabin and up a narrow flight of rickety steps.

The door creaked open. The single room inside was small, warmed by a fire blazing in the hearth that took up most of one wall. The sparse furnishings included a bearskin-covered bed and a square wooden table, the surface scratched and worn. Two shelves on the wall near the table held several bottles, two wooden mugs, and a frying pan.

"I'm guessing you know I'm Samuel Whittle?"

Longmeadow raised a bushy gray eyebrow and nodded. "Sit."

Samuel tugged the single chair away from the table and watched Longmeadow take a pipe from the mantel and light it using a twig in the fire. As he drew on the pipe, he gazed at Samuel through the puffs of smoke surrounding his face.

"The reverend said you might be able to help me end the curse."

"The curse, eh?"

"Yes."

"The ability to run with a demon's power, to know total freedom."

"You make it sound like a good thing."

Longmeadow shrugged. "Maybe. Maybe not."

Samuel's pulse raced. He was starting to lose patience. Standing, he said, "The reverend and a young woman are awaiting me in the woods. I'd like to get back to them as soon as possible."

"A young woman? Interesting."

"Who exactly are you?"

"Just an old man with older stories."

Samuel closed his eyes and sighed. A waste of time. Longmeadow didn't know how to break the curse. No one did.

"It's getting harder to control, isn't it?" Longmeadow asked.

"What?"

"What do you think?"

The wolf. "Yes, it's getting harder to control."

"Why do you suppose that is?"

"I don't know."

"Because you're getting used to it. You're starting to like it. Ain't ya?"

"I don't see what this has to do with—"

"But it does. Don't you get it? The longer you live with the demon, the more a part of you it becomes. There will come a time when you won't even care about being human anymore."

"How do I stop it?"

"By keeping your humanity."

"How am I supposed to keep it when I'm constantly becoming the wolf?" Samuel demanded. Even now, he felt the creature inside him. Oh, it was asleep, resting deeply, but not for long. It would rouse soon enough. Come the next full moon it would be growling to get loose and taste blood.

"The only way is to keep what makes you human close to your heart. You see, your heart is the one thing that's truly yours. The beast wishes it could destroy your heart, but if it does, then it will die as well. The heart keeps you alive, Mr. Whittle. If you can listen to it, even when the wolf takes over, then you have a chance."

"There has to be more to it than that."

"If you keep your heart and your humanity, then you might be able to convince a person—particularly a person you care about—to touch you, even in that savage, destructive form. Then you got a chance to break the spell—or so I heard. You see, Mr. Whittle, the demon hates gentleness. That touch, by someone who cares for you enough to risk themselves to save you, should drive the demon out and leave your heart intact."

"Touch me." Samuel nearly laughed. Such a thing was impossible. "You mean, rest a hand on me when all I want to do is tear things apart?"

Longmeadow nodded, his eyes narrowed as he puffed on the pipe. "You see, Mr. Whittle, the demon is made of human hatred. Every time an act of violence is done, it creates sort of a spirit of its own. Those spirits attract one another, melt together, and travel all over the place, just looking for somewhere to land and bite. Once bitten, the victim is infected with violence. The demon couldn't be happier because it once again has an outlet to the violence it was borne of. Around the time of all those battles, there was plenty of violence and hatred floating all over the colonies, plenty of spirits looking for a place to cause more trouble."

"How did you learn about these spirits?"

"From my grandfather."

"How did he know?"

"He was a student of what some call the dark arts. They can be dark or they can be light. What matters is how you use them."

"Some people believe such studies are evil." This entire conversation unsettled Samuel. Everything about John Longmeadow, from his primitive home to his piercing eyes, spoke of powers outside the mortal world. Powers that resembled the man/wolf curse too closely.

"Don't I know it. How do you think my family ended up living in these woods? It was my grandfather who built this place around the end of the last century. I grew up here with him and my parents. Now I'm the only one of us left. Long ago in Salem, there were some witch trials you might have heard about?"

"Yes."

"Nobody on trial really knew anything about the craft, but Grandfather was the real thing. He knew there were some folks getting ready to accuse him next. Late one night, he took his family and came here. Before he died, he taught my mother, father, and me everything he knew."

"Aren't you afraid of letting people know?"

"The reverend is the only one who even knows I'm here. One night about twenty years ago, he was visiting with a family who farms a few miles from here. He had a riding accident. When I found him he was half-dead. Ended up staying with me for the better part of a month. He's never betrayed me yet. Just keeps trying to convert me. That's why when he asked for my help with you, I knew it had to be the real thing."

"So all I need is for someone to touch me in my wolf form?"

"Yes, but you touching them won't work, so don't try cornering some poor person and hoping you'll earn release. The touch must be by someone who cares for you, and you must willingly allow it."

"I don't think I could without killing them." Samuel ran a hand through his hair and sighed. "This will never work. Thank you for your help, anyway."

Longmeadow nodded. Samuel felt the man's gaze on him as he left the cabin and stepped back into the winter chill.

It seemed he would be cursed forever — or until death.

Chapter Seven

Maggie sighed and stroked the horse's neck. She pulled her hood more snugly around her and strained to see any sign of Samuel. He'd been gone for quite a long time, or so it seemed.

"It's starting to snow," the reverend noted, edging his horse closer to Maggie's. "We should wait for him back home."

"I'm not leaving without Samuel."

Before the reverend could protest, Samuel stepped into the clearing. In spite of his companions' questions and curious glances, he swung silently onto the horse. Maggie felt odd stiffness in the way he held her and sensed whatever he and John Longmeadow had spoken of had upset him.

"Well?" asked the reverend as they headed out of the woods. "What did he say?"

"Nothing of use."

"Surely he had something to tell you?" Maggie glanced over her shoulder. She tried meeting Samuel's gaze, but it remained fixed on the path ahead.

"He said the only way to break the curse is for someone to touch me in wolf form."

"Touch you?" The reverend's brow furrowed. "But, Samuel, there's no getting near you when the demon takes you. Unless there's some way to render you unconscious and—"

"It won't work. According to Longmeadow, it must be a caring touch that I willingly allow."

The reverend shook his head and murmured, "Pity. What a pity."

Maggie remained silent, her pulse racing. Gently she rested her gloved hand atop one of Samuel's which held the reins in front of her. Touch him in wolf form. That's all it took. A single touch and he'd be free.

By the time they reached home, snow was still falling lightly. The reverend had left them at the bend in the road and returned to town.

"Something wrong, Maggie?" Samuel asked as they dismounted.

"No. I'll go fix supper."

She took a step toward the house, but he grasped her waist with one arm and tugged her close. "Look at me."

Gazing into his eyes she drew a deep breath and released it slowly. Samuel had kind eyes. Strong eyes. In spite of all they'd seen, there was no bitterness in them, only a flicker of sorrow. Warmth from his body flowed into hers, even through their layers of clothes. His breath fanned her lips and cheek.

"Tell me what you're thinking," he said.

She shook her head. "It's silly really."

"What?"

"I was wishing that Mr. Longmeadow might have an instant cure, that you'd walk into the woods a half-wolf and return a whole man."

He smiled. "That's not so silly. I was hoping for the same thing."

Sliding her arms around his neck, she stood on tiptoe and kissed him before walking to the house while he tended the horse.

By the time he returned, the snow was falling more heavily outside, but the kitchen was warmed by the stove and the parlor heated by the fire.

Samuel stepped into the house, stomping snow from his feet.

"I'll take your cloak." Maggie reached for the heavy, wet wool garment as he shrugged it off. Ice crystals sprinkled his hair and eyebrows. The sharp ridges of his cheekbones were tinged red from the cold and when he grasped her arms and tugged her close for a kiss, his lips felt cool. They warmed beneath the gentle stroking of her tongue.

Maggie's eyes slipped shut. Had it not been for the wet cloak pressed between them, she might have forgotten about supper and chores and accompanied him directly to the bedroom.

As he released her, he stroked her face with his fingertips and gazed at her with such intensity that her stomach clenched and moist heat seeped from her pussy. Her nipples tightened and her pulse throbbed. How she wanted to feel him between her legs, so strong and hard like an untamed stallion. She could almost feel his lips and tongue teasing her nipples, licking, circling, tugging, rubbing.

"Warm yourself by the fire," she said. "There's still some time before supper."

Maggie hung his cloak on the hook by the stove. As she turned back to the parlor, she crashed into Samuel's bare chest. Gasping, her heart raced with surprise and stirrings of desire. The sight of his broad, well-muscled chest covered with curling hair made her mouth go dry.

"Sorry, Maggie. Didn't mean to frighten you."

"Just surprised, that's...all." Her voice faded as he stepped back, offering her a view of his nude body. His lean waist, strong hips, powerful legs, and best of all, his heavy balls and thick, semi-erect cock that seemed to grow before her eyes had her clit throbbing without so much as a touch.

"You said we have time before supper." His lips slid into an arousing smile as he gently grasped her arms and tugged her close. "I thought of a few ways we might spend it."

She drew a deep breath and unfastened her apron. He took it from her hand and tossed it aside, then removed her dress. The fabric pooled at her feet and she stood before him in her shift, her nipples poking against the thin material. He bent and captured one nipple between his lips. Using his teeth and tongue, he teased it through the shift. The material grew so wet that it almost felt as if the nipple was bare to his carnal motions. Desire shot through her, tingling and teasing.

Maggie's eyes slipped shut as she clutched his head closer, her breathing ragged. "Oh, Samuel. It feels so good, so —"

He stood suddenly and hoisted her onto the square wooden table in the center of the room.

"Not here." Maggie was aghast. Yet in spite of her modesty which protested the improper position, arousal coursed through her. How good it would feel to sate their passion on the hard wooden table like a couple of animals unable to control themselves. "But —"

His mouth covered hers, silencing her protests as he raised her shift and spread her legs. Long, gentle fingers slipped into her drenched pussy then circled her clit. His tongue thrust into her mouth in time with his stroking fingers. Faster, faster, faster. The climax built, burning Maggie from the inside out. Tightening, pulsing, stealing her sight and hearing, save the pounding of her heart.

Just when she was on the verge of shattering, his fingers left her. Dragging her to the edge of the table, he entered her with a long, slow thrust. Inch upon inch of his steely rod filled her while his thumb rolled over her clit. The sensations were almost unbearable. This was too much pleasure. She couldn't wait. By the time he reached the hilt, she burst in orgasm. Her pussy throbbed and squeezed his cock until he groaned.

Yet, when her eyes opened and her senses returned, he was still buried deep inside her.

Gazing into his eyes, Maggie took his face in her hands. "I can do it, you know." When he narrowed his eyes in question, she continued, "I can touch you and break the curse."

"No." He pulled back a bit, his cock sliding out partway. "It's too dangerous."

She wrapped her legs around his waist and jerked him close, deep inside her once again. "It's worth the risk."

"Not to me. How could I bear it if anything happened to you, if I hurt—or worse—killed you?" As gently as he could, he pulled away. Running a hand through his hair, he paced the room. His worry and confusion was almost a tangible thing. Maggie pulled down her shift and approached him. She rested a hand on his arm and he paused, his gaze meeting hers.

"You say you can remember things when the demon takes you. You're chained. If you can control it for even a short time, we have a chance."

His powerful chest expanded against her breasts as he drew a deep breath and shook his head.

"Do you plan on staying like this for the rest of your life?"

"No." He murmured. "This will be the last time."

"What do you mean?"

"I'm asking Paul to use the bullet."

"No." She sank her nails into his shoulders as panic gripped her. "I will not lose you, Samuel."

"Maggie, please. Don't make this more difficult than it has to be. I have until the next full moon. I want to share those weeks with you, or as much of them as I can. I know the closer to the change the more difficult I become to live with."

"Why are you so willing to die but not take the chance to live?"

"Because I won't trade your life for mine."

"If you're set on this, then why not let me try just once? If anything goes wrong, Paul will be there with the bullet, ready to—to kill you, if that's how it must be."

He held her gaze and stroked her face. "I'll think about it."

"I'm not going to let you go easily, Samuel."

"You'll be taken care of. This house, my inheritance, it will be yours, Maggie."

"I don't care about those things. I want you."

"And I want you safe. You're the only person who has stood by me through every moment. You've never abandoned me, Maggie. Even through the worst times."

"That's why I know I can help you, if you'll let me."

"I don't know what will happen when the wolf comes, if I'll be able to control myself enough to let you touch me."

"I can't imagine how hard it must be for you," she murmured. Even as the full moon neared, he became wilder and prone to uncharacteristic bouts of temper. "I also know how strong you are, Samuel. You've endured this for years. I know you can control yourself enough to let me touch you."

"You have more faith than I do." He wrapped his arms around her and rested his cheek against the top of her head.

Maggie stroked up and down his back. She gripped his shoulders then slid her hands down his sides and grasped his buttocks. The hard, warm globes felt so good against her palms. His cock pushed against her, still so hard and ready.

Pressing kisses over his chest and his flat, firm stomach, Maggie slid down his body and sank to her knees.

"Maggie." His voice was husky with longing.

"Hmm," she purred, clasping the velvet-skinned rod and guiding the smooth, ruddy head between her lips. Closing her eyes, she enjoyed his texture and scent as she rolled her tongue over and over the head. How marvelous he felt, so thick in her mouth and hard in her hands. Sucking on his cockhead while lashing it with her tongue, she moved one hand from shaft to balls. She squeezed and rolled the warm, hair-dusted sac.

"Maggie, my love," he rasped as her sucking quickened and her stroking hands increased their pressure and tempo. His entire body stiffened as he thrust his hips forward. She sensed he was keeping a tight harness on his passion or else he would have thrust her across the room. Unable to resist, she moved her hand from his balls to his buttocks. The muscles were rock-hard and so, so arousing. She stroked the backs of his flexing thighs, then his inner thighs. Samuel groaned, his breathing ragged.

"Stop," He gasped, his fingers tightening in her hair, but Maggie had no intention of stopping. She clung to him, her lips and tongue working on him while her hands squeezed, kneaded, and stroked. Her fingertips pressed the sensitive flesh between his balls and buttocks, then pushed against the sphincter itself.

With a wild cry of rapture, Samuel's entire body stiffened then pulsed as he came. At the last moment, his cock popped free of her mouth and splattered both of them with a seemingly endless stream of cum.

"Maggie, oh, God," he gasped, dragging her to her feet and into his arms.

Resting her cheek against his chest, she listened to the slowing rhythm of his heart.

Come the next full moon, my love. Maggie languidly stroked his back. *Come the next full moon...*

Chapter Eight

Tapping sounded on the kitchen door. Maggie finished drying a china dish and placed it in the cupboard. Tossing her cloth aside, she opened the door and found herself staring into Clay Stratford's leering face. Her gut twisted with disgust. Clay was the only son of Edgar Stratford, the same man who, just a week ago, had led the group of townsfolk to Whittle House, bent on killing Samuel. The Stratfords owned the store in town from which Samuel bought food and other supplies to keep the house running smoothly. He paid a ridiculous price for the goods to be delivered, since the citizens dispersed every time he walked into town. For a while, Maggie had gone to town instead, but the people's whispered remarks about her soon turned to outright ridicule. She never told Samuel what happened. Only when she returned one afternoon with a cut and bruised face where some hidden coward had struck her with a rock did he realize that his curse extended to her as well. Rumor was only an evil woman could stay under the same roof as the man-wolf.

Most everyone in town hated Samuel. Only good, old-fashioned greed prompted the Stratfords to continue selling to Whittle House.

"Got your supplies out there on the wagon." Clay leaned a shoulder against the door, his cracked lips parting as he ran his tongue over them. "Want me to bring 'em in?"

"Yes, please."

"Gonna pay me extra for the service?"

"I believe you get paid enough, sir."

"It's cold out here, Maggie." Clay reached out and grasped a lock of her dark hair between his dirt-encrusted thumb and forefinger. "Thought you might ask me in to warm myself by the fire, then maybe you and I could—"

"You thought wrong." Maggie knocked his hand away and shoved him. Rage boiled inside her at the man's audacity. She was tired of women, especially black women, being treated with such disrespect, especially from contemptible bastards like Clay.

"Calm down, sweetheart. I thought your kind of woman was used to spreading your legs and breedin' on command."

The door opened and Samuel stepped inside. His gaze fixed on Clay like a hawk's ready to swoop in for the kill. The younger man took a step backwards and cleared his throat. "Mr. Whittle. Got your supplies."

"Then why are you standing here? Get them." Samuel's voice was just short of a growl.

Clay nodded and walked away.

"Did he give you a problem?" Samuel approached Maggie and rested a hand on the small of her back.

Gazing up at him, she felt mildly unsettled. She recognized his expression. The wolf was on its way. Awakening, yawning, preparing for the kill soon to come. His eyes looked sharper than normal, their expression just a bit harder than the Samuel she loved. Stubble dusted his jaw and his teeth gleamed white against his lips. Part of her wanted to tell him about Clay's harassment, but another part of her, the one that knew what the wolf was capable of, stopped her.

"There was no problem." She smiled slightly and returned to drying the dishes. Samuel stepped outside.

Through the window over the sink, Maggie saw him join Clay in unloading crates and barrels of supplies. Together the men carried them to the pantry.

When they'd finished, they stood in the kitchen where Clay collected his fee from Samuel.

"Same time and same supplies next month?" Clay asked before he left.

"Yes, except for one thing. Do you have any bolts of forest green silk?"

"Forest green silk?" Clay narrowed his eyes. "Maybe. If we don't, we can see about getting it."

"Do that." Samuel passed Clay extra bills to cover his additional order.

Nodding, the tall, skinny man left the house. Maggie closed the door behind him and glanced at Samuel. "Green silk?"

"You like green, don't you?"

"Very much."

"Good. You can make yourself a new dress."

"But silk? It's so expensive, and where would a servant wear silk?"

"You're more than a servant, Maggie. You know that. If you don't want the material, I can—"

"No." Maggie smiled. "I'd like it very much. I've never worn silk before."

He stroked her face and traced her lips with his fingertips. "I can scarcely wait to see you in it."

Samuel tugged her into his arms so swiftly she gasped. The surprised sound was stifled by his kiss. Cupping the back of her neck, he held her close while his other hand caressed her back and hip.

Maggie closed her eyes and tightened her arms around Samuel's neck. Leaning against him, she allowed him to support her almost completely as their tongues stroked one another.

Samuel jerked away suddenly and again Maggie started, her heart pounding. "What's wrong?"

She followed his gaze out the window to where Clay sat in his wagon, staring at the couple. A sick feeling wound its way through Maggie's stomach. The young man curled his lip before turning away and slapping the reins against his horse's back.

"Peeping little bastard," Samuel snarled, striding toward the door.

"Samuel." Maggie grasped his arm, frightened by the look in his eyes. "Forget about him."

"Who does he think he is, watching in windows? You know how his people love to spread rumors—"

"Samuel, he doesn't matter. Please."

His gaze turned to Maggie. Some of the wildness faded. He forced a slight smile and kissed her brow. "You're right. Everything is irritating me this morning. I think I'll go chop some wood for awhile. Maybe it will help me expel some of this damnable energy."

Maggie nodded and kissed his cheek. "That's a good idea."

As he left the kitchen, she drew a deep breath. It was only just beginning. The nearer the full moon, the wilder Samuel became. It would be different this time. So different. She and Samuel had never been lovers before. In the past, when he threw his temper fits or went wild, she would carry on her work, making herself as invisible as possible and by hiding in her room as often as she could. Would she be able to do the same now? Probably not. As the full moon approached, Samuel would often disappear at night. When he returned, he carried the heavy scent of brothel perfume. Sometimes she washed blood out of his shirts. One morning when she'd accidentally seen him after he'd finished his bath, there had been raw scratches on his back.

Samuel was a gentle lover, but the wolf seemed to infect his carnal appetite as well. Would that savage sexuality now be turned to her? Inside she trembled, but to her dismay, it wasn't simply from fear. Something about sex with the wolf thrilled her. Would he possess her? Would he be very rough? Perhaps he'd fling her to her knees, wrap an arm around her waist, and take her from behind, wolf-like.

Maggie's breathing had quickened and her pussy was wet with passion. Shaking her head, she concentrated on her work, but always her thoughts returned to savage, animal sex with the man-wolf.

* * * * *

Maggie stoked the fire in the parlor and glanced at the clock on the mantel. It was nearing midday. The meal she'd prepared was just about ready to serve, so she hoped Samuel would return from wood chopping soon.

Placing aside the fire iron, she straightened her apron on the way to the kitchen. She was about to stir the stew when Samuel stepped in through the back door. Her stomach fluttered and her pulse raced just looking at him. Several locks of his long, dark hair had loosened from the ribbon binding it at his nape and clung to his perspiring face and neck. His white shirt was untied, exposing a good portion of his throat and chest.

Glancing at her with a smile, he stomped slush from his knee-high black boots and removed his waistcoat, tossing it aside. The shirt beneath was transparent with sweat, revealing every curve of muscle and the dark mat of hair covering his chest. "The food smells excellent."

"It'll be on the table straight away. Change out of those wet clothes before you become ill."

"Maggie, I haven't been ill since the curse. It's as if I'm immune now that the demon's in me."

"Then that's one good thing about it."

An amused expression shone in his eyes as he pulled off the boots and left them by the door.

"I'll bring some water to your room," she said, glancing at him as he left the kitchen. Her temperature rose at the sight of his wet shirt clinging to his broad shoulders and powerful back.

Moments later, she stepped into his room. He stood by the window, gazing out with a far-off expression but turned to her almost immediately. Placing the pitcher of water by the washbowl and cloth on his nightstand, she stared as he slipped off the shirt and used the garment to wipe his face and chest.

"Looks like you got plenty of work done," she said.

Nodding, he approached and poured the water into the basin. Maggie's mouth went dry as she stared at his gorgeous torso. Heat emanated from his body. Resisting the urge to squirm with desire, she reached for the washcloth and dipped it in the water.

She noticed a quickening of his breath as she ran the wet cloth over his chest and down his ribs. Maggie's clit throbbed as she washed his arms and the small of his back. Her nipples tightened as she wet the cloth again and swept it across his broad shoulders. Unable to resist, she pressed soft kisses down his spine, sinking almost to her knees. She moved to his front and ran her tongue from his navel to his breastbone. He was such a handsome, irresistible man.

"Raise your arms," she whispered.

He stretched the long, rock-hard appendages overhead, the motion tightening his sleek muscles even more. Maggie soaked the towel and ran it under each of his arms. Rivulets of water trickled down his sides. Tossing the towel into the basin, she ran her hands over his chest and ribs. Her pulse raced and she panted with desire. The washing had cooled his flesh a bit, but it warmed beneath her hands and lips as she covered his chest and flat belly with kisses. His stomach clenched when she lapped it with the flat of her tongue while using her hands to caress his inner thighs. She cupped his bulging crotch. His cock and balls were far too big for her hand. She kneaded and squeezed as much as she could hold.

"God, Maggie." His voice was practically a growl as he flung her on the bed and began unfastening her apron and dress. She relished his enthusiasm and the rising power of the wolf. His fingers, usually so deft, fumbled with the buttons and ties. He cursed under his breath.

"Let me help you," she murmured.

He pushed her hands aside. With a swift tug, he ripped the dress down her body. Buttons flew across the wooden floor.

Maggie's eyes widened and she drew a sharp breath. "My dress."

"I'm sorry," he breathed against her lips before crushing them with his. She closed her eyes and yanked the ribbon from his hair. The kiss was demanding yet tender. His tongue stroked and thrust against hers. His mouth didn't leave hers as he grasped the front of her shift and tore it in two.

"Samuel, what are you doing?" she gasped.

He sat up, continuing to rip the shift down the entire length of her body. When she tried standing, he pinned her to the bed, licking and kissing the hollow of her shoulder. Maggie's pulse raced. It was the wolf inside him, thrusting forward to appease his lust. It frightened her but she loved it. It felt so good to be claimed, plundered, and desired by him.

Samuel cupped one of her breasts and rolled the nipple between his thumb and forefinger, teasing it to a hard peak. Passionate quivers coursed through her from head to toe when he slid down the length of her body and took her nipple in his mouth. He sucked it and teased it with his tongue while dipping a hand between her legs and sliding two fingers deep into her wet pussy. Using the tip of one moist finger, he circled and stroked her clit as he continued laving her nipple. Within moments Maggie convulsed, trembling and moaning in orgasm.

As she quivered, he covered her body with his and entered her with a long, swift thrust. Grasping her hands and pinning them above her head, he stroked into her fast and hard while rimming her lips with his tongue. Maggie panted and thrashed beneath him, her body aflame. Her nipples, so hard and tight, rubbed against his hair-roughened chest. Wrapping her legs around him, she thrust her hips in time with his.

"Ahh, Samuel," she panted, her tongue meeting his. He gently nipped her lower lip then laved her neck with the flat of his tongue. Maggie's moans turned to high-pitched cries of passion as she neared her peak again.

Kissing her deeply, he thrust faster. Exquisite sensations flooded Maggie's body. Just before she shattered, he released her hands. She clung to him hard with arms and legs. Her fingers gripped his hot, damp back. Her heels drove into his steely calves.

"Oh, Samuel," she whispered, gazing at him through half-open eyes as she caught her breath.

With a wolfish grin, he pulled out almost to the tip of his cock then slid in slowly.

"You taste so good, Maggie. You feel so good."

She clung tighter to his neck. "I wish we could stay like this forever."

"I love you," he said against her lips before kissing her. His cock shifted in and out of her hot, aching pussy. It seemed he was in the perfect mood to satisfy her desire over and over again.

His thrusts were slow and steady. Even as her climax built, he refused to speed his movements. Maggie felt hot enough to burst as she gasped and wriggled beneath him. She clung to his neck and tugged on his rock-hard shoulders. He growled and continued those frustratingly slow and oh-so-delicious thrusts.

"Please, Samuel," she gasped, closing her eyes and wrapping her arms around his neck. Rather than drag him closer, she only succeeded in raising herself off the bed. "Faster, please. Faster."

Laughter rumbled in his chest, but he obliged. Her pulse pounded as her entire body exploded in wave after wave of orgasm. With a savage cry, he rammed into her with a long, hard thrust and came, surging into her wet, throbbing pussy.

Chapter Nine
One Week Later

Maggie glanced at the clock she polished without really seeing it. Her worried thoughts focused on Samuel. With less than two weeks until the full moon, he seemed more out of control than ever. Last night she'd leapt awake to find him thrashing in the bed beside her. Growling, he tore apart sheets and splintered the nightstand. Maggie's first thought was to flee. Instead she'd shouted his name until he awoke. His gaze had fixed on her. Rage turned to sorrow, though the wildness never faded completely. Grasping her arm, he'd dragged her to her room and told her to lock the door.

She'd heard him pacing until dawn when he left for the stable. He never returned for the breakfast she cooked. Horse tracks led from the barn across the snowy field and disappeared into the horizon.

When Samuel had returned about an hour ago, both he and the horse were drenched in sweat. He's scarcely spoken to her as he rubbed the animal down, so she'd returned to the house.

Fear greater than any she'd ever known filled her heart. Not fear of remaining with Samuel. She'd endured his curse alongside him for too long for it to drive her off. Her fear was that, when the time came, she would not bring herself to touch the beast. In order for her to reach him, Samuel would need to muster the greatest self-control imaginable. Still in the form of a man, he already seemed to be losing to the wolf's savageness.

She placed the polished clock back on the mantel. For a moment she stared at the brick hiding the silver cuffs. She removed it and grasped them, running her fingertips over their smoothness. The workmanship was perfect. Paul's finest.

Strange that touching these tools of restraint, she felt an almost erotic thrill. Knowing that they harnessed the wolf's power, held him as he panted, strained, and raged in the throes of his violent hunger, excited her.

"Thinking of the beast?"

Maggie jumped, her pulse racing, as Samuel's arm encircled her waist while his other hand covered hers around the cuffs. He'd moved so silently—like a predator—that she hadn't heard him enter the house.

"Yes," she said.

"What were you thinking?"

"I wondered how these cuffs held him."

"Oh." Samuel spun her so she faced him. The rich brown beard covered his jaw and his eyebrows seemed to extend a bit longer off toward his temples, giving him a look of demonic beauty. He leaned closer, his finely shaped nostrils flaring a bit as he sniffed her neck and cheek. The tip of his tongue traced the shape of her ear before he spoke into it in a gruff whisper, "Curious how it feels to be restrained, are you?"

Maggie thought her heart might explode both from terror and arousal. Good sense told her to push him away, try to force him back to reality and far from the wolf's desires. A woman of good sense wouldn't have chosen to remain, the only servant, in the house of a cursed man, no matter how bewitching he was.

"Well, Maggie?" This time his husky words were whispered inches from her lips.

"Yes. I'd like to know."

He smiled, his teeth gleaming white in contrast to his dark beard. Tearing the cuffs from her hand, he tossed her over his shoulder and walked up the steps.

Maggie dangled down his back, already panting from desire and apprehension. She slipped her hands down his breeches and grasped his bare bottom, feeling the hard muscles tighten even more with every step he took. How she wanted him.

In his room, he dumped her on the bed and tore off his clothes. Maggie did the same, grateful he wasn't bent on destroying another dress and shift. She didn't have many clothes as it was.

Kicking off her shoes and stockings, she faced him, naked. He stood at the foot of the bed, gazing at her, his jaw clenched and his eyes more piercing than ever. Just looking at his well-muscled, nude body had her insides quivering. He held the silver cuffs in one hand while lashing them into his opposite palm.

Maggie waited, her lips parted as she drew sips of air. He sprang on her so suddenly she cried out. A knee resting on either side of her, he straddled her body. She inhaled deeply, loving the scent of his thick, erect cock just brushing her lips. The smooth head felt so wonderful she couldn't resist a lick.

He growled as he wound the heavy chain through the design in the wooden headboard and snapped the silver cuffs on her wrists. As he did this, she sucked and licked his cock. Her tongue swirled over the head and traced the underside. Samuel braced his hands on the headboard and closed his eyes, panting and thrusting his cock deeper into her mouth. She continued laving and sucking. When it brushed the back of her throat, she prayed she wouldn't choke, but he didn't push any further. Slowly, he pulled out and covered her body with his.

He licked her lips and kissed her, his tongue stroking hers.

"Do you like being bound?" He dropped kisses from her jaw to her navel.

"Ye...yes," she gasped as he licked under both breasts then took a nipple between his lips and sucked hard, as she'd done to his cock. The sensation was incredible. Perhaps it was knowing she was tied, but every lick, kiss, and touch seemed more thrilling and her body felt more sensitive than ever before.

Cupping a breast in each hand, he kneaded them, squeezing and rolling the nipples, as he licked his way down her belly.

"Oh, Samuel," she gasped as he nipped her hip—not hard enough to draw blood, but enough to send a thrill of pleasure/pain coursing through her.

Suddenly his mouth covered her clit, his lips tugging upon the plump, aroused flesh. Using the very tip of his tongue he ran it up and down one side then the other, repeating the motions until her breath came in frantic sobs and she strained against the silver bonds.

"Please, Samuel," she moaned when he stopped just before she shattered in climax. "Please, don't make me wait."

"Wait for what?" he snarled.

"You know what."

"Tell me."

"That feeling…"

"Tell me what feeling," he demanded, pressing kisses to her inner thighs. His beard scraped her soft, smooth flesh in the most erotic manner. He acted so animalistic, almost brutal, yet he never crossed the line of causing her pain. Samuel was still there. The man who loved her lurked beneath the wolf, holding him back, keeping him human. "Tell me in great detail, Maggie."

"I want to feel your tongue on me in that throbbing, aching place between my legs."

"More."

"I want…Oh, God," she cried as he lapped her clit with several fast, delectable strokes then stopped. "I want to feel your lips on the same place. Pulling, kissing."

She uttered a high-pitched mewl of desire as he obliged.

"Talk to me, Maggie. Tell me everything you want. I want to hear you while you climb toward perfection. I want to hear you at the moment of explosion."

Maggie's pulse raced. Her breasts heaved with each marvelously tortured breath. What he asked was impossible.

How could she talk and feel such wonderful things at the same time?

"Tell me," he roared, running a long finger down the length of her clit for emphasis.

"I want your tongue inside my entrance. Licking the outer lips… Sliding inside… Thrusting. Oh. Ohh, Samuel. Yes. Yes…" She gasped, her eyes tightly closed and her voice trembling as he pushed her writhing body towards a shattering climax. Still, she needed more. Just a little more. "I want you to lick between my legs. That little nub of flesh that's so sensitive. Push the flat of your tongue on it… Oh. Just like that… Don't move your tongue, but stick your fingers inside me, too."

Maggie thought she might faint from excitement. He'd done such things to her before, but never tied up, never by her instruction. She was feeling exactly what she wanted to feel, exactly where she wanted to feel it. Nothing could be this good.

"Keep rubbing. Keeping licking. Keep…keep…" She could scarcely talk anymore. Her breath came in harsh gasps. Heat enveloped her entire body. Blood pounded beneath her flesh and her heart knocked hard against her ribs. Suddenly another idea struck her. Something she'd never felt but knew would be incredible. "Between…my…quim…"

"Uh?" She heard the laughter in his inarticulate question. He couldn't use words of course. His lips and tongue were far too busy with her clit.

"Between my…quim and…bottom. The flesh…there. Oh, there," she moaned. His thumb found the soft, sensitive skin of her perineum. He pushed upon it gently. He stroked and tickled it with feathery touches while his fingers thrust into her pussy, his tongue lapped her clit, and his free hand pinched and caressed her nipples. Maggie couldn't endure anymore. With a shriek that left her hoarse, she came, writhing and bucking, her body misted with sweat, her wrists straining against the silver bonds.

The orgasm seemed to last forever. As it ebbed, she lay, panting and drained, enveloped in darkness but decadently fulfilled.

He freed her hands and stretched out on the bed beside her, gathering her to his chest as he stroked her hair and kissed her forehead.

"I love you, Maggie," he whispered.

"I love you, too, Samuel." Sighing with contentment, she cuddled close to his warmth.

Chapter Ten
The evening before the full moon

Maggie tried keeping her hand steady as she raised the spoonful of soup to her lips. Her attention focused on Samuel who sat across from her, devouring a chicken leg. The juice stained his chiseled lips, making them shine. His sharp white teeth tore tender flesh then gnashed the bone in a manner that almost made Maggie jump.

He paused, licking his lips and gazing at her with eyes that seemed to glow.

Over the past weeks, she'd grown accustomed to dining with him. At first she'd protested sharing a table with her employer. It went against all accepted rules, but Samuel had been adamant about it.

"You're no longer just my servant, Maggie," he'd said. "When and if we get through this, we will share everything as man and woman. Everything."

His implication filled her with joy, yet such happiness and such a promise came at a price.

Both were paying it now, Samuel doing his best to cling to humanity and Maggie fighting to remain calm and not flee from his unsettling presence.

"What's the matter?" He tossed the clean bone aside and drummed his fingers on the smooth, wooden tabletop.

"Nothing."

"You're a liar."

Maggie drew a deep breath and placed her spoon beside her dish. "Perhaps you should lie down. You look a bit —"

He laughed, a most humorless sound. "Lie down? My dear, I feel like I could run from here to Boston, or fight a bear. That's the only thing I miss about having King George's army around. A fresh supply of redcoats to clean my teeth on."

"You don't mean that." At least she hoped he didn't.

"Don't I?" Samuel stood, nearly toppling over his chair. Maggie's heart pounded when he grasped her arms and dragged her to her feet. "Maybe I can sate myself with you, instead." He thrust his pelvis against her. The hard bulge of his cock pressed against her belly.

"Samuel, this isn't you. It's the wolf. You must fight it."

"You're afraid of me." He buried his face in her shoulder and inhaled deeply. "I can smell it."

"Samuel, please."

"The last time you said 'Samuel, please' you were flat on your back with your luscious body wrapped around mine. Don't you want it again, love?"

"Yes, but not like this."

Her gaze held his for a long moment. His jaw tightened and he swallowed audibly. Brushing her mouth with a tender kiss, he loosened his grip on her arms and caressed her face. "I'm sorry, Maggie."

"Samuel. Where are you going?" She chased him to the door where he grabbed his cloak off the tall wooden rack and flung it over his shoulders as he stepped outside. "Samuel."

"I'm going to town. I can't stay here," he called, trudging toward the barn.

Town. To the whores. The ones he paid to claw his back and heaven knew what else.

"No." She chased him, not caring that she wore no cloak though the snowdrifts were almost to her knees. "Samuel, don't."

He turned and caught her up in his arms. "Are you crazy, woman? You'll catch your death out here."

"Don't go to town."

He glared at her, his teeth bared, as he carried her back to the house and placed her on the chair in front of the fire.

"Samuel, fight this demon." She took his face in her hands. Pouring all her affection into her gaze, she prayed he would listen to her pleas. "You can do it, Samuel. I believe in you."

"Maggie." He embraced her tightly. Too tightly. He tugged away, his eyes blazing, and spoke to her through clenched teeth that were far too pointed. "I must go."

This time when he left, she remained in the chair by the fire, staring at the leaping flames.

* * * * *

A little over an hour later, Maggie walked to her room and stoked the fire there. With a last, hopeful glance toward the road leading to town, she drew the heavy drapes and undressed. Barefoot, wearing only her shift, she removed the pins from her hair and shook out the thick, black tresses. Sitting at the foot of her bed, she brushed her hair and wondered what Samuel was doing. Part of her didn't want to know while another part of her wished she'd had the courage to demand he vent his passion on her. Of late their lovemaking had been incredibly wild, sometimes a bit frightening, but always fulfilling. Only today had she felt any real terror of him. The wolf was almost here. Tomorrow, there would be little, if any, of Samuel left.

At the sound of hoofbeats, she leapt off the bed and raced to the window. Samuel was back.

Her brow furrowed upon seeing a strange chestnut horse, bathed in moonlight, standing in front of the house. The rider, tall and thin, dismounted. His hood fell back, revealing Clay Stratford's elongated features.

Maggie drew a deep breath, apprehension clutching her breast. What did *he* want?

He pounded on the door. Something told her it was best not to open it to him—not with Samuel in town.

She opened the window and shouted, "What do you want?"

"Maggie?" Clay took a step back from the door and stared up at her, a leering grin on his face. "Let me in. It's cold out here."

"Come back tomorrow. Mr. Whittle is not taking visitors right now."

"Of course he's not. He's in town. Saw him ride in. I can give you a little sample of what he's doing, love." Clay parted his cloak and grabbed the bulge in his breeches, jouncing it a few times.

Disgusted, Maggie slammed the window shut and reached for her robe. She walked across the hall to Samuel's room where he kept his rifle. At the sound of an enormous bang from downstairs, she nearly screamed. She was loading the bullet when Clay stepped into the room.

"Well, what's this?" He grinned, stepping forward and snatching the rifle's barrel.

"Get out of here."

He tried yanking the rifle from her, but Maggie was stronger than he imagined. She kicked him hard in the shin and he punched her square in the face, sending her flying onto her back.

Blood gushed from her nose and her eyes filled with tears so she could hardly see.

Clay dragged her onto the bed. Maggie struggled, kicking, clawing, and biting, though she couldn't clearly discern where she struck due to her watering eyes. By the sound of Clay's grunts and gasps, she was hurting him as much as he was hurting her.

Suddenly he was wrenched from her. Wiping her eyes, she saw Clay on the floor, his face and clothes ripped from her nails, his eyes unfocused as he struggled to his feet. Samuel stood over him, his legs spread apart, his eyes glowing and his teeth bared. He growled, the sound not quite human, not quite animal.

"What the hell are you doing?" Samuel bellowed, dragging Clay to his feet and punching him before he could reply. The blow sent the younger man crashing into the window. Glass broke and Clay nearly fell out.

"She's a whore." Clay pointed a trembling finger in Maggie's direction. "She invited me—"

Clay raised his hands to defend himself, but he was no match for Samuel.

Samuel grasped him by the throat and flung him out the door. He pounced, wolf-like, landing in front of Clay.

In his terror, Clay rolled backwards, down the flight of stairs. He landed with a crash at the bottom. Maggie stood in the doorway of Samuel's room, her heart pounding and her head throbbing, both from Clay's punch and the terror that Samuel might do something drastic.

"Whoever touches my woman dies," Samuel snarled, leaping down the steps and landing in a crouch. Clay staggered out the door, bleeding and limping.

"Samuel," Maggie shouted.

He glanced at her then back at Clay. He headed for the door and Maggie did the only thing she could think of.

"Samuel, help me." She dropped to her knees, covering her bloody face with her hands. Better to play the part of a weasel, just for a little while, than for Samuel to tear Clay apart and have the entire village chasing him down.

He raced up the steps and pulled her into his arms. Carrying her to the bed, he placed her on it.

"Let me see, sweetheart." He gently moved her hands from her face. "I think the bleeding has stopped. I'll get some water."

She nodded, wiping blood on her hands as he left. Thank the Lord he hadn't murdered Clay outright, not that the vicious swine didn't deserve it. Moments later he returned with a bowl of water and a clean washcloth. Tenderly, he bathed her face.

"Your nose doesn't appear broken," he said.

"I think I'm fine."

"I should have killed the son of a bitch," Samuel growled, picking up the chair and hurling it across the room. The wood splintered.

"Will you stop it," she shouted. "I've had enough for one night, damn it."

Maggie leapt out of the bed and stomped toward the door. He caught her arm and tugged her to his chest.

Staring at her with blazing eyes, he shook his head. "I'm sorry. I'm—"

Drawing a trembling breath, Maggie wrapped her arms around his neck. "If you have excess energy, Samuel Whittle, burn it in a way we both can enjoy."

His lips parted and his breathing quickened. His cock pressed against her belly. "Haven't you had enough excitement for one night, Maggie?"

"I see." She gritted her teeth. Rage overcame any fear left over from Clay's attack. "You've spent yourself in town with those harlots."

His brow furrowed and he growled. "What are you talking about?"

"You think I don't know about the whores, Samuel? Don't forget, I'm the one who washes the blood and disgusting perfume out of your shirts. Don't think I haven't noticed the scratches on your back that you just happen to receive on those nights nearer the full moon."

"You're right, Maggie." His lip curled and his broad chest expanded with each agitated breath as he threw off his cloak. His boots, breeches, waistcoat, and shirt followed. "I did go to town to rut the hell out of the roughest whores money can buy, but I didn't do it this time. I left with a cock harder than a bayonet and a need so great I felt like ripping off my own skin. Why? Because all I could think of was you."

Maggie licked her lips, her pulse racing and her gaze fixed on him. God, the man did things to her she'd never imagined possible and couldn't find the words to explain.

She wrapped her arms around him, one hand buried in the hair at his nape, the other clutching a handful of his tight buttocks. In panting whispers, she said against his lips, "Then fill me with your hard cock and rut the hell out of me."

Samuel swept her into his arms and claimed her lips in a kiss that stole her breath. He walked to her room and placed her on the floor by the fire. While she shrugged off her robe and tugged her shift over her head, he licked and stroked the length of her legs.

Maggie sprawled on her back, her breasts heaving with each excited breath as he licked the joining of her thighs and hips then took one of her nipples in his mouth and sucked deeply.

She ran her fingers through his hair and clutched his shoulders and back.

"Hard," he demanded.

She sank her nails into his flesh and raked as he entered her with a swift thrust and howled, a sound that both thrilled and terrified her. It was pure and wolfish, though the body covering hers was warm and distinctly human male.

"Oh, Samuel," she gasped when he pulled his cock out of her and rolled her onto her stomach.

Clutching her hips, he hauled her against his erection, pushing and rubbing it against her bottom cheeks. Maggie's fingers gripped the carpet as he entered her from behind. Inch by marvelous inch, the hard, velvet-skinned rod slid into her.

As he pumped, she thrust her bottom backwards, matching his rhythm.

"Yes, yes, oh, yes," she cried.

He thrust faster, harder, driving her hot, throbbing body headlong into orgasm. Maggie's world turned black. She pulsed from head to toe, her wet, quivering pussy so wonderfully full of him.

Suddenly he released a howl that sent carnal ripples down her spine. He stiffened and came, his hands tight on her hips, his ragged breath filling the room.

Maggie collapsed on the carpet, Samuel atop her. After a moment, his warm, wet tongue lapped from her nape all the way down her spine. The action was sensual, animal-like, and she smiled with bitter joy. Unless their plan succeeded, this might be the last night they ever spent together.

Chapter Eleven

Muffled cries of agony sounded from the hidden room below Whittle House.

Maggie placed her sewing aside and stood, pacing in front of the parlor fire. Her hands twisted and she whispered prayers for Samuel and for herself, that she would find the strength to help him break the spell.

A glance at the clock told her it was nearly eight. The moon had risen hours ago, but just within the past moments had she heard the evidence of Samuel's change taking place, of the wolf taking over.

A particularly ferocious bellow caused her to jump, her pulse skipping. That afternoon Samuel had chained himself in the room below. Maggie hoped the new cuffs would hold him. Paul waited with him, his rifle loaded with the silver bullet, just in case.

The pounding of hoofbeats outside momentarily blocked out the growls from below. Maggie raced to the window and glanced out. Fear struck her like a fist. Edgar Stratford, the reverend, and a large group of townsfolk armed with rifles, muskets, and torches stopped in front of the house.

"Whittle. Samuel Whittle. We've come for you, you murdering son of a bitch," Edgar roared.

Maggie dragged on her cloak and stepped outside. Lifting her chin, she stared, unfaltering, at the crowd and said, "Mr. Whittle is not here."

"Where is he?" shouted a man from the back.

"I'll tell you where he is," bellowed Edgar, his face pale and eyes shining. "He's prowling the countryside like some rabid animal. He's out for more blood, just as he was out for Clay's."

"What are you talking about?" Maggie demanded.

"You know, slut."

"Edgar," snapped the reverend, glancing at Maggie with concern in his eyes.

"Explain yourself, sir," Maggie stated.

"When my boy Clay came here last night to ask Whittle about additional purchases from our shop, you were waiting for him. You slithered over him with your evil body and carnal touches and when he finally succumbed to your power, Whittle nearly tore him apart."

"That's not true," Maggie shouted.

"Isn't it? When my boy came to me last night, he was cut and bruised like a man who'd survived a battle. He told me Whittle said he'd kill any man who touched his slut."

"Clay broke into this house last night and attacked me."

"Liar."

"Why would she lie, Edgar?" the reverend asked. "I feel for you in your hour of pain, having just lost your son, but Clay had a tarnished reputation with the ladies of the town."

"This is no lady," Edgar roared. "She's a demon's concubine. A dark witch for the man-wolf to hump."

Maggie's eyes widened and she trembled. "What do you mean Clay is dead?"

"That demon Whittle killed him."

Maggie drew a sharp breath. "No. It's not true."

"The boy got drunk and drowned in the lake, Edgar," the reverend said. He glanced at the crowd. "All of you know it's true."

Several murmurs of agreement passed through the group.

Edgar's pale face reddened with fury. He shook the torch gripped in his fist. "He died of fear. Terror that the beast who calls himself Samuel Whittle would come after him and finish what he started last night. That's what drove him to the drink."

"What drove him to the drink was his unquenchable thirst," the reverend snapped. "You know he had a weakness for women and whiskey, Edgar."

"You bastard." Edgar turned his rage on the reverend. "And you call yourself a man of God. There's a demon right here in our town and you protect him."

Terror rose inside Maggie as the crowd roared, their fear almost tangible. For years they'd been terrified of Samuel and the stories of his curse. Even if Clay's death had been accidental, it was a fine excuse to rid themselves of Samuel.

"My boy is dead." Edgar glanced at each of the faces surrounding him. "Yours might be next. Or maybe your daughters. Rutted by the wolf and made to carry his evil whelp." The crowd uttered a collective gasp that urged Stratford on. "I'm going to scour this wilderness, find him tonight, and kill him. Are you with me?"

"We're with you," the crowd bellowed.

Maggie sighed with relief. At least they were leaving the house alone. Suddenly she screamed as Edgar lifted her into the saddle.

"Let me go." She jammed her elbows backwards.

Edgar grunted with pain but managed to press the nose of his rifle to her ribs. "Stop moving or you die right here and now, bitch."

Maggie remained still except for the furious rise and fall of her breasts. She'd had more than her fill of the damned Stratfords and the townsfolk.

"You're coming with me. I know the wolf will come for his slut. As long as I have you, more than likely I'll be the one to kill him."

"Good thinking, Edgar," shouted one of the men. "Let's go."

The crowd kicked their horses to a gallop and dispersed.

In spite of her rage, Maggie sat quietly. Keeping Edgar and the others riding over the countryside was better than having them lurk around the house. At least now, as long as the chains held, Samuel would be safe at home.

* * * * *

Samuel's agonized scream turned to a canine wail as he strained against the silver cuffs cutting through his wrists. The change took several moments, but during that time he experienced pure hell. His throat ached from screaming. Every bone and muscle in his body burned like hot coals. His racing pulse filled his ears.

Convulsions struck him as he writhed on the floor, unable to move far due to the bonds.

As his thoughts and memories faded and pure instinct took over, the pain vanished, replaced by incredible power and savage hunger. He needed to run. He needed to chase down his prey. He needed to—

The wolf's gaze fixed on the man standing in the far corner of the room. The scent of his fear was heavy on the air, yet the hands clasping the rifle were steady.

"Easy, Samuel," the man said. "I made the cuffs solid this time. You won't get loose. In a few minutes, Maggie will come down and we'll break the curse. Just stay calm."

Though unable to completely understand the words, something in the man's voice calmed the wolf's rage just a bit before blinding fury overcame him again. Howling and growling, he flung himself against the bonds in an attempt to reach his prey.

Suddenly the wolf paused, trembling, and sniffed the air. Through the layers of thick carpeting covering the little room and the wood ceiling dividing him from the main house, he caught the faint scent of townsfolk. Some were familiar scents, others were not. One stood out above all others. A beautiful aroma, feminine and sensual. He couldn't think of her name, but he discerned one primitive and raw emotion—love.

His ears twitched, picking up the sounds of arguing. Then the woman—*his woman*—screamed "*let me go*". Hoofbeats pounded then faded.

She was in danger. They were taking her away. Fresh rage overcame the wolf and he howled and growled, throwing his entire weight against the bonds. The silver burned through his flesh and hair, the pain almost unbearable, but not as unbearable as the thought of *her* in danger.

With another massive pull, the chains ripped from the wall. He was free. Leaping at the door, he burst through and raced up the narrow steps, his back legs striking the man who attempted to follow and knocking him down the stairs.

* * * * *

Maggie's nostrils curled at the reek of Edgar's rancid breath blowing against her from behind. His attention focused on the path leading through the trees.

She waited patiently for him to relax his hold on the rifle pressed to her side. If he did, then maybe, just maybe, she could escape and lose him in the woods.

Suddenly a tall bearded man appeared from behind a tree. He gazed at her and Edgar.

"Can I be of help?" he asked.

"We're looking for a wolf," stated Edgar. "A big one. If I were you, Mister, I wouldn't wander around these woods tonight."

"A big wolf you say? Haven't seen any."

Edgar grunted and nudged his horse forward.

The bearded man grasped the animal's halter.

"Get your hand off my horse." Edgar turned the gun from Maggie to the stranger who grasped the nose of the weapon and jerked. Maggie managed to keep her seat as Edgar tumbled to the ground.

"Ma'am." The bearded stranger nodded at Maggie as he fixed the rifle on Edgar. "I got the feeling you didn't want to be riding with him. You looked a bit upset."

"You bastard. I don't know who you are, but you have no idea what you've done. I'm telling you there's a mad wolf roaming loose and—"

Edgar stopped speaking and stared in horror as his captor shoved the nose of his gun against his lips.

"Why don't we have some quiet?" the bearded man said. "These here are my woods. You're invading my privacy. I don't like that, Mister."

"Thank you for your assistance, sir," Maggie said.

"You can call me John. John Longmeadow."

"Mr. Longmeadow." She smiled. So, they finally met. "I—"

"Shhh." He glanced in Edgar's direction and shook his head. "Wouldn't do to talk now. Why don't you take that horse and find what you're looking for?"

"Yes. Thank you, sir." She turned the horse down the path heading out of the woods towards home and Samuel. There was still time to break the curse.

* * * * *

The wolf had nearly reached the woods when he saw a rifle-toting man charging over the hillside.

His feet flew, scattering ice and snow as he bounded through the drifts.

Suddenly a shot rang out from behind. Pain exploded in the wolf's shoulder, but he ignored it, focused on his prey.

The man ahead glanced over his shoulder, his face stark with terror as he lifted his rifle, but he wasn't fast enough. The wolf pounced on him. The pungent scent of the man's fear and the wolf's own blood filled his nostrils.

"I don't have her, you evil bastard," his captive shrieked in fear. "Look for Stratford. He's the one you want"

Suddenly he caught *her* scent. Glancing up, he saw her standing just outside the woods. A horse loomed behind her, blowing icy breath on the night air.

The wolf stared into her face. *Love. Love. Love.*

He raced for her and several more shots exploded, ripping through his fur and flesh. The wolf howled in agony and collapsed onto the bloody snow.

Moments later she was beside him, her tears falling onto his muzzle. "No, no, no."

He tried lifting his head, but weakness and pain overcame him. Above the agony floated the comforting sensation of her hands on his side, stroking and caressing.

I love you.

"I love you," she buried her face in his furry neck. "I love you so much…"

Chapter Twelve

Pierce jerked awake, his heart pounding with such ferocity he thought it might explode. He panted hard.

Pushing himself to his knees, he ran a hand through his wet hair. Disoriented, he glanced around the old-fashioned room and narrowed his eyes at the flames leaping in the hearth.

"Whittle House." He glanced down at his shirt plastered to his sweat-drenched body. For some reason, he'd expected to see blood. "God. That was—"

There were no words for what he'd just experienced. Common sense told him it had been an intense dream, but the feeling in his gut told him otherwise. Somehow, he had been given Samuel Whittle's memories and been allowed to experience his life through some strange, psychic experience.

For a long time he sat, staring at the fire, filled with more emotions than he'd ever thought to experience. Most clear of all was love. Samuel's love for Maggie, love that Pierce would never have understood without their help.

"This is crazy." He sighed, his throat constricting. The last time he'd cried he'd been six years old. His mother had dumped him off on his father's doorstep with a kiss on the cheek and he'd never seen her again.

Shaking his head, he fought for control and won—somewhat. At least he wasn't going to sit here and cry like a damn wimp.

Suddenly, he remembered something. A snowy morning shared with a woman he cared for more than anything. Pierce's eyes slipped shut as he imagined what it felt like sitting on the horse, his arms around Maggie, loving her, feeling her...

He opened his eyes and noticed a flashlight shining in the foyer. The brightness struck him in the face.

"My God, Pierce." Tabatha approached, kneeling beside him. "Are you all right?"

He nodded.

"Here." She slipped an arm around him and helped him to stand. "Are you sick? You look terrible."

"Not sick. I don't think so." He didn't need her support, but for some strange reason, he wanted it. Her body felt good so close to his. Comforting.

Her sneaker-clad foot kicked an empty bottle across the floor and her brow furrowed. "You're drunk?"

"Yes… I mean, I was, but not now." He sat on the couch and drew a deep breath. She tried moving away, but he tugged her beside him and stared deeply into her eyes. Beautiful, brown, familiar eyes. "Tell me what happened to Samuel Whittle?"

Her brow furrowed. "What?"

"The guy who owned this house, the accused werewolf. What happened to him?"

"Supposedly there was a shootout not far from here. Legend has it, he changed from wolf to man before the eyes of the local reverend and several of the townsfolk and the curse was broken."

"Yes." Pierce closed his eyes for a moment. "That's how it happened. She loved him. She touched him."

"Pierce?" Tabatha rested a hand on his knee. When he looked at her, he noted her eyes were wide and her face had gone a shade paler. "What are you talking about?"

"After that what happened to him?"

"It was said that he and Maggie Springfield, a free black woman working as his maid, moved to Pennsylvania where, at that time, interracial marriage was allowed. Thirty years later, they took a risk and returned to Whittle House where they spent a reclusive life with their son, Andrew. Records indicate that Andrew kept the house until his death in 1899. After that, the Jones Historical Society took possession of the house until they dissolved, then we at Philmore took over its care."

Pierce couldn't help smiling. "He did marry her."

"What do you know about it? Pierce? What are you doing?" Tabatha followed him to the fireplace where he moved aside the clock and tugged at one of the bricks.

"Oh God." Tabatha covered her hands with her mouth as the brick came loose and Pierce reached behind it. He tugged out a pair of broken silver cuffs. They were tarnished with age, but the workmanship was excellent. Several tufts of coarse, gray hair were trapped in the chain.

"How did you know about that?" Tabatha reached out a trembling hand and touched the cuffs. "We... I mean *they* hid them after that night."

"What night?"

Tabatha stared into his eyes. She tried pulling away, but he held her fast. "The last night."

"Tell me something, Tabatha, and don't lie. What were those cuffs for?"

"To restrain the...the werewolf." Her voice was scarcely audible. Tears glistened in her eyes.

Pierce nodded slowly. He released her and cupped her face in his hand before tugging his cell phone out of his pocket. He dialed.

"This is Pierce. I'm calling off today's auction at Whittle House. I know it's short notice, but that's how it is. Also cancel the contractors for the new building. Whittle House is staying."

Tabatha stared at him, her mouth open in shock. "Why did you do that, Mr. Durant?"

"I have to get home and shower." Pierce headed for the front door. "I need to talk to my lawyer and get things settled.

You'd better get on the phone with whoever is in charge of Philmore."

"Why?"

"I'd like Philmore involved in the operation of it."

"Operation of what?"

Pierce stopped in the foyer and smiled at her. Something about her tugged at his heart, a heart freshly awakened from a long, cold slumber. "I'm reopening Whittle House as a museum, so everyone can have a taste of post-Revolution history and remember the people who lived here."

"Why the sudden change?"

Pierce took a step closer to her and placed his hands on her shoulders. "Because something happened to me tonight. I'm not sure what it was, but it woke me up. Life is short and I'm wasting it making and hoarding money that will be here long after I'm dead. I have to go. Thank you." He kissed her cheek.

Tabatha lifted a hand to the spot he'd kissed, a half-smile on her lips. "What did I do?"

"You cared."

His heart pounding and his mind whirling with upcoming plans, Pierce jogged to his car and hurried home.

* * * * *

Tabatha glanced at herself in the full-length, brass-rimmed mirror in the corner of her room. Her hair hung, soft and full, around her lightly made-up face. A sleeveless pale green sundress draped provocatively over her generous curves. Gold sandals, reminiscent of those of an ancient Greek goddess, adorned her feet.

She drew a deep breath and tried to control her racing heart. Any minute Pierce would be picking her up for dinner. A week ago, she was certain she'd never again go out with the arrogant self-centered bastard. Something inexplicable had happened to Pierce Durant. She didn't doubt it had something to do with the morning she'd walked into Whittle House and found him, dazed, on the floor.

His words and actions had been strange, yet painfully familiar. That same night, she'd had the most startling experience. She'd been so furious about the house being destroyed and its contents auctioned off that she couldn't sleep, so she'd sat in the living room watching old movies to get her mind off her problems. The next thing she knew, she was living the life of Samuel Whittle's maid, Maggie. The strangest thing was Maggie had no recollection of Tabatha. Only when Tabatha awoke, in tears and shivering as if in the middle of a frozen field, did she realize what had happened. *Realize.* She *still* couldn't explain it. She tried passing it off as a dream, but the feelings had been too strong, the experiences too real. She had to go to Whittle House right then and see it before it was stripped of its contents and destroyed.

When she'd walked in and found Pierce in a state of distress, she'd nearly panicked. Only when he'd gone to the fireplace and retrieved the silver cuffs did she begin to suspect the impossible. Was it true? Had she and Pierce somehow gone back in time and lived the lives of Maggie and Samuel? Perhaps they *were* Maggie and Samuel reincarnated?

Tabatha shook her head and squeezed her temples. Thinking about it gave her a headache.

Still, she couldn't deny the possibility, especially since Pierce had changed so much. As promised, he'd called off Whittle House's destruction and moved the new condos to an undeveloped location. He left the house in the care of Philmore Historical Society with the understanding that they would open it to the public as a nonprofit museum.

Tabatha had been surprised when he'd phoned her with a humble apology and an invitation to dinner at a small restaurant outside of the city. Hesitantly, she'd accepted. There had to be something wrong with a rich handsome man who suddenly turned from the Big Bad Wolf into Prince Charming.

She swallowed hard. Maybe that was a bad comparison, considering the history they were dealing with.

Her doorbell rang and she drew a deep breath before answering it.

Pierce stood, his super-long legs covered in black pants, his broad-shouldered, well-muscled torso draped in a dark blue shirt a shade lighter than his eyes. He looked like the cover model on one of those hot books that made her want to reach for a vibrator. His dark hair was arranged as neatly as the thick, curly mop allowed. A lock of it formed an endearing ringlet on his forehead. Those deep eyes, once cold and unwelcoming, had warmed so much.

He offered her a bouquet of red roses. "These are for you."

"They're beautiful. Thank you." She held the roses to her face and inhaled their scent. "Come in while I put them in water."

He followed her to the kitchen and leaned against the doorjamb, watching as she filled a vase with water and arranged the flowers.

"I'm glad you agreed to go out with me again, Tabatha. I acted like a jerk before."

She glanced at him and smiled slightly. "It's all right. We all get jerky sometimes."

"Not sometimes. I've spent most of my life being a jerk."

"Pierce—"

"No. I have to say it. I don't know why I felt the need to be that way. I guess it was because it was easier. It's simpler to avoid feeling for people than it is to risk getting hurt."

Tabatha drew a deep breath and folded her arms beneath her breasts. She approached, her gaze on his. "Wow. This is some pretty deep conversation for a second date."

He chuckled. "I guess so. You must think I'm some kind of nut."

"I didn't say I minded deep conversation."

His smiled faded and his eyes met hers with intensity that made her heart pound and her nipples tingle. God, he was handsome, and when he acted normal and human like this, she actually liked him. A lot.

"Pierce, I want to ask you something."

"What?"

"I want you to tell me the truth as you know it."

"All right."

"Those silver cuffs from Whittle House?"

"Yes."

"What were they used for?"

"To restrain the wolf."

"And?"

He swallowed hard and approached, stopping so close that she felt heat emanating from his body. His lips were so finely shaped and looked so soft and kissable. *Please give me the right answer, Pierce. Please.*

"And Samuel used them to tie Maggie to the bed when they made love."

Tabatha's head spun and she was filled with elation such as she'd never known. She slipped her arms around his neck and closed her eyes as his mouth claimed hers. His warm lips moved gently against hers while their tongues loved and caressed one another.

When the kiss broke, Pierce's arms were wrapped tightly around her, supporting her entirely as she stroked his nape.

"I'm telling you right now, Tabatha Lane or Maggie Springfield, I'm in love with you. I was then and I am now."

"I love you, too. From now on things can only get better for us," she said.

"It happened, didn't it?"

"Yes, Pierce or Samuel, or —"

"The name doesn't matter." He smiled. "Only love does. You know, I didn't leave all the antiques in that house."

"No?"

He shook his head and brushed her mouth with a kiss. Reaching into his pocket, he withdrew the cuffs, the silver freshly polished and gleaming.

"I figured these really belonged to us. Paul wouldn't mind."

"No." She grinned, sliding her fingers over the smooth metal. "I don't believe he would."

"Would you like to go to dinner now?"

She shook her head and slipped the cuffs from his hand. Stepping into the hallway, she glanced at him over her shoulder. "I'd like to see if they'll fit through my headboard."

A smile touched his lips and his sapphire eyes gleamed. "Just tell me what you want, love. Tell me in great detail."

Once in her bedroom, Pierce tugged her into his arms and kissed her neck. Tabatha clung to him, relishing his scent and the warmth of his lips against her flesh. Funny how everything about him seemed so different. Their shared psychic dream into their past lives had brought them closer than she ever imagined possible. Memories of all they had shared as Maggie and Samuel flooded her. More than anything, she longed to feel his cock driving into her pussy.

"Oh, Pierce, I want you so badly," she panted, tugging his shirt from his pants and unbuttoning it with deft fingers.

"I want you, too, Tabatha." He unzipped her dress and let it spill to the floor.

Standing before him in nothing but her bra and panties, she should have felt a bit apprehensive, yet somehow this seemed so right. He quickly discarded his clothes and rolled on a condom, but even that seemed like too long for their bodies to be parted.

Tabatha reached to unhook her bra, but he grasped her arm and turned her around. Pressing warm kisses to her neck and back, he unfastened the bra and flung it aside. He reached around and cupped her bare breasts. Tabatha's eyes slipped shut and little sighs of pleasure escaped her lips as he gently squeezed and caressed her breasts. His thumbs ran over her nipples, teasing them to stiff, aching buds of desire.

He removed one hand from her breasts and seconds later the cool silver cuffs brushed against her belly. He trailed them up between her breasts while running his tongue along her shoulder.

"I feel like I've waited forever to be with you like this," he breathed.

A slight smile tugged at her lips. "It has been a few hundred years."

"Yes. It has."

He turned her to face him and cupped her face in his hand. His callused palm felt good against her cheek. Tabatha's heart fluttered. She wanted him so badly and had no desire to wait a moment longer. Grasping his face, she covered his mouth in a searing kiss. Her tongue traced the shape of his lips, then slipped between them. His met it, stroking and exploring her, desperate yet at the same time gentle.

Tabatha ran her hands up and down his back, then cupped his backside, relishing its tightness. His body was so lean and powerful, even more beautiful than she had imagined. Every sculpted muscle was a pleasure to touch. His arms wrapped around her waist, pressing her close to him. The sensation of his hair roughened chest against her breasts sent a thrill of passion coursing through her. If possible, her need for him increased even more. Her clit ached and her pussy grew wet with need.

"It's almost magical, this feeling I have for you," she whispered.

"It is magical." Suddenly he swept her into his arms and carried her to the bed. Placing her on it, he gazed at her with lust and affection. With the utmost tenderness, he took her wrists and used the cuffs to bind them to her headboard.

Tabatha's pulse raced. She drew a deep breath and released it slowly, watching him through half-closed eyes. Parting her legs, he positioned himself between them. He caressed her hips, then slid his hands beneath her buttocks. His warm breath teased her clit for several seconds before he used his tongue to caress the sensitive flesh. Tabatha's hands tightened into fists and she resisted the urge to moan. Over and over his tongue caressed and teased her. He used the tip of it to stroke along the side of her clit, and the flat of it to caress her flesh in a rhythmic pattern that soon had her writhing.

"Oh, Pierce. Don't stop. Please don't stop." She squirmed with pleasure and strained against the silver bonds. Each stroke of his tongue drove her closer to what she knew would be a shattering climax.

Still lapping her clit, Pierce reached up and caressed one of her breasts. His palm circled the fleshy globe. Taking the nipple between his thumb and forefinger, he pinched it, not enough to hurt but with just the right amount of pressure to send waves of pleasure coursing through her. As if reading her mind, he knew exactly how to touch her.

Tabatha gasped, her eyes tightly closed, enjoying every sensation of his lapping tongue. Increasing his speed and a slight bit of pressure, he drove her to orgasm. Massive pulsations of pure pleasure rocked her from head to toe. She thrashed and moaned his name, longing to break free of the bonds so that she could cling to him. He licked with gentle strokes until the last ripple coursed through her.

For a moment, Tabatha lay still except for the wild beating of her heart and the rise and fall of her chest as she caught her breath. Pierce unfastened the cuffs and tossed them aside. She slipped her arms around him and tugged him closer, gazing deeply into his eyes.

"That was great," she purred, "but I want more."

"Oh, I'll give it to you, love." He brushed her forehead with a kiss, then covered her lips with his. The sensation of his powerful body against hers ignited her passion again.

Kissing her deeply, he slid his thick cock inside her. Inch by marvelous inch the velvet-skinned staff filled her until he was buried to the hilt.

They lay for a moment, their breaths mingling and their gazes fixed on one another.

"Tabatha," he murmured against her lips. "I don't know how I could have been so stupid. All my life, this is exactly what I wanted."

"Sex with bondage?"

A smile flirted with his lips. "No. To be loved."

"I do love you, Pierce. We were meant to be together, just like Samuel and Maggie."

His mouth brushed hers in a tender kiss. Tabatha ran her fingers through his hair, loving its thickness, then splayed her palms across his back, gripping tightly.

He took her slowly, teasing her with long, smooth strokes that stirred her deep inside. All the while he gazed into her eyes, his expression reflecting his wonder at his newly discovered emotions. Suddenly his movements increased and his eyes darkened with passion.

"God, Tabatha, I can't wait any longer. I need you so much."

"Take me, Pierce. I'm so ready for you."

Thrusting her hips upward to meet his frantic motions, she clung to him tightly. His body heat seeped into her, stirring her even more.

"Pierce. Pierce. Oh, Pierce, that feels so good," she cried out, clinging to him harder. The tightening in her pussy became almost unbearable, then she exploded, her internal muscles squeezing his cock until he burst inside her. His sleek body strained against her, and she relished his strength and tingled in the knowledge that she brought him the same pleasure as he brought her.

For several moments, she listened to his ragged breathing close to her ear and enjoyed the sensation of his hot flesh against hers.

"I've been hiding so much for so long, Tabatha, ignoring needs I didn't want to believe I had. Thank you for setting me free."

She tenderly took his face in her hands and kissed him. There was still so much they had to learn about each other, so much they were destined to share. She looked forward to every moment of their life together.

The End

About the author:

A lifelong fan of action and romance, Kate Hill likes heroes with a touch of something wicked and wild. Her short fiction and poetry have appeared in publications both on and off the Internet. When she's not working on her books, Kate enjoys dancing, martial arts, and researching vampires and Viking history.

Kate Hill welcomes mail from readers. You can write to her c/o Ellora's Cave Publishing at 1056 Home Avenue, Akron OH 44310-3502.

Also by Kate Hill:

Shadow-Time Lover

R. Casteel

Chapter One
Romania
1350 A.D.

Zolona sat on the window seat of her second-floor bedroom, looking out over the vast estate of her father, the lord of Garlanzo Castle. It was the first night of the full moon when evil walked the land. She knew it was not so. Bright moonlight kept the true evil away, driving it into hiding until the light began to wane.

The deed must be done in the shadow-time. It was for this hour she waited, alone in the darkened room. She was frightened of the evil but sought to embrace it. If she went too early it would mean her death, too late and the evil would pass into her and be perpetuated for another generation.

The door opened, the dim light of the torch outlined the bent and bony form of the seer. "My child," she screeched in a high-pitched, irritating voice. "Ya are the last virgin daughter within the castle walls. Yer father has been wise ta keep ya pure. Yer deceitful sisters refused ta do their duty and took lovers between their legs."

"I know what I must do," Zolona answered quietly.

"Have ya prepared yer body with the oil of the rose to mask the scent of yer fear?" The creaking of her old bones grew louder as she approached the window.

"Da, Seer, I have done as ya instructed." She turned her face back to the moonlight. This was her destiny, to rid the land of the evil curse.

"Ya have yer gown ready?" The seer's voice grated on her nerves. The claw-like fingers of the old hag dug into her shoulder.

117

"Woman," she snapped. "Do yer ears sag like yer breasts so that they too are useless? Go! Be on yer way. Leave me at once."

She heard the woman wheezing and the shuffling of her feet as she moved across the floor. Zolona did not know how old she was, nobody did. It was rumored her life was tied to the curse. The gods knew she had been an old sourpuss for longer than anyone living could remember. It would be worth the sacrifice of her virginity just to be rid of the crone.

The door closed and darkness came from the far corners, filling the room. Zolona stood, opened the window, and stepped onto the balcony. The howl of a wolf echoed through the valley and a chill caused her body to shake. She raised her arms to the sky and her robe dropped to the cold stone. Moonlight bathed her naked body and a breeze swirled around her, carrying the scent of roses off into the night.

She offered up a prayer to the gods that they might look favorably upon her. To the Moon God that he might soon hide his face, and the god of morning whose star lit the sky before dawn, that he might accept the offer of her virgin blood. Last, she set her eyes upon the Warrior in the sky and prayed for courage and a strong heart, lest fear pave the way for failure.

The moon continued on his course to the sea and the entrance to the land of death and darkness. The time was at hand. She must make the final preparation.

Turning, Zolona stepped through the window-paned doors and crossed the darkened room to her bed. The white, sheer gown seemed to glow with a mysterious sheen against the deep burgundy of the thick comforter. The old woman had given her the material with a strict warning not to put the garment on until this very night.

Picking up the silk-like material, she slipped it around her shoulders and tied the thin sash below her breasts. It clung to her upper body like a second skin and bellowed out into a sensuous cloud around her feet. Her body lost the chill of the night air and began to warm. What spirits were at work this night that this see-through, apparition-like garment gave her body heat?

Her bare feet made little noise as she crossed the stone floor. Zolona pulled the heavy oak door open and the dim light from the torch in the hall spilled into the room. With what might be her last look at her comfortable bed, she turned and headed down the wide, drafty passage to the stairs.

An eerie silence hung over the interior of the castle. Dark ghosts danced on the walls as the burning torches along the way sent fingers of fire and black smoke toward the ceiling. It was as if the castle walls themselves were in league with the spirits that walked in the shadow-time of predawn.

She heard a noise behind her, but dared not turn around. Her eyes could not look upon another human face until the power of the curse broke and moon's face began to change.

Zolona descended the stairs. The faces, woven into the tapestries hanging on the walls, seemed to follow her with their eyes. If they could speak, would they tell her of their own daughters' failure to free the land of evil?

She reached the main floor. Several torches were out, increasing the darkness within the castle. Even the servants were in hiding, fearful of meeting her face-to-face. No doubt once she stepped through the outer door, they would begin to scurry around catching up on their daily duties. The last barrier stood before her.

A figure clothed in black from the hood over his face to the hem of his long flowing robe, slipped from the shadows, and stood before her. "It is time. I go ta break the evil curse upon this house and land. Release me, my father, ta my destiny and pray the gods will be appeased with the sacrifice of my virginity."

He turned, pulled the door open, and stepped aside.

For the first time since her first bleeding, Zolona stood outside the castle walls without an armed guard. If not for the hour at hand, she would have danced for joy on the dew-covered grass.

Going down the cobblestone lane, she turned onto a well-trodden path. She knew the way well and hurried beneath the canopy of trees. Night animals scampered through the fallen leaves. An owl, disturbed by her presence, dropped from a branch overhead and flew deeper into the woods.

A wolf's sinister howl split the night and dread crept up her spine. Her heart began to race beneath her breast as she glanced from side to side. Tension mounted with each quiet step.

She broke out of the trees and into a small clearing beside the lake. The moonlight cast a white shimmering path across the placid surface. Dew from the grass covered her feet. Wildflowers pulled at the hem of her gown and brushed the calves of her legs like the sensuous caress of a lover.

The gazebo stood by the water's edge, lonely and forlorn with neglect. She stepped inside the columns that once supported the roof. It was gone, as she first remembered it years ago as a child, leaving the large flat stone in the center open to the sun, moon, and stars. The stone had drawn her in fascination from the beginning. Its smooth weather-beaten surface still kept the discolored stains of blood, which time alone could not wash away.

A sudden tingling along her spine caused her to gasp. She could feel the evil staring at her from the dense underbrush at the edge of the clearing. In her mind, she saw it circling around her, sniffing the air, and waiting.

As the moon slipped farther from the sky, long finger-like shapes spread across the field. Something flashed through the grass, disappearing into another area of growing darkness. A long howl burst forth into the clearing and caused her to jump. Her hand flew to her mouth to cover her startled cry. Zolona tried to hide her fear and remain calm but her palms were moist and her eyes darted to and fro.

It was shadow-time.

The moon dropped below the mountains and the light faded. She thought she could hear the hiss as it dipped into the distant sea, or was it the wind whispering through the trees.

The sinister presence of evil settled around Zolona. She stood next to the rock; the backs of her calves touching the cold damp stone. The phosphorus glow of the gown grew brighter and she saw its light reflected from the greenish eyes of the evil one. It was there, with her, inside the gazebo. Its harsh breathing roared like a mighty storm within her head.

With trembling hands, she loosened the sash. The garment parted and the night air sent a chilling breeze across her breasts. Her nipples tingled with expectation, but was it out of fear, or the result of some perverted, immature childhood fantasy dream? Only this time, as she sat upon the large rock, it was not a vision she could wake up from and be back in her own bed.

As Zolona lay back on the bloodstained surface of the stone, the evil leapt to the rock and straddled her body. Savage lust gleamed in its eyes. Long white strands of salvia dripped from its fangs to fall upon her breasts. *Have I come ta early after all?* The thought flashed through her mind as its foul, hot breath washed over her face and the harsh satanic growl from its throat sent shockwaves of fear coursing through her body. *Has it all been for nothing?* She closed her eyes, unwilling to watch the approaching hand of death.

The beast sniffed along her body from her throat to her toes. Its cold, wet nose brushed her skin and plunged between her legs. Zolona bit back the scream. With nostrils flared, the beast continued back up her body. The razor-sharp canine teeth came closer to her face. Its thick rough tongue licked her throat.

Strong jaws closed around her throat. *I have failed.* She felt the pain as its teeth broke her skin and her hot blood began to flow down her neck. Suddenly, the pressure at her throat lessened. She opened her eyes.

The beast rose up before her. Pain flashed across its face. The long, coarse hair covering his body began to change. From the wolf she recognized, he became some half-beast, half-man creature from the land beyond the dead. Zolona looked down the length of its hairy body and stared with wonder and awe at the size of his swollen genitals.

Better ta kill me quick than tear me in two with the hard lance between his legs. The thought flashed through her mind even as the tip of his shaft descended towards her womanly core. With one quick brutal thrust, the beast entered her, tearing her maidenhead and penetrating deep inside her body.

"Nooooooo!" The white-hot, searing pain closed her throat, choking back further sound. Tears filled her eyes, blurring the image of the lust-crazed man-beast. Over and over, he thrust into her ravaged body.

Somewhere along way, in the midst of all her pain, she felt her body responding to the attack. Her own body betrayed her, meeting his hard driving thrusts with her own. Zolona stood atop a high pinnacle reaching for the Morning Star. The star burst into a brilliant flare of light and she was falling, falling…darkness descended over her, covering her in a shroud of blissful sleep.

Filip stood looking down at young woman lying in her virgin's blood on the Rock of Sacrifice. Knowing it was necessary did nothing to ease the pain and burden of knowing he was responsible for the oozing stain of crimson between her thighs. It was no small consolation knowing she could have easily died.

"Come quick." An anxious voice called from the shadows of the approaching dawn. "There is still work ta do and little time left."

He gathered Zolona up in his arms and hurried after the old woman. She stood straighter. Gone were the haggard look and slumping shoulders. Her steps were sure and quick through the forest. With each moment of passing time, she gained more strength.

Filip followed her to a hidden cave. Inside a fire burned within a circle of stones. Near the fire a black kettle sat, steam rising from a foul-smelling mixture of herbs and spices known only to the old witch. He placed his young burden on a bed of sweet-smelling heather, jasmine, and lilacs.

Her long tresses spread across the bed like golden honey. The firm mounds of her breasts barely moved as she hovered near the realm of death. His first image of her as he changed back from the beast had been one of shock and revulsion written across her face. Now, she looked so peaceful and beautiful.

The old witch brushed him aside and took a handful of the thick paste from the kettle. Spreading Zolona's legs apart, she packed her raw and bleeding flesh. "This will stop the bleeding and bring healing. The curse has been lifted with the taking of her body, but ta find yer rightful place within the castle walls, ya must win her heart as well."

He watched her hair go from a dull, dingy gray to a bright copper, glowing like fire in the first rays of the sun streaming through the cave's opening. "I have sought this day with longing since I laid my husband ta rest in the castle's mausoleum. Promise me this one thing; bury me next ta my husband that I may rest in peace." She hurried away, running through the woods over the path they had followed to the cave.

An evil, hysterical laugh danced on the wind. "What hideous secret does yer evil heart carry ta thy tomb, ol' witch?"

Filip turned and knelt beside the sleeping Zolona. The essence of rose oil still clung to her body. Her body was young, tender, but every inch a woman at eighteen years. He grew hard looking at her and chastised himself for wanting her so soon. His memory, foggy from the transition, recalled little of the actual mating. He hoped hers would be as kind.

Kneeling beside her, he lifted his hand to her face and his fingers skimmed lightly across her velvet-soft skin. "Sleep, my love. I shall return."

Filip crept through the forest to the small stone house he and those like him had used for generations. He dressed quickly and retraced his steps to the lake and the stone gazebo. There, lying on the Rock of Sacrifice, lay the body of Helen Garlanzo, beloved wife of the first patriarch and lord of Garlanzo Castle. She lay on what had been Zolona's bloodstained gown, only now it was nothing more than a crumpled pile of old decayed cobwebs.

Filip picked her up and carried her to the castle door. It opened immediately upon his knock. The family stood inside the door and he saw the relief wash over their faces at the sight of the fiery copper locks. He followed the present lord and master of the house out to the estate mausoleum. There, in the dark and dreary vault, a casket had been opened in preparation for receiving the body, four hundred years after the curse had first plagued the land.

The Lord of the Manor looked down at the woman whose beauty had been restored in death. "My daughter is well?"

"She is." Filip closed the lid to the coffin. "Zolona is resting. I will bring her home soon. Do not be frightened for her."

"Did she suffer much?" He helped Filip secure the lid and shove the coffin back into its rightful place.

"She is alive." He turned away from the crypts and hurried to the door.

"Ya will stay with her until she is well enough ta travel?"

Filip paused, "Da."

"That is good. I will prepare food and clothes ta take with ya, and give ya my finest horse ta carry her home. Please, come inta the house for a glass of wine while all is made ready."

They walked in silence for several minutes. "Young man, may I ask yer name?"

"For now, Filip will do. My surname for now is unimportant." They entered the castle walls and the Lord of the Manor offered him a seat in the kitchen.

The family hovered in the background while the servants rushed to do the bidding of their lord. He caught some of the hushed, behind the hand comments.

"My, but he's a handsome brute..."

"I wonder who he is. I haven't seen him in the village."

"…the beast." Laughter followed. "Him? Don't be daft."

Filip feigned a cough to hide his smile. *May ya never learn the truth, dear lady.*

"Here is more wine, sir, for yer cough. Ya must have caught a cold in the damp early morning hours."

"Thank ya, miss." He took the wine and swirled it in the goblet. The blood of the grape reminded him of his shameful deed at the gazebo. Filip drained the sweet liquid in one long swallow.

He stood, stretched, and took the bag of food and clothes outside. "I shall return with yer daughter within the full moon." Filip shook his hand, sprang to the back of the saddled horse, and rode off down the cobblestone path. The sun, well past its zenith, cast a long shadow across the way as he left the trodden path for the obscure cave.

The bed was empty when he arrived at the cave. He ran down the path to the stream and stopped at the sight before him. Zolona stood in a small pool, water to her waist, a light melody lifted from her lips and blended with the soft babbling of water flowing over the rocks.

She looked up and a moment of shock registered on her face only to be replaced by a smile. "Ya came."

"Ya know who I am."

"Not yer name, but I've seen ya many times…in my dreams." She left the pool. Water droplets on her skin glistened like rare jewels in the sun.

"Are ya a witch?" he asked with some growing fear.

"A witch," her melodious laughter rang out through the trees. "Ya mean like the old crone at the castle? Nu, I am the seventh daughter of the seventh generation. Many a lonely night, ya have come ta me upon my bed and whispered in my ear."

He smiled. "And what were these whispered words?"

"That ya would be my shadow-time lover, but first, I must set ya free."

Filip looked into her eyes for some signs of loathing. Instead of hate, he found compassion and understanding. Did he dare ask the question that burned within his heart? She stood within his easy reach in all her natural naked glory. Dripping wet like a siren fresh from the sea, her beauty drew his hand up to softly touch her face.

"My lovely Zolona, dare I ask what of thy response?"

The brightness of the morning star radiated from her face. "The same now as then, as will be tomorrow. Come, my dearest, my shadow-time lover, and lie between my breasts."

Filip drew her within his arms and sealed the words of hope and promise with a kiss. He held her as they watched the sun slowly sink behind the towering mountains and fill the skies with gold and purple hues, bathing them in the last fleeting rays of light.

Zolona began trembling in his arms, sweat dripped from her brow like blood. He recognized the horror in her eyes. It had been his constant companion until only this very morning. There was nothing he could do but step back away from her.

She fell to the ground. Her screams of pain cut through him like a two-edged sword, they pierced his heart. "I am sorry, Zolona. I wish ta the gods I had known. Better ta have slain ya than this."

Anger flowed through his veins like the mighty Danube at the deceitfulness of the witch. Filip remembered her evil laugh. She had indeed taken a vile secret to her grave.

Her creamy white skin began to change, long dark gray hair appeared from every pore, and her terrified screams turned into those of a tortured animal as her muscles ripped and tendons tore. The bones of her body shifted in size and shape, disfiguring her into a beast of Hades until she appeared, as he had been himself, the cursed of the land and terror of the night, the Werewolf of Garlanzo Castle.

Filip knew only too well the nightmare. Human by day, wolf by night and hiding for fear that he would be found out, while praying he would. With his nights ruled by hate, he ran; killing whatever crossed his path, be it man or beast. For years, he had been hunted ruthlessly through the mountains and valleys of Transylvania.

Only the old witch had known who and what he was. In her deceit, she spoke only half-truths. The curse had indeed been lifted from him, only to enter into the body of Zolona.

She crouched in wariness, her long fangs bared in a snarl as she sniffed the air.

"I'm sorry, Zolona." He knew any movement could very well be his last. Filip slowly sat on the ground. "I know ya can understand me. Ya have every right ta hate me."

The wolf, twice, almost three times the size of a normal animal, took a cautious step toward him.

"Ya were so brave, facing me in the gazebo. I despise myself for this evil curse upon ya. Let me be yer first victim. Revenge yer thirst for the ol' witch upon my body and put ta rest the agony I feel for the pain I have caused ya."

He bowed his head in shame, tears flooding his eyes, as he waited. Filip felt the hot breath of the beast across his face. Slowly, resigned to his fate, he raised his head and looked into her eyes. Her tongue licked the tears from his face. He had never known in all the years that it was possible for the beast to cry, but her eyes misted with compassion. She rubbed her head against his face and Filip placed his arms around her broad muscular shoulders and wept.

"Would that I had died, than bring this curse upon ya and yer family. How can ya not hate me?"

She moved back away from him. "Da, go. Avoid those who would kill ya. I will build a fire and stay throughout the night. When the shadow-time of morning stretches across the land, return ta me, my lovely Zolona."

She dried his tearstained cheeks with her rough tongue, turned, and ran off into the encroaching darkness. The moon rose over the crest of the mountains. Filip stood, gathered wood and tinder for the fire, and turned towards the witch's cave.

Dropping the load of wood beside the fire ring, he glared at the witch's iron pot. Blackened by years of her foul, evil use, the Garlanzo crest appeared to be but a faded outline. He picked it up, "Damn ya!" With all the force of his pent-up anger, he hurled it against the stone wall of the cave. "If ya had not died, I would take great pleasure in killing ya myself."

On a ledge, he found a piece of flint, an old rusted striker, and in a wooden box, a small pile of hemp fluff the old crone used for starting fires. Within a few minutes, a small thread of white smoke drifted up. Gently blowing on the smoldering hemp, a tongue of flame leapt magically from his hand.

Filip placed the burning tinder within the fire ring and slowly added dry slivers of bark and grass. As the flames grew, he added still larger pieces of wood, thankful for the heat against the encroaching chill of the mountain night air.

In all the years, this was his first night without food or the possibility of having any. Better to be hungry than feast upon the flesh of some unsuspecting stranger passing through. Turning his head, Filip gazed out of the cave's opening and watched as the light of the rising moon gave the area an eerie glow.

For an hour, he fed fuel to the greedy flames until a bed of coals winked at him in the darkness. His eyes turned suddenly to the cloth sack he had brought from the castle. *Zolona will have nu need of the food her father provided.* Filip ate greedily of the meat and bread and drank from the firkin of wine.

There was not a man nor animal alive able to stand against the wolfen beast, nor escape the death grip of its jaws. He had not prayed in years, not since the old woman had made him realize the futility, but he prostrated himself before the opening of the cave.

"Oh, Lord of the moon, guardian of the night, have mercy on Zolona and prevent her from taking human life. Spare her from sharing my guilt from feasting on mortal flesh."

Picking up the small iron kettle, Filip took the knife the witch had used, sliced his skin, and let his blood drop as an offering into the cold blackened pot. Instantly, it sizzled, sending a choking, biting tendril of vapor into the air. The cave spun as he staggered to his feet and groped for support. His feet tangled with the bed and with his arms outstretched he fell onto the mat of flowers. The faint perfume of roses drifted through his mind as darkness closed about him.

Chapter Two

Leaping over boulders, fallen trees, and across swollen streams, he ran beside the she-wolf through the night. At the crest of a small knoll, he paused... There below him on a small plain of grass a flock of sheep lay sleeping, unaware of death stalking the night. An unwise herder lay sleeping beside a fire. Zolona burst from her hiding place, charging into the night, scattering the sheep, and making straight for the one who slept unaware. Helplessly, he watched the scene unfold, his scream of warning, frozen in his throat.

The mouthwatering aroma of cooking meat and the sizzling of fat on the fire brought him up from the black nightmare of his sleep. Zolona knelt before flames, turning a leg of lamb on a crude spit. Her hair hung damp on her bare shoulders and he watched the muscles moving across her back. Lily-white skin contrasted with the dark gray of the cave walls and his eyes lowered to the smooth round cheeks of her ass.

"Ya came back." The rough material of his pants grated across the head of his cock as it hardened. His hunger for her shoved aside his need for the food she fixed.

"Where else could I go?" She shifted on the balls of her feet and turned towards him. "Ya of all people should understand."

"What of the sheepherder who watched his flock?" He realized it had been a dream, but it had been so real.

"How did ya know the herder was there?" Her eyes took on a confused, searching glare. "He ran off inta the night, screaming that the gates of Hades had opened and for the gods ta save him."

Relief flooded over him. He exhaled a sigh, lay back upon the bed, and said a silent prayer of thanksgiving to the gods for answered prayer.

"Ya were afraid the beast would kill him."

He turned his head to answer but her beauty, as she stood and walked toward the bed, stilled his voice. Her smile promised the heat of passion. The fullness of her young breasts drew his eyes as they rose and fell with each breath. Slowly they lowered to her trim waist and the small field of darker curls at the meeting of her thighs.

"I should have, for he was a thief." She sat on the bed beside him. "For years, the herds of my father have been raided. We thought it was the work of the beast, for there was always blood upon the ground. I know now, ya were not the evil stalking my family. It is the work of a two-legged beast, an acquaintance who sits at our table, while his hirelings do his treacherous bidding."

"I am grateful ta the gods ya spared the life, even though he deserved less." Filip reached out and placed his fingers lightly on her leg.

"I will not be so kind ta Lord Gravely next time we shall meet." She returned his gesture by placing her hand on his leg. Her fingers inched upward leaving a trail of fire, towards his loins.

Zolona fixed her eyes on his thickening cock. Her breathing increased and her tongue traced the fullness of her lips.

"For years, the pompous fool has vied for a union of our families. He begged Papa not ta waste my childbearing years on an old woman's senile ranting, but that I should marry his anemic and pathetic son."

She grasped his cock and squeezed. "I have made my choice." She lowered her lips to his. "It is better ta be with my shadow-time lover and accept my fate, than be shackled in a loveless marriage ta a man I despise."

Her lips were tender, full, and sought his with a building desire. Zolona grew bolder, parting her lips, and teasing him with her tongue. Fingers pulled at his rough clothes, deftly undoing the buttons of his pants. "I am nu longer a virgin," she spoke against his lips, "so do not play silly, coy games. The hardness of yer shaft excites me and fills me with desire."

She swung her leg across his waist, placed his cock inside the lips of her pussy, and drove it deep inside her wet and eager flesh. Zolona gasped and bit back a cry of pain. Her eyes grew large, questioning. "This is not supposed ta hurt. My sisters told me after the first time there would be nu more pain."

"Yer sisters should know." His fingers caressed her cheek.

She glanced down at the base of his cock. "I am bleeding…again, but the pain is almost gone."

"I will be gentle," he whispered.

"Nae, I do not want gentle." Zolona tightened her muscles around him. "I may be found out tomorrow or the next, and we both know what that would mean."

"Ya have little ta fear, my lady." His hands covered her breasts; the dark pebbles of her nipples grew warm against his palms. "Ya will find as the beast, ya will not be easy ta catch, much less ta kill."

"Ahh! But as a woman, I have been captured and even now the tip of yer cock-lance points ta my heart." She began to rock back and forth. Her head rolled upon her shoulders sending long stands of flaxen hair dancing across his hands.

Moving with her, his fingers twisted and pulled at her distended nipples. Her eyes, a sliver of white, glistened between her long, thick lashes, gazed unseeing at the roof of the cave. Soft moans from her parted lips, filled the air, and fueled his desire to please and satisfy her frenzied need.

Her face began to blur as he struggled to meet the wild rocking of her hips with his thrusting cock. Filip ceased to exist as a single person. There was no more he or she, but one, climbing higher on the lofty peak of passion.

His low panting grunts lifted from his throat, mixed with hers, and fell back to his ears sounding like the melody of a shepherd's flute drifting over the valley on a long and lonely night.

He balanced on the edge of the precipice, waiting. Zolona's body stiffened, tightened around his, and he dropped over the edge with her. One moment he plunged helpless towards the ground, the next he soared with her on the wings of passion as his world around him exploded, in a rush of heat.

For several seconds, Zolona lay panting, collapsed on his chest. "Oh, my," she kissed his neck and began giggling. "My oldest sister must be doing it wrong, or else she lied ta me."

A chuckle rumbled from his chest. "And, what makes ya think of yer sister in this way?"

She rose up on her outstretched arms. Her hair tickled the flesh across his chest. The wild passion of her eyes took on a soft, warm glow. "She told me, 'Zolona dear, having a man inside ya is disgusting. With their pawing at ya, pulling at yer breasts like the teats of a cow and sticking their filthy little cock inside ya, why, it is downright shameful, but it *is our duty* as women'."

He laughed as she mimicked the haughty tone of her sister and her speech of suffrage and duty for the continuance of the human race. "I take it then," he pulled her down to lie on his chest, "ya do not agree with the wisdom of yer sister?"

Zolona took his lips in an openmouthed seduction. Her tongue dueled with his for dominance and possession. She broke the kiss and whispered in his ear. "What do ya think?"

"I think yer sister is doing it wrong." The heat from her laughter warmed his skin.

"Come, my shadow-time lover," she slipped from his arms. "Ya must eat ta keep up yer strength." She looked over at the skewered meat. "Ya have two choices, regular lamb or..." The corners of her mouth turned down and her shoulders slumped, "very well-done."

Filip rolled to his side. The portion of meat closest to the fire had burned black. "The lower half resembles my own cooking." He tried hard not to laugh at her. "It will do fine, my lady."

She got up, took the spit from the fire, and carried it back to the makeshift bed. "Ya never did tell me yer name." Zolona tore off a large piece of meat and handed it to him.

"I am Filip." Sinking his teeth into the meat, he waited. How would she handle the news?

"Pray tell me, from which family?" She laid her hand on his thigh, inches from his cock. "Please, after today's events, let us not have any secrets between us."

"I am from the Garlanzo family, as was the old woman."

Her face turned pale as the color drained from her skin. Dropping the food, her hand flew to her mouth in shock. "Then ya are…" Her eyes grew large, apprehensive.

"The only living heir of Garlanzo Castle."

Chapter Three

His words were like an angry fist, pounding her heart and mind with no mercy. She gained her feet, staggered to the opening of the cave, and leaned against the sun-warmed stone. *What have I done? What of my parents, my sisters, and their families? What will become of them?*

"What troubles ya, my love?" Filip stood beside her; she tipped her head and stared into his eyes.

"Ya dare ta call me yer love? This is the reason I was chosen, is it not? So that after all these years, ya could regain the castle, the lands, and the title. Tell me, when did ya and the witch begin ta plan this deceit?"

"Any deception involved came from her. Any virgin would have lifted the curse from me." He reached out to touch her, but she brushed off his hand and stepped away.

"Oh, really," she scoffed. "Then why is it, the stone in the village carries the names of so many virgins who did not survive on the altar?"

She saw sadness and heartache flash across his face before he turned away and stared out over the land. "Do ya not realize the guilt I alone must bear for all those deaths?"

"And is there nu guilt that I now bear the curse?"

His shoulders slumped. "More guilt than ya can possibly know." His voice, soft and broken, drifted to her on the mountain breeze.

"Ya feel guilt now, but how soon will it end and ya stake yer claim ta the title?"

He turned towards her. "So long as the curse rests upon ya, I will make nu claim for land or title."

"Ya say that now," she derided. "But what of the long winter nights when ya are huddled by the fire? Will ya not think ta yourself, 'I am the rightful lord of Garlanzo. Why do I sit here and freeze my balls, when the imposter warms himself by the fire'?"

"That will not happen." He stepped in front of her.

Even now, she wanted him again. What power did he hold over her? "How can I be sure?" *I want ta believe ya.* She lifted her hand and placed it on his upper arm. She could feel the nervous tension of his taut muscles.

"Upon the word and honor of a Garlanzo, I make this my solemn vow. For so long as the curse rests upon ya, I will make nu demands for title or lands."

"I accept yer vow of honor Filip, rightful heir of Garlanzo and lord of the land." Her arms went around his neck and she sealed the vow with a kiss. *So be it, by yer own words, ya shall never lay claim ta my father's land.*

"Come, we shall bathe in the stream and return ta our meal." Zolona took his hand and walked beside him the short distance ta the small pool.

His size dwarfed hers with his broad muscular shoulders and thick barrel chest. Hair black as midnight, hung to his shoulders and the day-old growth of his beard darkened the lower half of his face. For being such a big, powerful man, Filip was a gentle, passionate lover.

I could have done worse in taking a man... She thought of the person who, had it not been for the curse, she might have already married. *Much worse indeed.*

The water, from the high snowcapped mountains, sent a shiver up her back. Zolona waded out to where the water reached her mid-thigh and began scrubbing the dried blood from between her legs. After a couple minutes, her teeth were chattering. Looking up, she found his eyes were fixed on the small patch of hair below her waist. Letting her gaze drop, she marveled at the hardness of his cock.

"It would appear my sisters were indeed keeping secrets." He slipped a finger inside the soft outer folds of her pussy. "They told me they were *thankful* a man could not get it up more than once a day."

"Then their beauty must pale beside yours, or they only mate in the dark."

She began to laugh. "Maria is different, but my sisters would never think ta wash in front of their husbands, much less ta actually 'do their duty' in the light of day."

He wadded out to stand in front of her. "Then I am glad it was ya who had the courage ta face the beast."

Reaching up, she touched his face and trailed her fingers down his flesh 'til they came in contact with his hard cock. She wrapped her fingers around the shaft and squeezed. "I too am glad. I would not care ta lose my sisters to the beast."

Filip lowered his head and took her lips in a long, passion-filled kiss. The chill of the water seemed to vanish before the flame of his desire. His cock throbbed within her hand.

She broke the kiss. "I will bathe ya, feed ya, and lay with ya upon the bed."

"I promised yer father that I would see ya home." His fingers pinched and pulled at her nipples. A low moan escaped her lips.

"Time enough until tomorrow ta see Papa. It will be difficult ta explain why I can live nu longer under his roof." She splashed water across his skin. His quick, indrawn breath brought laughter to her lips.

"Laugh ya little wench."

Ice water covered her breasts. She retaliated with more water, splattering it across his face. Filip lunged for her and Zolona stepped aside, slipped on rocky bottom, and fell. Submerged, she grabbed his feet and pulled bringing him down beside her.

Their arms and legs intertwined and she struggled to free herself. As they broke the surface, his mouth captured hers and all the play stopped. Her arms lifted around his neck, her breasts flattened against his chest, and she wrapped her legs around his waist.

"Take me, here, now, beside the pool."

"With pleasure, my wolfen queen." He carried her out of the water and gently lowered her to the grassy slope.

The intensity of his eyes lit a fire where they touched her skin. "Please!" she whimpered. He knelt between her legs and she looked down at the hard shaft of his cock with excitement. This time, she knew there would be no pain, only pleasure.

His fingers brushed the hair between her legs and she licked her lips in anticipation. Filip parted her flesh with his finger and stroked the hard, sensitive nub. Lightning flashed across her flesh and she rocked her hips for more of the same. His low, husky laughter added fuel to the fire of her need.

"Ya torture me with yer...games." Zolona savored the pleasure of his finger deep inside her, but she wanted more. "Yer finger feels better than my own, but," she gasped as he slipped a second finger inside her, "yer cock is...bigger. Ohhh!"

Soft, kitten-like moans filled the air. Her fingers clutched at the grass, ripping it from the ground. "Mmmmmmmm," she whimpered at the sudden emptiness.

She opened her eyes to see his face inches from her own. Placing her arms around his neck, she pulled him closer. Their lips met and parted. As his tongue invaded her mouth, his cock slid past the outer folds of her pussy and plunged deep inside her.

Her hips lifted off the grass and ground against his. His cock throbbed inside her, filling her with his heat. "Da! Oh, Da." She buried her face in the hollow of his shoulder, wrapped her legs around his waist, and held on as his hard, pounding shaft continued to send ripples of pleasure to every nerve.

His breathing labored, his body quivered and jerked. Liquid heat exploded inside her, sending her over the edge with a muffled cry. Zolona shook with the force of her own climax.

As the waves of pleasure subsided, she opened her eyes. A dark purple bruise and several teeth marks discolored Filip's skin.

"Ya have been branded," she kissed the discolored skin.

Filip turned his head and looked at the mark. "So it would seem." He stood and stretched out his hand. "Come. We shall eat and then ride ta the castle. I promised yer lord I would have his daughter home."

"I fear it is too late, the day is far spent." She took his hand and Filip pulled her to her feet. "I must be gone from there before the time of shadows reaches the valley."

"We shall be." He held her hand as they started back up the path. "Once we are outside the castle walls, ya will be safe when the time comes."

"Ya do not know my family," she laughed. "Were I ta show up in the afternoon, Mama would bar the gates if I should try ta leave. Alas, she may anyway."

"Then we shall finish our meal, and then go ta my place." He led the way into the small cave, sat on the bed, and picked up the remainder of the meat. Tearing off a portion, Filip handed her a piece.

Zolona watched him eat. In the back of her mind, a nagging suspicion kept rearing its ugly head. "How old are ya, Filip?"

He paused and looked at her—or, she felt, through her—as if she were not even there. For several long moments, she did not think Filip was going to answer.

"Why?" He let out a heavy sigh. "Does it matter?"

"Nu." She turned her eyes back to her food.

"How old do ya think I am?"

"I...do not know," she answered in truth. "Ya look ta be in yer early twenties, maybe twenty-four or twenty-five. But something tells me ya are *much* older." A knowing smile lifted the corners of his mouth.

"Which do ya prefer, my lady, twenty-four or -five?"

"I think…I like older men, so I will say five." *He is not going ta tell me his real age. Everthing is so different now. Maybe I do not want ta know.*

"Good choice." Filip laughed, stood up, and offered his hand to her.

"Come then, we shall be going. We have some distance ta go and in places, it is difficult."

"Will we make it before the time of shadows reaches the valley?" She took his hand and rose to her feet.

"Da, but we must hurry." Filip gave her a quick kiss and turned away. "There are some clothes for ya in the things yer father sent."

Finding the clothes, she noticed her father chose wisely in their selection. The special riding skirt she had made had caused uproar in the home and a scandal in the village. She did not really care, as long as she could ride astride through the open meadows of the estate.

Filip reached down and picked up the small iron kettle that the witch had used. "Do we need ta take it with us?" She knew the value of a good iron pot. Even a small one, would be of value to a poor shepherd's family. Zolona, however, sensed some lingering presence of evil that surrounded this pot, and she wanted nothing to do with it.

"I share yer misgivings." He tossed the iron pot into the shadows. Picking up the sack, he turned to the cavern entrance. "Are ya ready ta see yer new home?"

"As long as ya are with me," she smiled, "I am ready."

She rode in front of Filip, keeping her horse at a steady gait to prevent overtiring the animal. They moved up the valley, skirting the small stone houses of her father's tenants and the shepherds tending their flocks. After crossing the meandering stream several times, he pointed to a smaller creek to the left.

"Follow this inta the mountains."

With a slight tug of the reins, the horse turned.

Zolona followed the thin trail beside the creek, but pulled up short at the rocky cliff. "Which way now?" she asked in confusion.

With a smile on his face, Filip pointed to a small fissure in the rock face. "Through there."

Her horse had other notions and it took her several tries to get it to enter the narrow opening. Their feet brushed the rock wall, and once she had to pull her legs up out of the way to make it through.

They finally reached a small finger of green valley on the other side and she let the reins go slack in her hand. Leaning forward, she pushed her ass against his growing cock. His hands moved along her legs, up under the loose shirt she wore, and cupped her breasts.

Dropping the reins, she let the horse choose its own path and undid the buttons on the inside of her thighs.

"What are ya doing?"

"It should be obvious." Zolona reached behind her and undid the buttons of his trousers.

"I have ta wonder how ya ever made it this long and still be a virgin." His laughter sounded low and sensuous in her ears.

"I had a bodyguard who was with me everywhere I went." She grabbed his cock, flipped up the back of her riding skirt, and rubbed against him. "He came out of Egypt and had served his life as a eunuch."

He brushed her hand away, took hold of his cock, and placed it between her soft outer folds of womanly flesh. Sliding backwards and lowering her hips, Zolona sighed as his hard shaft delved deep into her. Grasping the long flowing mane of the horse for support, she slid up and down on his cock.

Filip grasped her around the waist, and with each backward thrust of her hips, countered with his own.

Her horse began prancing in the field adding to the movement of his cock and depth of penetration inside her. With the long hair of the horse's mane wrapped around her fingers and her knees pressed against its side, Zolona rode out the rising tempest. The muscles in her legs quivered with each pounding thrust of his cock. She felt the surge of liquid heat flow from his cock and with a cry of passion collapsed on the horse's neck as her climax washed over her in breath-robbing waves.

"Oh! I shall never be able ta ride again...without comparing it with this one." Her breathing slowed, her pounding heart quieted, and she loosened her grip on the horse's hair. Taking the reins, she slowed the horse to a walk.

"And when I see ya on a horse, walking through the tall meadow grass, I will grow hard with remembering the passion of this ride."

The stone face of a house set against a towering cliff came into view. "We are home, my lady. It is not so grand as ya are use ta, but it is comfortable and dry."

"It looks wonderful. I will be honored ta share it with ya." She brought the horse to a stop with a slight backward pressure on the reins, swung her leg over, and hopped lightly to the ground.

Filip dismounted, took her hand, and led her to the front door. "My lady, yer cottage awaits." He opened the door and bowed out of the way.

Zolona stepped across the threshold and looked around in wonder. The house continued as part of a cavern deep into the side of the cliff. She could tell much time and effort had been taken in building his home.

"This is more than adequate, Filip. It's lovely." Turning, she slipped her arms around him. "Thank ya," she whispered, and gave him a soft kiss on his cheek.

"It is nearing the shadow-time, hold me until I must leave," she begged.

Filip scooped her up in his arms, carried her to a solid homemade chair, and sat with her in his lap. "I will be outside the walls of Garlanzo Castle in the morning. Meet me by the fruit orchard and I will have yer clothes."

Giving him one last embrace, she stood. "I will be there at first light. I do not need remind ya of the dangers of arriving too soon. The transition back is worse, and I fear for even yer life at the hands of the beast within." Her fingers brushed his cheek. "I must go now." Zolona ran for the door removing her clothes as she went.

Just minutes after the door closed behind her, Filip could hear the heartbreaking scream as the beast emerged. Blow after agonizing blow, his fist pounded the table. "Damn ya! Damn yer evil soul ta hell."

Filip lit a fire and fed kindling to the hungry flames. The wood cracked and popped as the reddish-blue fingers clawed their way over it and sent a shower of sparks up the chimney. Lighting a candle, he made his way into the cave. He stopped at a heavy wooden door kicked it with all his strength.

Wood cracked, the sound echoed around him. Again, he slammed his foot into the door. It exploded open, banging off the wall. Taking the candle, he entered the witch's room, and put the flame to a candelabrum.

The added light sent shadows dancing along the wall. A thin pallet lay in the corner. A small table and chair were the only furniture in the room. Several old books, covered in dust, sat on a crude shelf. *Maybe I will find what I am looking for in one of those.*

Picking up the books, he carried them to the front of the cavern and sat near the fire. Shifting through the old yellowed pages, Filip grew discouraged. He found pages of chants and spells, magic potions, poisons and cures. Frustrated, he started to close the book when a word leapt off the page. This had to be it. Nothing else came close to describing the evil curse.

"So, ya thought yourself ta be a powerful witch." He began reading it again, slower. The title alone sent a shiver up his back. *The Revenge of the Wolf. This is a spell used against those who have transgressed against a powerful and dominant witch. The casting of this spell should not be done in haste. If cast by a lesser witch unjustly against a dominant one, it will be returned upon the head of the caster threefold, with dire consequences for generations ta come.*

There was more, but it would have to wait. The night had passed quickly and he would have to hurry to meet Zolona in the grove at daylight.

Chapter Four

The morning shadow-time had passed. The dew covered her naked body as she lay in the tall meadow grass surrounding the grove of fruit trees. She rose up to where she could see and scanned the area for any sign of Filip. If she were caught like this, how could she explain her lack of clothes to her parents? Her poor misguided sisters would feign shock, and then mock and ridicule her behind her back. She sighed. *They probably will anyway.* The thought did nothing to lessen the resentment towards Filip at being late.

A flash of black through the trees caught her eye. In the middle of the grove, the rider brought the horse to a walk. She recognized Filip and whistled. He stood in the stirrups and looked in her direction. Zolona stood, waved and started towards him.

With a swift kick to the ribs, he sent the horse charging through the trees. He reached her side in a matter of moments and pulled up sharp on the reins. The head of the horse came up and his hindquarters dropped to the ground as he slid to a stop in the wet grass.

"My father would not approve of his prime livestock being mishandled," she scolded. "Yer late. Suppose one of the serfs from the castle had come ta the grove this morning, or worse yet, one of his knights decided ta take a morning stroll."

"My apologies, my wolfen queen." He stepped down from the saddle, stood in front of her, and adjusted the growing bulge in his pants. "Ya look lovely with the morning dew sparkling like diamonds in yer hair."

Without warning, he picked her up, swung her around, and gave her a resounding kiss. She started to respond to his sensuous lips. "Ya think I'm excusing yer tardiness with a few flattering words and kisses." Placing her hands on his chest, she pushed him away.

"It is far too open here in the meadow. Follow me. Someone may have seen ya approach the castle and send a watch ta check." Using the horse to shield her from the prying eyes, she led Filip through the grass and into the surrounding forest.

"How was yer night, my lady?"

"Interesting," she turned her head and smiled. "I daresay, the beast can cover an amazing amount of distance in one night."

"Pray tell, where did the beast take ya?" Filip reached out and took her hand.

"Ta the far north end of the estate, over the mountain, and onta land of Lord Gravely."

He halted in his tracks and grabbed her shoulders. "It is far too dangerous for ya ta be leaving the valley. Promise me, ya will not do it again."

"I can not make such a promise, Filip. The man is a thief." She shrugged off his hands and entered the tree line. "While he sits his fat arse under the table of my father bemoaning the sad state of his affairs, the size of his herd grows faster than the rabbits our cook keeps for food."

"I hope ya were not seen." He tied the reins to a small hickory tree.

"Why the concern over the lie'n pig?" She placed her hands on her hips and waited.

"Over the years, he has grown stronger, his knights grow bolder and now patrol the hills in large numbers throughout the night."

"I observed his fearless knights, huddled around a campfire, swilling down their grog and fornicating with scared peasant women." She spat on the ground. "They are mere highwaymen and gypsy trash."

Filip took her into his arms. "Enough of Gravely and the affairs of his lands. Have ya eaten?"

She smiled, "Da, thank ya, my lord, for yer concern. I feasted quite well last night."

A groan rumbled in his chest. "The knights did not chase ya?"

Zolona laughed, "They were too busy a pulling up their pants and trying ta catch their horses."

"I am worried for yer safety." His fingers threaded through her hair. "I think ya take too many chances."

"As a woman, I can do nothing ta stop Gravely from robbing me father blind." She rested her head against his shoulder. "But as the beast…there is much I can do."

"Ya will end up on the tip of a lance and the trophy of a knight before it is over."

"Would it matter ta ya if I did?" Zolona whispered against his neck.

"Da, very much so." His lips brushed her hair and then left soft fleeting kisses along her ear.

Turning her head, her lips met his in a tender, almost hesitant caress. "I think ya mean that." She felt the hardness of his cock pressed against her leg. "If ya wish ta lie with me, Filip," she grinned and stepped away, "ya best do it now. Once inside the castle walls, ya will not be getting another chance."

His fingers flew to the buttons of his homespun trousers. Warm desire spread through her at the sight of his swollen cock. She reached out and wrapped her fingers around the rigid shaft.

Kneeling on the ground in front of Filip, she looked up and smiled as she placed a kiss on the head of his cock. She felt a slight tremor as his legs stiffened. Growing bolder, she parted her lips and took him in her mouth, caressing him with her tongue.

His breathing quickened, the muscles in his legs quivered, and he rested his hands upon her shoulders. She lay back on the soft pine needles and patted the ground beside her.

Lying beside her, he lowered his head and took her nipple between his lips. As his teeth gently grazed the sensitive flesh, her back arched from the ground and a low sensuous moan floated from her throat.

"Oh!" she gasped. "Do not make me wait," she pleaded. "I ache ta have ya inside me."

He slipped between her legs and she felt the tip of his cock penetrate her flesh. His mouth took hers in a searching, probing attack. Pain flashed through her like a knife. Her cry swallowed up inside him.

Zolona broke the kiss, "Why, Filip? This is the third time with pain. The first I understand, but yesterday and now today." She buried her face against his neck. "Tell me this is not part of the curse. Am I ta suffer pain every morning ta have yer pleasure?"

"I am sorry, my lady." He rested his forehead against hers. "I…am afraid this may well be the truth of the matter."

"An unfair lot I have drawn, my lord."

"Da, that it is." He started to pull out and roll off of her.

"Where do ya think ya be going? Ya will not cause me the pain without giving the pleasure. I will not let ya."

He settled his weight back on her. "Are ya sure, my love?"

"The pain has lessened, my lord." Wrapping her legs around him, she arched her hips, and wiggled her ass to hurry the union.

She exhaled a contented sigh as his cock slowly entered the blood-slick walls of her pussy. Frustration began to mount at the carefulness of his movement.

"Ya do not need ta be so careful. I will not break," she chided. "If ya cannot bring me pleasure, then I will find a man who will."

A moan escaped her lips as he drove his hips hard against hers. "And who would ya find, the foppish son of Lord Gravely?"

Her eyes closed as she savored his wild abandon. "Nu...only my shadow-time lover can please me... I want nu other."

His lips met hers in an open-mouth exchange of passion as their tongues touched and danced in rhythm to the savage thrusts of his cock. Her fingers raked across his back and grasped the cheeks of his ass. With heart pounding and her vision blurred, she rode the tempest of their climaxes. Gasping for breath, Zolona lay content with the weight of his body pressed against her breasts.

"My lord, I fear the vassals and serfs will soon arrive in the orchards and fields. It would not do ta be caught in such a compromising position."

"Yer right, my lady. It is time ta go."

Filip pulled out of her and she cleaned her thighs with dew-laden grass. Taking the clothes he brought her, she dressed and crossed to where he waited with the horse.

He lifted her with ease into the saddle and swung up behind her. She leaned against the solid wall of his chest, thankful for his strength and support.

At the far end of the orchard, they were greeted with cheerful waves, calls of good morning, and many a backward glance as they went on their way.

"By nightfall," she laughed, "the whole village will know I returned at dawn with a strange man."

"Da," he joined her laughter. "And with pine needles in ya hair, they will not be a wondering what ya were doing."

"I do not." Her hand flew to her hair, searching for the offending needles.

"Da, my lady." Filip took it from her hair and held it out for her to see. "I fear we have been found out."

"Oh, my." Twisting around, she looked into his eyes. They were bright with laughter. "I am afraid my sisters will never tire in reminding me of my wanton ways."

His gaze held a deeper emotion, one she was loathe to put a name to. The future before her held too many uncertainties to look beyond the shadow-time of day.

The guards at the castle gate stared as they rode through. Chickens scattered, a dog barked at them, and several women gawked openmouthed at the sight of her riding in such a compromising way. "Tongues will be sure ta wag over breakfast porridge."

"Then, my wolfen queen," he whispered in her ear. "Shall we make it worth the effort ta indulge in so arduous a task at break of day?"

She turned her head and gazed into the dark pools of his eyes. "Da." She touched her lips to his and felt the longing desire to turn and flee, to spend the day naked in his arms.

The crash of broken pottery sounded in the courtyard. With regret, she broke the kiss and turned her eyes to the well. "Good morning, Sister Letty. Close yer mouth, girl, before ya swallow a fly. Papa will not be pleased with ya for breaking the water pitcher."

Letty lifted her skirt and ran to the kitchen. The door swung wide and out poured a horde of women she affectionately referred to as twits. They stood in a half circle around them, starring at her as if she were sprouting another head.

"Good morning, dear sisters, Maria. Good morning, Mama. I'd like ya ta meet Filip."

There were several guarded glances from her sisters to Mama. Some not so guarded. "Mama, what is the meaning of this? Ya said Zolona was sick and not ta be disturbed. Does Papa know she has been out all night fornicating like some tavern wench?"

Zolona felt his arm tighten around her waist. Lowering her eyes, she could see the knuckles of his clenched fist were white against his dark skin.

"Maybe if ya spent a little more time with yer legs open and yer mouth closed, dear Charline," she rebuked her sister, "yer husband would not spend his time at the tavern."

Charline turned red, stomped her foot, and ran back to the kitchen.

"Zolona, ya owe yer sister an apology," the voice of her mother crackled with irritation.

"I owe her nothing but a swift kick in the arse for what she said ta me. If there be any apologizing done, she will be making it ta me. Where is Papa?" She leapt from the horse and turned to Filip. "Come, ya must be hungry. If my family has forgotten their manners, I have not.

"Letty, set another place at the table...and try not ta break anything else." She gave her mother a kiss on each cheek. Taking Filip by the hand, she led him into the family house, down the long passage, and to the large table in the dining hall.

"Good morning, Papa," she kissed each cheek. "I've told Letty ta set another plate. It is good ta see ya again. I shall leave Filip ta yer care while I run ta my room, freshen up, and change. I will not be but a moment."

She turned and ran from the room.

"Thank ya for bringing Zolona home." He motioned for Filip to take the seat beside him. "I have had the devil of a time keeping her absence a secret."

"My lord, I commend ya for the delicate handling of this awkward and difficult time."

"The curse has been lifted. We must go on from here and restore the estate's holdings," he paused. "Something troubles ya, my son? Tell me in truth, has the curse been lifted from Garlanzo Castle?"

"I am sorry, my lord. It has not." Filip turned his face away from his lord's visible disappointment. "At least...not completely." Looking around the room, he lowered his voice. "My…the old witch deceived us all. The curse transferred, my lord…ta another."

The lord looked briefly towards the door Zolona had gone through. "Tell me," his voice broke. "Does the curse now rest upon my…?"

"Da."

The Lord of the Manor slumped, his head sagged, and when he lifted his face, his eyes were glazed with unshed tears. "Tell me Filip. Do ya bring any word of hope ta bind up the soul of her father? Can the curse be lifted from her?"

"There is always hope, my lord."

* * * * *

Zolona gasped at the sight of her father. He seemed to have aged a dozen years. She turned a questioning gaze at Filip. His somber expression answered the question she was afraid to ask out loud.

Her feet carried her to Papa's chair. He turned, buried his face against her middle, and wept.

"Papa, do not cry for me." Silent tears flowed down her cheeks at the distress of her father. "Because of this, I have found out the lies of Lord Gravely."

"And what lies does my future daughter-in-law accuse me of telling?" Lord Gravely stepped through the door. "Sir Weston will not take kindly his wife-ta-be is spreading discord so close ta the day of yer betrothal."

"Leave us," he addressed Filip. "I have matters of urgent business ta discuss with Lord Garlanzo."

"I have nu desire ta discuss business this morning. We are ready ta break the morning fast. Whatever it is ya wish ta see me about will wait. I will have a plate set and later we shall talk." Lord Garlanzo patted her hand. "Tell the maid, Lord Gravely will eat with us."

Zolona cast a warning glance towards Filip and hurried to do as her father asked.

"Sir Weston sends his regrets at not making the trip, but we were attacked last night by the beast," Lord Gravely sighed. "It scattered my flock and ran off my knights' horses. I came upon what remained of one on yer land as I rode through."

"Were none of yer knights slain by the beast?" Zolona asked as she reentered the dining hall.

"Nu, they chased the evil away," he boasted. "The beast is big as a lion. There was nothing more they could do."

"My word!" Zolona covered her mouth to hide her grin. "Yer knights are so brave ta attack such a monster on foot."

"There will be nu more talk of monsters and evil beasts at the table." Lady Garlanzo announced as she and the rest of her daughters entered the hall. "My girls have delicate dispositions and I will not have them taking ta their beds."

"Zolona would not mind going back ta bed," Letty giggled. "Would ya, sister?"

"Well, I'm sure she can be excused if her fever returns." Lord Gravely spoke with heightened concern.

"Oh!" Charline quipped. "It was nu fever that kept her ta her bed. She had an itch, poor thing."

She heard the suppressed laughter from several of her sisters as they and their husbands took seats around the table. "Charline, dear," she smiled. "At least, I know what an itch is, and the remedy for it."

The face of her sister turned red and there were more giggles up and down the table. Zolona felt sorry for their husbands who looked in confusion at each other.

Father stood, and the table became silent. "I wish ta make an announcement this morning," he paused and looked from Filip to his daughter. "This is the last time I will have this privilege. I do here by announce the betrothal of my daughter Zolona ta…"

Lord Gravely sat up in his chair, his chest puffed up like a strutting cock.

"Filip Garlanzo, heir and rightful Lord of the Manor."

Lord Gravely sputtered, his face turned red, and he jumped to his feet. "This is preposterous!" he bellowed. "An insult of the worst order. This man is an imposter."

Filip stood. "Yer the imposter, Gravely. For years, ya have robbed this land and people of their cattle."

Shockwaves rolled down the table. Startled gasps from her openmouthed sisters mingled with the chilling glares of hatred from the men around the table.

"What lies this imposter tells," Gravely ranted. "He is the one who wishes ta rob ya of yer title and lands."

"Believe what Filip says, Father," Zolona stood next to Filip. "For I have with my own eyes witnessed what he says is true."

Her father turned to Lord Gravely. "Ya have used our acquaintance for evil, ta make yerself fat off our labor. Leave this house and these lands, never ta return. For if ya do, yer head will decorate the tip of my lance, and my sword will be drunk with the blood of yer kin."

At the murderous glares of the men, Lord Gravely left the room in haste.

"Thomas, assemble a guard and escort him ta the mountain pass and set a watch."

"My lord." Thomas looked with confusion between the two. "It is said the beast rules the mountains at night."

"Thomas, do not fear the night," Zolona spoke. Her soft voice seemed to echo in the large room. "The anger of the beast has been turned this day upon Lord Gravely's house. Let it walk where it will in peace."

"Would ya say these brave words," Letty asked, "if it were yer Filip and not my Thomas?"

"Da, I would," she smiled. "I have met the beast, face ta face."

The looks of doubt circled the table, but enough had been said already.

"Yer sister does not lie." The commanding voice of her father quieted the hushed whispers along the table. "The day is wasting and I have business ta tend with the new Lord."

"My lord, I have nu wish ta remove the title from yer name, nor move yer family from their home." Filip took Zolona's hand. "Yer daughter shall make her home with me in the mountains."

She could see the stark relief wash across their faces. They were not concerned about her, only that their life would not be changed. Catching the notice of her mother, she smiled.

"My dear, there is much ta be done before a wedding," her mother beamed, "but we should be ready within a fortnight." Her mother looked around the table at her other daughters.

"There will be nu wedding in a fortnight, nor any other night so long as the beast walks among us."

"But...Papa just announced yer betrothal?" Letty looked around for support.

Maria, her dearest and closest friend, looked up with a shaky smile, "At least ya will not be leaving us so soon."

"Dear Maria, I am sorry ta disappoint ya, we will be leaving before nightfall." She looked up to see her mother grasp her chest. Her eyes rolled to the top of her head and then she fell from the chair.

Zolona rushed to her side only to be shoved away by Charline. "Letty, bring the smelling salts. Mother has fainted." She turned on Zolona. "Have ya not done enough? If ya insist on bring the family shame, then pack yer things and go. Good riddance if ya ask me."

"Charline." The stern warning of her father filled the air. "Tend ta yer mother, and put a guard on yer spiteful tongue. Listen ta me, all of ya. Zolona knows what must be done in these matters. And I will not listen ta any more drivel about her causing shame ta the family. If ya have forgotten that three of ya were expecting when ya said ya vows, I have not."

"What about Lord Gravely? He will not be taking this laying down." One asked from down the table.

"Nu, and I hope he does not." A gleam flashed across his eyes. "Send runners ta every house. We must prepare for war, if we expect ta survive."

Zolona marveled over the transformation of her father. He had been given a direction, a new challenge to face, and a new enemy to conquer. The mundane chores of the estate suddenly took on more importance. The men sat up straighter in their chairs and offered sound advice in the defense of their home and family. Runners were sent to sound the call-to-arms and gather support against the pending war.

"Father, give Filip ten of yer most trusted archers. When Lord Gravely advances we will seal the pass behind him and attack his rear guard."

He turned to Richard. "Choose out nine men, fierce in battle, proven in courage and join with Filip."

"I will also go with them," Maria announced.

"Come, Maria, I will help ya prepare for we must be gone before nightfall." She took her hand and left the hall in a flurry of ruffles.

Chapter Five

"Filip, the day is far-gone and there is still much ta do in preparation," she whispered. "Even now, the beast begins ta waken."

"Go ta yer room, my wolfen queen. It will be best if yer family sees not the horrors of shadow-time." His fingers gently caressed her cheek. "Seeing the beast will be difficult enough for them."

She gave Filip a quick kiss and fled up the stairs. Reaching her room, she closed the door and leaned against it. The pain sliced through her, ripping a strangled cry from her throat.

Lord Garlanzo stood in the inner bailey looking up the closed bedroom door. As tears filled his eyes, he lifted his clenched fist. "Damn yer mother ta hell."

"Da," Filip turned to see the stricken face of Zolona's mother. "Tend ta yer wife, my lord."

"My lords." Richard approached, his eyes darting to the stairs. "The men are ready at last. My apologies for the delay."

"Very well," he turned to see curious, frightened stares of family members and servants hiding in the flickering shadows of the torches.

"Tell me, Richard," Filip sighed. "Had ya known what lie ahead, could ya have been ready sooner?"

"Nu, my lord."

"Then make nu apology for what could not be helped." He clasped Richard on the shoulder. "I will…" With a heavy heart, he ascended the stairs and stopped at her bedroom door.

Filip opened the door and stepped back. With a vicious growl, the giant wolf sprang from the room and landed in a weary crouch at his feet. As he descended the stairs, the beast stayed by his side.

Children screamed and hid behind the skirts of their mothers. Women fainted, collapsing in a flurry of lace. Their fear of the beast and their barely concealed hatred for him at bringing this curse into the castle walls weighed heavily on him.

He stepped outside and the courtyard erupted into a pandemonium of chaos. Dogs barked, horses reared, dislodging their riders in the dirt, and those whose horses didn't bolt, fought to bring their mounts under control.

"Open the gate!" Filip called to the watch.

The gate swung open and the beast disappeared into the darkening shadows.

Not knowing when, or if, Lord Gravely would attack, they rode hard through the night. He looked to Maria, and admired her courage and stamina. Dressed in a serviceable riding skirt, she rode beside Richard without complaint through the long hours.

Under the cover of darkness, they passed single file into the small valley. Filip could feel her nearness, but for now, all he could do was wait.

He dismounted and opened his door. "Richard, set a watch and bed the men down in the meadow. There is grass and water for the horses."

"Right away, my lord."

Richard led the men, his wife, and the pack animals away. He was left alone in the night. A chill crept up his back and a whisper of wind kissed his face. A smile lifted his worried frown.

He stepped inside but left the door open. The heavy breathing of the beast filled his ears, and all was quiet. "Hunt well, my wolfen queen."

* * * * *

Horses whinnied in fear of evil as the gentle mountain currents carried the scent of the beast across the narrow valley. The piercing cry of a tortured animal rent the stillness of the predawn shadows. For several minutes afterward, the silence closed in around him, isolating him from the world. Slowly the birds resumed their morning songs as the skies lightened and the shadows turned to flee.

The dim outline of the open door disappeared and the soft thud of its closing filled the room. "Good morning, my lady. Did ya feast well on the flock of Lord Gravely?"

"Da, my lord." She lay beside him on the bed. "They are not as fat as those of my father and I was forced ta slaughter several for a meal."

His arms sought her in the darkness. "What of his fearless knights?

"The ones outside the castle walls were shaking in fear and pissin' in their boots at the howl of the beast." Her fingers stroked the hard shaft of his cock and a low moan floated from his lips.

"What of the ones inside the castle walls? Do they prepare for war?" His lips found the nipple of her breast and he drew it into his mouth.

"Da, I heard the sounds...ahh, of preparation all the night."

Leaving the sensuous peak of her breast, his tongue left a wet trail to the flat plane of her belly. "Then there is little time before the battle is joined." Sliding lower, his chin brushed the soft curls below her waist.

"Da, ohhh!"

He parted her soft outer folds and blew on the hard nub of her clit. Her fingers grasped his hair as her legs tensed. Filip licked her creamy soft flesh, tiny tremors shook her, and she lifted her hips off the bed.

"Da, oh Da!"

A low whimper filled his ears as he left the sweet musky flesh of her pussy and crept up her body. "I will be gentle my wolfen queen, but there will be some pain."

"Da, but nothing compared ta the time of shadows, my lord." Zolona took his mouth in a passionate kiss. Their tongues touched, retreated, and then touched again.

He slipped inside her wetness and again, felt the thin barrier blocking his way. "I'm sorry, my lady." In the dim light, he watched the pain flash across her eyes and heard the light catch in her breathing.

"Do not be sorry, Filip. What pain I feel soon subsides and is well worth the pleasure of yer cock inside me."

With a slow, determined pace, he moved inside her, plunging to the limit of his erect shaft and then edging out again.

"Ya tease me, Filip. I am not a new colt ya have ta break ta ride."

She heard a giggle from across the room and a husky male voice, "Hushhhhh."

"Maria, what are ya doing awake?"

"How do ya expect anyone ta sleep, with as much noise as ya were making? Course, ya will make more when ya will have yer pussy licked." The male voice was muffled and difficult for Zolona to hear.

"Maria, what ya doing?" Zolona laughed against his neck.

"Zolona dear, if ya must know...I had me Richard's cock in my mouth. Now hush."

She bit Filip's shoulder to smother her laughter and listened to the slurping sucking sounds coming from across the room. "Ya talk about me making noise, yer as noisy sucking cock as he is licking pussy."

Deep muffled laughter filled the room.

Filip began moving inside her, harder, faster with wild abandon. Locking her legs behind his ass, she met him, thrust for pounding thrust. Gasping for breath, she turned her face and watched in a blur, her dear friend Maria sitting on top of Richard. Her breasts bounced and her body bucked as she rode his cock.

Masculine grunts and softer moans mingled with the squishy sounds of wet pussy. Maria stiffened, her back arched and her passion-filled cry of release sent Zolona over the edge. Wave after wave of climax ripped through her pussy and spread across her body. She held on to Filip, her nails digging into his back.

When it did not seem possible to come anymore, his fire spread through her, setting off a final climax. Her body shook, her chest burned, and she lay panting, fighting to breathe. Filip covered her with his body and she felt the hard pounding of his heart against her breast.

Filip pulled out of her, stood, and crossed to the fireplace. He stirred the burning coals and a shower of sparks rose up the chimney. Adding more wood, he watched the flames lick along the dry bark. Taking a torch from the wall, he held it to the fire.

"Take this, my love. At the back of the cave, ya will find water ta clean yerself."

Covering her nakedness from Richard, she stood and took the torch. "Come, Maria, we will bathe and prepare the food. The men will be hungry after riding all night."

"Da," Maria giggled. "We had best fix extra, two of the men were ridden hard." They found the pool of water and waded in. Their squeals of shock at the cold echoed through the cave.

"Tell me…is it painful?"

"Da, pain like ya cannot imagine or describe. Ya think ya is going ta die, and then ya wish ya had." Zolona washed the blood from her thighs.

"Ya are bleeding, is it that time a month, or are ya hurt?"

"Nu, Maria." Zolona sighed. "It is part of the curse. Every morning it is the same as the first time." She stepped out of the water and began to dress. "Enough about the curse and my bleeding pussy. There is work ta do."

* * * * *

Filip and Richard rode into the meadow and watched the small band of men with their mix of longbows and short crossbows aiming at targets scattered across the field. Very few arrows failed to find their mark.

"Yer men are well-trained, Richard. Ya should be proud ta lead them ta battle."

"Da, they are the finest archers in the land." Richard smiled. "Gravely's men will have more ta fear tonight than the beast. The tips of our arrows will drink their blood and the beast will feast upon their flesh."

He knew it was going to happen, but hearing Richard put it into words saddened him. "Whither her guilt will be as great as mine for spilling human blood, I know not...but Zolona *will* carry the guilt all her life."

"Da," Richard clasped his arm. "We all carry our ghosts; some are just greater than others."

Filip sighed, "Da. Come, we shall eat and then rest." They trotted their mounts to the house. "Tonight will be long and difficult."

* * * * *

A hurried knock on the door brought them from their beds. "It is time. Lord Gravely's men approach the pass. The watch has ridden ta warn the castle."

"Very well, alert the men ta be ready." Filip dismissed the guard, turned to the fireplace, and took a large sword from the wall.

"Forgive me, my lord, but have ya any practice with the claymore? I mean, it being a Scottish weapon an all."

"Da. It is a gift from a Highlander for saving his life. He taught me well in its use." He held the long blade in the air. The polished steel glowed red, blue, and orange for the fire.

"And when was that, my lord?" Richard asked.

"A long time ago," he sighed. "Before the curse."

Zolona gasped, "But that was over…"

"Four hundred hears ago," Maria placed her hand over her mouth in shock.

"Da, I was twenty-four years of age when my mother, Helen Garlanzo, brought the curse upon the family." Filip belted two short swords to his waist. "It is time."

"Maria, my lovely wife." Richard caressed her cheek. "I leave in yer hands the lives of my men. Bind the wounds of the injured and comfort the dying as though it were me." With a last tender kiss, he picked up his sword and crossbow and went to his men.

"Be careful, my shadow-time lover," Zolona held him tight. "Come back ta me."

"I have not lived all these years ta die at the hands of cutthroats and thieves." Taking her lips in one last embrace, he followed Richard.

"Come, Maria, I will help until the shadow-time and then I too must go."

Time slipped by in nervous silence as she worked beside Maria, preparing food for the hungry men when they returned, and bandages for their wounds. "Nu!" she screamed. The pain flashed through her causing a moment of blindness. "Run, Maria! Do not look upon the beast." She collapsed on the floor as her tortured cry filled the cave.

Chapter Six

Lord Gravely's men spread out in typical marching fashion with the mounted soldiers up front. "Not much of an army," Filip commented.

"Gravely is not a warrior, only a self-righteous thief." Richard spat on the ground. "Never did care for him. We will wait to make the first attack. Let them grow lax and tired. They won't feel like chasing us."

"If they grow more complacent, they will be asleep." Filip shook his head in disgust.

"Da, but our arrows will soon wake them up." Richard smiled.

They returned to their small band of men, hidden deeper into the woods, and followed the advancing army.

A twig snapped up ahead and Filip drew one of his shorter swords. With a flash of steel, the battle with the rear guard exploded around them. He parried the blade and lunged. His sword pierced the thick leather jerkin, and the shock of failure and of his own imminent death spread over the face of the man as he looked at the sword buried in his chest.

Filip heard the heavy twang of a crossbow and looked up to see the fleeing messenger fall from his horse. It was over for now, but would soon begin again in earnest. A hand clamped on his shoulder.

"Well done, Filip. We have the advantage now. Lord Gravely will rely on their rear guard for warning," Richard laughed. "The only warning they will get is the screams of the men dying in their midst."

"Da." He looked down at the man he had killed. "It is time to press home the attack. Ready the longbows, Richard."

They crossed the meadow, each man bending low over the neck of his horse and spread out riding abreast in a single line. Filip felt his heart pounding. His palms started to sweat and he wiped them dry on his woolen pants.

Richard halted the men. Filip raised his arm and ten bows pointed their shafts to the sky. He dropped his arm and death filled the air. A second and third wave of arrows followed the first in quick succession. Confusion and disorder broke out in the ranks as men screamed and fell.

"I believe they know we are here," Richard laughed. "Our arrows were thirsty, nu?"

"Da, but let us not forget, they are eager ta spill our blood as well." Filip pointed to a group of armed riders approaching. "We have company."

"Crossbows ta the ready!" Richard ordered. "Hold fast...hold...fire."

With his broadsword held at the ready, Filip charged the remaining riders. A clash of steel rang out across the valley and a helmet rolled through the grass. The sightless eyes of the man stared to the sky.

Filip ducked a slashing blade, and with an outward thrust sent his blade into his attacker. His horse spun and he ducked. Richard's arrow whizzed by his head and felled another of their enemy.

"Retreat!" Richard ordered.

Filip took one last swing with the massive claymore and a severed arm dropped to the ground. Digging his heels into the flanks of his horse, he joined his men.

"It has been a long time since yer blade has feasted." Richard yelled. "Next time, my lord, do not be so anxious to die. The night is still young."

Darkness crept across the valley and still their enemy pressed forward, fewer in number, but wiser, and more watchful than before.

With the castle in sight, Lord Gravely halted the advance and campfires began to twinkle in the night. The howl of the beast sounded in the still mountain air and a hush descended over the meadow.

The twinkling fires grew brighter as they added fuel. "They seem ta be a little nervous," Richard chuckled.

"Da, and with good reason." Filip crouched and made his way through the tall grass.

The field came alive around them with screams, yells, and the clash of steel. Filip slashed, parried, and countered with his broad blade. The enemy pressed him on every side, trying to get past the claymore as it danced upon the night. He felt a tug and an intense burning rose up his arm.

The beast came out of nowhere to stand beside him, and faced those who attacked his rear. She lunged, going in under the tip of a sword and ripped open his throat with her razor-sharp teeth.

Twisting in midair, she snatched a spear thrown at Filip and let it drop harmless in the dirt. Attacking at whatever extremity she could reach, the beast charged through the horde. Limbs snapped like twigs, blood dripped from her mouth and face. Panic spread through the enemy forces and those whose hearts and minds were not frozen in fear dropped their weapons and ran.

Lowering the claymore slowly to the ground, Filip took in the carnage. Men lay dead or dying around him. His hands, covered in the drying blood of the fallen, lost their death grip on the long wooden handle of his broadsword and it dropped onto the crimson-stained grass.

The bitter metallic taste of blood filled his mouth and assaulted his senses. The sounds of the battle around him lessened, as did the moans and cries of the dying. Refusing to support him any longer, his legs buckled and he sank to his knees.

"Come, Zolona, I can hear the panting of the beast." With great effort, he raised his arm. A moan of protest rumbled in his chest. "It is over. For now we have won."

The beast towered over him. Her hot breath bathed his face. Filip reached out and touched her, running his fingers through her matted, sticky hair.

"Thank ya. I was starting to think I would never see ya again."

She licked his face and Filip smiled. "I am not the only one who needs a bath."

"Filip!" Richard called to him from the night.

Through the moonlight, he saw a shadow walking through the killing field. "Over here, Richard."

"We have won." Richard sank to the ground beside him. "Praise ta the gods, we have won."

"Da, for now," he took a deep breath and sighed in exhaustion, "but it will soon be light. When Gravely sees we are but few, he will attack in force."

Richard's joyous laughter filled his ears. "He is dead. True, I saw him with mine own eyes. The enemy has broken and fled."

"Surely ya are mistaken." The beast pushed against him and he fell on the ground. "Zolona, I am too tired for games."

"Nu! When the battle started, Lord Garlanzo opened the castle and attacked from the front as well. Weston Gravely has surrendered what little of his army he has left."

"Then…it is truly over."

"Da," Richard clasped him on the arm and he winced. "You are injured. Come, I will get you ta the castle."

"It is nothing, I will…" Filip felt like he was floating. Thick dark clouds passed over the moon, shutting out the light.

* * * * *

Sitting beside her bed, Zolona held Filip's hand. With Maria's help, they had bathed him, bound up his wounds, and laid him in her bed. Time seemed to stand still, as she and the beast kept their vigil. None of her sisters remained close. They following Charline and avoided her like the plague.

"Zolona." His weak voice brought giddy relief and a smile to her face.

"It is about time ya decided ta wake up," she chided. "Ya had us worried." She leaned over and kissed his lips.

"How long have I been here?" His eyes roamed the room.

"Three days." Lifting his hand to her lips, she placed a kiss on his fingers.

He started to get up and she pushed him back to the bed. "Wherever you think you are going, forget it. Ya need ta eat so ya can get yer strength back. I will have Maria bring ya some of the broth she has been keeping warm."

"Broth?" His mouth turned down, his nose scrunched, and his face wrinkled. "There be nothing wrong with my stomach. I was injured in battle, not suffering from some unknown affliction of my bowels. I need something ta sink my teeth into."

"Ya will take the broth, even if Maria has ta hold ya down while I pour it down yer throat," she teased.

Filip sighed, "Da, I will take the vile stuff, but only if ya promise me something more substantial later."

"I must warn ya," she laughed. "We have eaten fowl for two days. Maria was not sure how many birds it would take. She killed all the birds that were too old ta run, and long past the time of being tender. Trust me, you are getting the better meal."

"Are ya badmouthing my cooking again?" Maria walked through the open door, crossed over to the bed, and sat down. "I see ya finally decided ta join us. Welcome back ta the living, Filip."

"Thank ya. It feels good ta be back."

"Zolona, ya haven't left the room hardly in three days. Run down and get Filip his broth. I'll sit here and make sure he behaves."

"If yer sure ya don't mind." She stood and stretched. "I will be right back."

Maria waited until she left the room. "Filip, I found a book at yer place, and from what I am able ta understand, the third part of the curse can only be broken by ya, on the Altar of Sacrifice."

Filip closed his eyes against the truth. "Then we are doomed, for I feel she will not willingly allow it ta happen."

"Why would she wish to remain as she is?" she questioned.

"Because of my promise ta not seek the title for as long as the curse remained."

"Then you spoke foolish, my lord. Though ya seek it not, it is yers by birth."

"Father is relieved ya are awake." Zolona entered the room, "and the cook is happy ta be finally getting rid of the broth."

He took a look at the large steaming bowl. "It smells wonderful, but if I take all that I'll, ah…overflow the chamber pot."

Zolona laughed. "Ya need not be embarrassed, Filip. Who do ya think has taken care of ya at night while ya were taken ta the bed? She knows yer body as well as she knows that of her husband, or almost as well."

"Then I am in debt ta ya, Maria."

She waved off the notion. "It was nothing. As the betrothed of my dearest and closest friend, I consider ya part of the family, even if there be nu plans for the wedding."

He finished eating and noticed the light through the window beginning to fade. Shadows crept slowly across the floor. His glance at the window and then at Zolona did not go unnoticed.

"Ya can relax, my lord." Maria laid her hand on his arm. "I have witnessed the horror of the change. It is never easy, seeing her suffer the hell of the beast, but knowing there is hope to break the curse helps."

"What is this about breaking the curse?" Zolona questioned with alarm in her voice.

Maria turned her head away. "I am thinking, since it was lifted from Filip, there is hope for ya, too."

"Then ya hope in vain, Maria, for I…"

Zolona doubled over, grabbed her stomach, and fell to the floor. Blood flowed from her lip in a feeble attempt to stop the agonizing cry as the beast emerged.

Maria covered her face with her hands, "Is there any cost too great, my lord, ta have her set free?"

"Nu." He looked upon the beast with a heavy heart. It walked over, sniffed the bed, and licked his face. The wolf turned and ran from the room.

"She will be back. She goes to kill the animal set out for her." Maria slipped off the bed. "Do not, I pray, let yer promise interfere with what ya know is right ta do."

"Ya place me in a most difficult path, Maria." He ran his hand over the three-day stubble of his beard. "If I go ta the Altar of Sacrifice ta meet the beast at the morning, she may kill me to protect her family. If the curse is broken, then she will hate me and never speak to me again. I would rather share her with the beast for I care not ta live without her."

"Lord or nu, ya be a selfish man, Filip. I thought ya were different from your *mother*." She turned and left the room without a backward glance.

Her words were a slap in the face. Had she been a man, he would meet her on a field of honor. Mother was evil, not selfish. It was difficult to remember the beginning of the curse. Her desire for position over the then Lady Gravely started her seeking powers she did not understand. In four hundred years, she never gained the poise and elegance of Lady Gravely.

Bitterness and envy had sprouted evil and only in her death did she find peace.

The beast entered the room on silent feet, crossed to the bed, and laid her head on the bed.

"Ya were right about the broth. I feel my strength returning." He scratched the black head behind the ears.

"Maria says I am *selfish* like my mother. What do ya think? Am I like her?"

Her long, rough tongue licked his face.

"Ya knew her better than most people. Whenever she came ta visit, she always talked about you. How ya were so *perfect*. She hated your family; course she hated every family that lived here."

Filip swung his feet out of bed and sat up. "I feel like going for a walk."

The beast growled.

"I have been in bed long enough. Ya can walk with me. In truth I would like ta have ya with me." He found his clothes, dressed, and crossed the room to her door where the beast blocked his way.

"There is only one way ta stop me from leaving, my wolfen queen." He stared the beast in the eye. Slowly she lowered her head and moved aside. The beast fell in behind him as he descended the stairs.

At the outer door, he turned. Maria stood in the flickering light of a torch. Her accusing silence stung worse than her words of rebuke. He opened the door and entered the courtyard.

Old habits died hard. Although the beast had fought for them, those outside scurried away in fear. A small child wandered into view only to be snatched up by a terrified mother and hauled to safety. *Is this the life ya want for her; living with the rejection of her family and forced into hiding like ya were?*

His feet took him down the cobblestone path, through the trees, and to the lake. Stars filled the heavens with a dazzling brilliance like millions of torches burning in the distance. Shadows of the waning moon were softer, turning the ruins of the gazebo into dark fingers lifting out of the earth. An owl called to its mate, the song of the whippoorwills filled the night, and across the small lake, the smack of a beaver's tail echoed across the water. The high-pitched scream of a night cat brought the beast's head up. A momentary hush settled over the area.

It should have been peaceful, but the turmoil tearing him apart from within, marred the tranquility.

"Go, my wolfen queen. I will rest here, and await yer return." She hesitated briefly at his command, turned, and disappeared into the night.

Sitting by the water's edge, he drew his knees up to his chin and wrapped his arms around his legs. An old acquaintance, loneliness, sat down beside him. *Why the troubled heart? You are free at last to enjoy life.*

Da, I am, but at what price? His mind questioned. *Ta grow old watching Zolona remain young, trapped within the curse.*

Have not I been yer faithful companion through all these past generations? Do not be concerned with the beast. When ya are gone, I will keep her company.

He lowered his head to his knees. *Yer presence was never welcomed and even now, I grow weary.*

Then ya know what ya must do.

"Da, I know." Filip picked up a stone and threw it into the water. The ripples spread out across the smooth surface. From the center of the circles, the water began to boil with an evil hiss; steam rose and formed a small cloud that hovered inches above the surface. It glowed bright against the darkness and slowly moved towards him. The crackle of a demonic laugh filled the air.

Chapter Seven

Anger and resentment welled up inside of him. "Go back ta *hell* where you belong, Mother."

"Ya dare ta try ta destroy the curse? Ya cannot do it, I will not allow it." Lightning flashed within the cloud and the pungent odor of brimstone filled the air. "They must be made ta suffer, as I have all these years."

"Nu!" He jumped to his feet. "It is time ta end the curse and the hatred yer foolish pride caused."

"I have had my revenge on the House of Gravely. Now I will have it on those who sit at my table as though they have the right ta what was mine and is yers by right of birth."

"I will break the curse or die trying," he said with growing conviction.

"Then ya shall join me," she promised. "For ya shall not succeed."

"I love Zolona, and for this reason alone I must try."

"*Love!*" her sarcastic cackle echoed across the lake. The hovering mist lifted and he was alone once again.

His words surprised him. Did he love Zolona? To be honest, the word was foreign to him, as was the emotion. "Love." The full extent of its meaning wasn't clear. He mulled the word over, let it roll off his tongue, and found to his delight it was sweet to the taste and pleasant to the ear.

Filip turned from the lake and strode through the grass to the old ruins. The moonlight had faded, even now the eastern sky held the faint glow of the approaching sun. He loosened his trousers and let them fall to the cold stone.

The beast stood on the other side of the gazebo as if unsure and leery of being inside the circle of stone pillars. With cautious steps, she approached, giving the large flat rock in the center a wide berth, and stopped in front of him.

Using her massive size, the beast blocked his way to the stone. Filip stepped to the left and then to the right. The beast countered each move, never taking her large eyes off of him.

Kneeling down, he lifted his hand to her head. She backed away, teeth bared and a low growl rumbled from her throat. "Ya do not want ta hurt me, Zolona. I am yer shadow-time lover. Remember, ya told me how I used ta come ta ya in yer dreams."

He stretched out his arm, her head became a blur, and her jaws snapped shut on empty air as he jerked his hand back. "Ya are not going ta make this easy, are ya?"

With every muscle coiled, he lunged, wrapped his arms around the body of the beast and stood, pushing it toward the stone. Pain shot down his arm as her teeth sank into his shoulder. The beast toppled backward on the altar taking him with her.

Filip felt the beginning of her change. Her tortured howl rent the shadowed predawn gray. Thrusting his hips against her, his cock pierced the flesh of the half she-wolf Zolona.

Hot human flesh filled his hands. Zolona's body shook with her sobs. Filip tried to rise up but his arm failed him and he fell to lie beside her. Blood matted her hair, covered her left breast. He struggled to sit up and blinding pain forced his eyes closed.

Her tears splattered on the Altar of Sacrifice. "I was willing ta live with ya forever. Why, Filip? Does the title mean that much ta ya?"

"I do not have forever. I would grow old and die, while you remained young. In time, we would have resented each other, and after I was gone, ya would have known the true lonesomeness and isolation of the beast."

He paused, as the altar spun, and the stone pillars danced in the morning light. "The why is easy, I love ya."

She opened her eyes and gasped, "Filip, ya are bleeding."

"A love bite, my lady," he tried to smile. "A small price ta pay ta set my betrothed free."

"Filip!" He collapsed on top of her, and she pushed his body onto the stone altar.

Evil laughter filled the old ruins. "Ya cannot have him!" She recognized the voice and ran for the castle.

Disregarding her nudity, Zolona burst through the courtyard and into the main living quarters of the castle. Servants stared, openmouthed at her blood-drenched body. "Where is my father?" she demanded.

One of them pointed to the dining hall and she rushed in. "Papa!"

"Child, what is the meaning of this and where are yer clothes?" He jumped to his feet and the chair toppled backwards with a crash.

"Filip is dying and the witch has returned for him. Papa, ya must do something."

"Where is he?" He was already in motion, heading towards the door.

"At the lake."

His booming voice filled the castle, as he called out to the servants.

"Get dressed," Maria ordered. "If his evil mother has returned for Filip, then ya alone stand between them."

"Me?" she questioned. "I am nu witch. I have nu power ta stop her."

"Da, ya do Zolona. Look inside ya and speak yer heart."

Running up the stairs to her room, she pulled a dress over her head and left without taking the time to have the back buttoned up. The wind tore at her hair as she ran. Tears streamed down her face at the thought of being too late. Her breath came in harsh labored gasps and her side burned as she entered the clearing at the lake.

A thick swirling fog surrounded the gazebo. Lightning flashed within the stone pillars. His face pale, her father stood rooted in fear before the fog. Zolona did not know what awaited her inside, but with her courage bolstered by the words Maria had spoken, she ran past her father and into the gazebo.

Helen Garlanzo hovered over the Altar of Sacrifice and the body of her son. "Ya dare ta think ya can stop me. Ya have nu power over me. Filip is mine," her evil cackle filled the ruins. Lightning danced across the floor and around the stone where Filip lay.

"I command ya to leave!" Zolona boldly took a step towards the body of Filip lying on the stone.

"Ya command me." Her evil laugh sounded like thunder. "By what authority do ya make such ridiculous request?" Helen demanded.

Look inside ya and speak yer heart. "I love Filip."

"Nu!" The cloud turned dark, blotting out the sun. "Ya do not!"

"I do." Her heart swelled with joy, "and Filip loves me. Yer evil cannot harm us."

Filip struggled to sit up. "Ya know in yer wicked heart what she speaks is true. Be gone from here back ta the fires of hell and may ya burn forever, in yer envy and hatred."

Zolona ran to him, placed his good arm over her shoulder, and staggered under his weight out of the gazebo. A pillar of fire rose from the center of the floor and engulfed the ruins. A large plume of black, rolling smoke towered overhead and a brilliant flash of light momentarily blinded them.

Her sight slowly returned. The ruins were gone. In its place, stood a gazebo made of white marble. "What has happened?" She stared at the beautiful structure. "Where did that come from?"

Filip chuckled. "It has been here all along, obscured by Mother's hate and the curse, for four hundred years. It was built for the day I would take a bride. According ta the lore of the land, if the marriage vows are said with the couple kneeling on the altar, the bride would bear strong children and the land would prosper."

"Is it true, or just a myth?"

"I do not know, but I am willing ta find out." Filip lifted his hand to her face. "If ya will kneel with me on the altar and be my wife."

Her heart swelled up with joy and she found it difficult to see. Turning her head, she took courage in the tear-blurred image of her father's smiling face. She lifted her face to his, "I do love ya, Filip, my shadow-time lover. I would be honored ta be yer wife."

His lips touched hers in a sweet, tender kiss.

Chapter Eight

Zolona sat relaxing in the bath and lifted her chalice as Maria poured more wine. With all the preparations for the wedding, this was a well-needed break. Guests arrived all day and the brother of Richard, Basarab Governor of Valachia, made a grand entrance to the castle and sleeping space soon included the floor of the great hall and the courtyard.

"I take it Filip is still determined ta live at the other end of the estate." Maria laid her head on Zolona's shoulder. "I shall miss ya living so far away."

Zolona sighed. "I am sure ya will, but it is *only* a short journey."

"I think all the fuss over this wedding is a waste." Charline replied with biting sarcastic malice. "After all, it is not like ya are a *virgin*."

"Like you were, Charline," Maria giggled and sat up.

"At least I did not run naked around the castle or come riding in at dawn with pine straw in my hair."

"Please," Zolona begged. "Can not this petty snobbery between us be put aside?"

Standing, she stepped from the pool. Light from the torches reflected off the water droplets clinging to her skin. Maria quickly rose, picked up a wrap, and draped it around her.

"Charline," Zolona paused to gather her words, "as a sister, I love ya even when ya are a pain in the ass."

The Charline's face turned red, and her hand flew to her open mouth.

With a smirk, Maria whispered, "How does it feel ta be on the receiving end for once?"

"Good night, Sisters." Zolona left the bath, made her way through the inner bailey, and climbed the stairs to her room. This night gave little chance of satisfying the craving of her body. Instead of sharing her bed with Filip, she was stuck with the sister of Richard and the portly wife of the Governor for bed partners. Making matters worse, the lady snored.

With her hand on the latch, she paused as the sound of continuous chatter reached her ears. Zolona leaned her head on the cold stonewall and groaned. Turning away from her door, she took the stairs to the castle wall.

She reached the darkened parapet and the night breeze cooled her heated flesh. The song of the whippoorwills along the river filled the air. Below, torches and campfires burned giving light and warmth to those who had not yet sought their bed. A horse whinnied in the corral and another answered. In the distance, somewhere in the mountains, a cat cried, a wolf howled for his mate, and the little foxes sang to the moon.

"Come ta me, my love," she whispered to the wind.

The soft tread of footsteps intruded into the peacefulness of the night and she held her breath. It would not do to be discovered alone on the wall so late at night, especially if the person had stayed too long in his cups.

"My little wolfkin," the low sensual voice of her beloved reached her ears. "Ya should not be up here." His hands clasped her waist and crept up and around her to cup her breasts.

"I am not alone, now." She laid her head back against his solid shoulder. "My shadow-time lover is with me." At the movement, she felt his body tense. "Forgive me, my love. In the joy of your presence, I forgot the injury the beast delivered."

"Think nu more upon the beast, nor upon the past." His fingers loosened the sash of her wrap and the material parted. The light touch of his fingers against her breasts sent a thrill of expectation to pool between her legs.

She lifted her hand to caress his face and her fingers raked through his hair, still wet from his bath. Her other hand slipped between them, her fingers crept inside his robe, and wrapped around the hard length of his cock. A low, trembling groan drifted across her ear.

"Can ya not wait one more night, my love?" she teased as her fingers stroked his throbbing flesh.

His hand dropped lower, fingers slid through the musk-dampened hair and into the wet folds of her flesh. "Ahhhh," her long tortured moan, although whispered, seemed loud in the dark shadows of the walkway.

"Is it my lady's request? Do ya wish me ta stop?"

Zolona rocked her hips against his probing fingers. "Nu, my lord." Turning her head, she sought his mouth and welcomed the fire of his kiss.

"Ya have made me a wanton woman." She let go of his cock and lifted her hand to the wall for support.

"Tomorrow, I shall make you my wanton wife, but for tonight I seek a woman ta satisfy my desire." His tongue captured hers and sucked on it.

"Seek nu further, my love." She ground her hips against him. The length of his cock pressed against her from behind and she leaned over the parapet wall.

Filip lifted the thin material of her wrap. She felt the probing head of his cock seeking entrance and then sliding inside her. Zolona bit back the cry of pleasure lest the guard below her hear and look up.

"Ya are so wet. Yer be well prepared."

His heat dispelled the chill of the stone against her flesh. The roughness of the rock against the aroused nipples of her breast clouded her thoughts. "Ya conspired…with Maria…ta seduce me?"

"Da," his low sensuous chuckle stirred her hair as he bent over her. "I followed ya from the bath, hoping ya would seek the shadows and we could be together."

"I asked the night spirits ta send ya ta me."

Filip drove her into the wall with his savage thrusts. The sensual slap of flesh on flesh filled her ears and drove the night sounds away. His low grunts brought a smile and she ground her hips against his. Fingers clutched at her hips, pulling her hard against him.

His legs trembled against hers and his body shook. Heat flooded through her. Zolona placed her fist in her mouth to keep from crying out as his climax triggered her own and lifted her up where the eagles dwelt, to the snow-covered peaks of the towering Carpathians. She soared on the winds of desire before falling into the refuge of the arms of her shadow-time lover.

Filip held her for several minutes before breaking away and pulling out of her. "Come, my love," he whispered against her hair. "It is with much regret I must return ya ta yer room."

"I do not wish ta go." She turned within his arms and placed her head on his shoulder as her arms snaked around his waist.

"Richard will soon be off watch and we will be discovered." He kissed her forehead and then her nose. "But after tomorrow, we will not have ta be apart in the night." His lips touched hers in tenderness, and with the promise of tomorrow.

His fingers quickly tied the sash of her wrap below her breasts. Taking her hand, he led her back inside the castle walls and to her door. With a final kiss, he turned away and the night shadows covered him.

Zolona finger combed her hair and straightened her wrap. Lifting the latch she entered her room. There was space on the bed but if she had to sleep with someone who snored like a man, that person better have a cock, too. No wonder it was rumored that the Governor and his wife slept in different rooms.

Quietly crossing the floor, she sat on the window seat and leaned against the sill, staring out into the night. She was happy and at peace.

* * * * *

A gentle hand shook her awake. The late morning sunlight brightened the balcony and spilled across the floor. Zolona lifted her head and gave Maria a kiss on the cheek.

"Come, and I will wash away the essence of yer night meeting with yer beloved."

Zolona took her hand, stood, and walked with Maria behind the privacy curtain. A tub filled with steaming water awaited her. Maria untied the wrap and it dropped to the floor.

Stepping over the side of the tub, Zolona eased herself into its encompassing heat and the sensuous fragrance of the rose. "Ah, it feels so wonderful," she sighed. "Thank you."

Maria washed her with care, preparing her for the wedding later that day. "We have good men."

"Da," Zolona answered in a soft relaxed whisper.

"They understand the close bond that be between us ever sense I came to live with ya after me dear parents were killed. They will not deny us our time together."

"Da," Zolona opened her eyes and smiled. "Ya think, perhaps they would like to watch?" She lifted her lips to Maria and took her mouth in a tongue-probing kiss.

Maria broke the kiss and ran her fingers across her breasts. "Perhaps."

She stood and picked up a towel. "Come, there is much to do before the wedding."

Maria dried her off and picked up a long white cotton gown trimmed with red lace, and short off-the-shoulder sleeves. Over the gown, she placed an apron covered with red and purple flowers, and golden feathers of the peacock.

"I have never seen this before." Zolona ran her hands over the tiny stitching of the design.

"It is my wedding present ta ya."

"It is very beautiful, Maria." She gave her a hug. "Thank ya."

Going down to the great room, she found servants scurrying around sweeping the floor, cleaning the table, and laying new reeds and flowers on the floor. Dogs sniffed the floor for bones hidden away in the bedding only to find them gone.

Outside in the courtyard, a sense of enthusiastic chaos hovered under the surface of growing tension. With the wedding only hours away the final preparations for the feast were well underway. Large spits, turned by young boys from the village, held sides of beef, pigs, and roasts of mutton.

Toddlers ran naked through the crowd playing and adding to the festive atmosphere permeating the courtyard. More guests arrived from the surrounding countryside and the activities spilled over outside the castle walls.

A special gift arrived from the Governor of Valachia, a wagon bearing three barrels of oysters straight from the Black Sea, and a barrel of his finest wine.

The wedding feast would last for days.

She wandered over to the chapel. Having been purged from evil with a liberal sprinkling of salt, the new priest stood before the altar confirming wedding vows, christening babies, and offering sacraments.

She watched for a while and turned away, confused seeing little difference between the priests and the old witch. If they were so powerful, why had the old woman been able to laugh at their Holy Water and eventually drive them from the estate?

"Wait, child."

Zolona looked up into the face of Lord Basarab, Governor of Valachia. "Da, Sire." She bowed her head and curtsied. She rose to her feet but kept her eyes lowered.

"What power broke the evil curse of the witch?" he asked.

She lifted her eyes to his kind face. There was no condemnation or rebuke, only a comforting smile. The words of Maria came to mind. "The power of love, my lord."

"So this love," he paused, "was more powerful than the evil?"

"Da." Had his lordship been reading her thoughts?

"The God of love, whom these people now worship openly, has shown mercy ta the land. He does not demand their allegiance, but waits for it ta be freely given, from the heart."

It was as if the sun had burst through the darkness of her confusion and she smiled.

"Will you go with me ta the priest, and give yer allegiance to the True Power, the God of Heaven?" He held out his hand to her.

"Da," she whispered and glanced around in apprehension. "If He will have me, I will."

"He turns none away." The Governor offered his arm and she placed her hand on it. He led her to the altar and knelt with her as the priest offered up prayers on her behalf.

She lost track of time as she listened to the priest. Feeling a tug on her arm, she rose with Governor Basarab, walked with him down the aisle, and stepped outside. Maria came running up to her.

"There you are." She clutched at her breast, her sides heaving. "I have searched for ya until I am near beside myself. We must hurry and dress for the wedding."

Zolona lifted her eyes to the mountains. Where had the day gone? "Da, I'm coming."

She turned to the Governor, curtsied, and kissed his hand. "Thank ya, my lord. Now if ya will excuse me."

Taking Maria's hand, they ran across the courtyard through the throng of guests.

* * * * *

Shadow-time quickly approached. Zolona came down the stairs wearing a wedding gown of imported dark blue Chinese silk and a wreath of edelweiss woven through her hair. Her father waited at the foot of the stairs and held out his hand.

"Ya make a beautiful bride, my daughter." He kissed her cheek. "The Governor and I feel it best if the name of Garlanzo never surfaces again, and Filip agrees. Everyone has been sworn ta secrecy and his true identity will never be known."

"Even Sister Charline?" she asked with great doubt.

"Da!" he laughed. "Even she has been warned ta hold her tongue. Although," he winked, "the task may prove too taxing for her."

He led Zolona out of the castle and paused. The scene before her had been altered dramatically. The animals were gone, except for the dogs looking for free handouts around the fire pits. Long tables filled the yard and the tantalizing aroma of cooked meat assaulted her senses. Placing her hand over her stomach, she waited for the butterflies to leave.

A path of flower petals led out of the castle and with her hand on the arm of her father, she left the castle and followed the flower-strewn cobblestone path. Torches burned along the way sending shadows dancing through the trees. The sweet perfume of their oil filled the air.

Stepping into the clearing, the heady fragrance of freshly cut hay hung heavy over the area and assaulted her senses with every step. The wedding chapel, awash with the light from a hundred torches greeted her. Inside, Filip and the priest waited at the stone altar.

Her father led her to the chapel and stepped inside. Kissing her on each cheek, he placed her hand in the hand of Filip and stepped back. Together they knelt on the stone altar.

The priest lit two large white candles, one on each side of the altar and began reading from the 127th Psalm. She had secretly hoped the ceremony would be short, but it was not to be, as the priest began to offer up prayers for each noble in attendance, and, it seemed, for every person living and dead the priest had ever known. Next he went through the church history from creation of Eve from the rib of Adam to the Christ dying on the cross. "…Blessed is the Father, and of the Son, and of the Holy Ghost, now and forever."

He paused and all those assembled sang "Amen".

He picked up the marriage crowns. Her sigh of relief of it being almost over changed to a whispered groan as the priest again started petitioning God for His blessing of the crowns. First by reminding Him of Adam and Eve in the garden, and progressing through the patriarchs and saints of the Holy Book.

She was only half listening to the priest, wishing the ceremony were over, when part of his prayer became very personal. "…bless Zolona and the fruit of her womb. May her children rise up and be great. Blessed is the Father, and of the Son, and of the Holy Ghost, now and forever.

Does he know I am with child already? She glanced to the side and looked at Filip. She had not even told her beloved. *I didn't even tell Maria.*

He paused and all those assembled sang "Amen".

I just wish I knew when. Before or after the curse was broken?

"Now, the Servant of the God, Filip Mircea marries the Servant of the God, Zolona, in the name of the Father, and of the Son, and of the Holy Ghost." The priest said this three times as if God wasn't listening the first time and then picked up a marriage crown and moved it in the sign of the cross in front of Filip.

Filip kissed the crown and then her father, acting as wedding godfather, and the priest placed it on Filip's head.

The priest went through the same words again, this time picking up the other crown and making the sign of the cross with it in front of her face. Zolona kissed the crown and her mother stepped forward to help the priest set it on her head.

"Oh God our Lord, with honesty and grandeur crown them." The priest took bread and wine, blessed them, and gave them to her and Filip. Picking up a *cadenita* of burning incense, he made the sign of the cross above their heads.

Filip rose and she stood with him as they began a procession around the altar called the Dance of Isaiah. She followed Filip, who followed the priest with the burning *cadenita* three times around the altar. Her father and mother followed behind her.

At the end of their third trip around the stone, the priest again asked the blessing of God upon Filip. At the end of his prayer, Filip made the sign of the cross three times and bowed his head. The wedding godfather and priest removed the crown and placed it on the holy book.

Zolona had to endure yet another lengthy prayer before she too was allowed to have the crown removed.

She breathed a sigh of relief when it was over and Filip kissed her for the first time as his wife. "I love ya, Zolona," he whispered.

"Nu less than my love for ya, my shadow-time lover." She gave him a hug. They followed the cobblestone path from the Wedding Chapel back to the castle and the beginning of the wedding feast.

Author's Note

For centuries, Romania has been a battleground, a chess piece upon the table of political power and economical plunder for surrounding neighbors. It wasn't until the Treaty of Trent at the end of WWI, and the Treaty of Craiova, at the end of World War II that the present-day Romania came into being.

In the early history of Romania, there were three main provinces — Valachia, Moldavia, and Transylvania. The majority of Transylvania was, after many years of bloodshed, controlled by Hungary/Germany. The remainder of Romania was sought after by the Ottoman Empire of Turkey and what is today Russia. Eventually, after years of paying tribute, Vlad Dracula broke Ottoman power over Romania in the 1400s. In 1477 Vlad Dracula was slain in a battle with the Turks.

This is a partial listing of the leadership history of Romanian Provinces:

Basarab I...1324-1352...Valachia

Bogdan I...1359-1365...Moldavia

Mircea the Old...1386-1418...Valachia (Grandfather of Dracula)

Vlad Dracul...1430-1477...Valachia (Father of Dracula)

Vlad Draculea (Dracula)...1448 (two months) He was overthrown and lived in exile in Transylvania and Moldavia until 1456 when he gained power and ruled Valachia until 1462. In 1462, he was imprisoned in Hungary. In 1476, Vlad was released to again rule over Valachia and fight against the Ottoman Empire. He was killed in battle two months later.

About the author:

Romance Author R Casteel retired from the US Navy in 1990. He enjoys the outdoors, loves to scuba dive, and is a Search and Rescue Diver. With twenty years of military service, which included experience as flight crewman, search and rescue, and four years as a Military Police Officer, it is of little wonder that his books are filled with suspense and intrigue.

As to his ability to write romance, Gloria for Best Reviews writes "I had thought Leigh Greenwood was the only man who wrote wonderful romance...I was wrong...Rod Casteel is right there too!"

Mr. Casteel lives in his hometown of Lancaster, Missouri, and would love to hear from you.

Mr. Casteel welcomes mail from readers. You can write to him c/o Ellora's Cave Publishing at 1056 Home Avenue, Akron OH 44310-3502.

Also by R. Casteel:

Mistress Of Table Rock
Tanieka: Daughter Of The Wolf
Texas Thunder
The Crimson Rose
The Toymaker

A Matter of Duty

Elizabeth Jewell

Chapter One

Piper woke slowly, a pale shaft of light touching her face. Today was the day.

Two years. As of today, she and Trey had been married for two years. Not perfect years, but she hadn't expected or asked for perfection. She had asked only for love, and had not been disappointed.

It had been unexpected, but the best things often were. When he had appeared in her favorite bar wearing the face of her dead lover, she had gone home with him on an ill-conceived whim, hoping for little more than a quick, mindless fuck, something to take her mind off what she had lost when Billy had killed himself. Instead she had found Trey.

The ensuing weeks had been strange, frightening, and exhilarating. Discovering Trey's true identity, his position in the secretive and highly organized shapeshifter community, discovering his gifts, seeing what he could do, what he was—she could now rate these as some of the most bizarre experiences of her life. And the most important, because they had brought her here. Here where she lay next to the man she loved, he wearing the face they had chosen together.

Two years. It was hard to believe, but it was true. She smiled to herself, treasuring the knowledge and the sense of comfort and safety it provided. Twenty-four months. 730 days. The warm bulk of him in her bed. His voice, his touch, the particular smell of his skin. Her Trey.

He moved next to her, rolling over to face her.

"Morning," he said, his voice languid and sultry. "Happy Anniversary."

She smiled back. There was nothing quite as beautiful as Trey in the morning, tousled and golden, with that bleary, not-quite-focused look in his eyes. She moved a little closer to him and leaned in for a kiss.

"Happy Anniversary."

She kissed him, slow and sleepy, taking her time. His tongue traced hers gently, without demands.

"I love you," he whispered against her mouth, and she smiled and kissed him again.

"Love you, Trey."

He put an arm around her, pulling her close. Content, she nestled into his chest and closed her eyes.

He didn't quite smell human. She had noticed this about him early on; there was a prickly tanginess to his scent, rather like a citrusy deodorant soap. It was subtle, she had barely even noticed it until they had moved in together. Now it seemed to permeate everything from the bed to his clothes to the very air of the apartment. It didn't bother her—it was just different. It was Trey.

She nestled into the familiar embrace, the familiar smell. She could honestly say she had never been so happy. Trey shifted, holding her closer, his hands sliding down her body.

"So," he said, and she could hear the smile in his voice, "who do you want this morning?"

"Trey. I want Trey."

He laughed. His hands moved up to cup her breasts, thumbs toying with her rising nipples. "We talked about this."

"I know we did. I wasn't really listening, though."

He slid firm, flattened palms down her belly until they lay nestled against her hipbones. "Anyone," he said. "Anyone you like."

"I like Trey." She was being deliberately stubborn; she knew it annoyed him.

"And Trey is glad for that." He snuggled her closer. "But today Trey wants to gift you."

Piper smiled. Trey's hips were tight up against her now; she could feel the ridge of his erection prodding into her groin. "Then Trey can start by gifting me with Trey." Before he could protest, she added, "We can see where it goes from there."

He nodded and kissed her again. His mouth was warm and firm and he explored her, lips and tongue moving rhythmically against hers. She opened to him, let him in. He tasted like early morning lust. Her fingers laced into his hair, shifting his head so that his mouth slanted against hers.

She delved into his mouth for a time, tasting the planes and corners. She loved the way he kissed, with enthusiasm and something almost like curiosity, though he'd kissed her a thousand times since they'd met. His hands moved over her body as if he were learning her, as if he'd never touched her before, the tips of his fingers drifting over her skin, leaving trails of longing in their wake. She looked into his eyes, into the clear, crystalline blue, the tiny mole on his lower left eyelid.

Every once in a while it still occurred to her to consider the artistry, the care, that had gone into the construction of this face. His true face, the raw, unformed Trey, was blank, hairless, blunt. It was second nature to them, though, to reconstruct a human form in every imaginable detail. Shapeshifters did it as easily as breathing.

He bent toward her and kissed her again. Perfectly detailed, down to the pattern of the taste buds on his tongue. He was perfection, but with all the necessary flaws to make him human. His mouth perhaps a little too small for his face, the lines across his forehead a bit deeper than one might expect in a man his apparent age. His hands were square and solid, his touch confident and sure.

She surrendered to that touch, letting herself go lax under his skilled ministrations. He knew exactly how and where to touch her—he always had, another skill inherent to his race. It was a kind of surface mind reading, the same skill that had allowed him to recreate himself as Billy when he and Piper had first met. It hadn't been quite enough, though, for him to discover that Billy was dead. Otherwise, he never would have worn the other man's face.

It had forced them together—the ancient rules of the shapeshifter community demanded that Trey basically give himself to Piper, once she understood what he was, and that he had approached her in false pretenses.

She didn't mind that he'd lied to her. She hadn't even then, because she'd known full well he wasn't Billy. She wondered from time to time what it might have been like if Billy hadn't been dead, if he had approached her in the guise of another lover, one who had only broken her heart. But if that had been the case, they wouldn't be together now.

He cupped her breast, his thumb pressing gently into her nipple, rolling it. Heat burgeoned in her at the touch. She shivered, warm, slick heat growing between her legs. She opened under him, embracing him with her legs. He settled down between her thighs, the hard ridge of his erection rubbing into her. God, but she wanted him inside. Now. Hard and fast.

Bending his head, he tongued her nipple, toying with the erect bud, scraping it gently with his teeth. He kissed down the side of her breast, to the valley between, then back up, until his tongue touched the other nipple. She closed her eyes as his tongue curled around her, feeling the soft friction, the slightly rough texture of his tongue. He sucked, laved, and fire flooded her, shooting down her body, straight to her groin. She pulsed there, her labia thick and heavy, her sex opening, ready. So hot, so deep…

He lifted his head from her breast and lifted himself over her, his tongue trailing up her neck, over her chin. His lips brushed hers, ever so lightly. At the same time, his hand slipped down her stomach, moving her nightgown out of the way, his fingers moving under the elastic of her panties. She pushed up toward him, drawing his fingers down, almost into her. He opened his eyes, sapphire glinting from between golden lashes. A smile curved his mouth.

"I want you," she murmured. "*You*."

He smiled a little. She knew she perplexed him in her insistence that he maintain his usual form when they made love. He could be anyone—the Hollywood hunk du jour, her greatest fantasy, the man she'd had a crush on in college... He didn't understand why she so rarely took advantage of that.

She wasn't even sure she could have given him a coherent answer, if he ever came out and asked. It seemed wrong to her, though, to want this man and that man, and not *the* man—the face he chose to present to the world—when they shared these intimate moments. It was like cheating on him. Except with him...

No point puzzling it all out, because it would never make any sense. Instead she closed her eyes and reveled in the sensation of his fingers gently invading her, separating the lips of her sex, dipping into the deep, hot core of her. She pushed her hips against him, drawing his fingers inside her. He put an arm around her shoulders and held her against him as she rode his hand, pounding herself down on him. He added a third finger, filling her deeply. Fire flooded her; he curled the tips of his fingers just so, finding the exact place inside her that made her entire body fill with harsh stilettos of desire.

"Trey—" she managed, but even the single syllable was lost as her body suddenly clenched, leapt, then flew, orgasm ripping through her from cunt to fingertips. She let out a deep, ragged moan.

She heard him laugh, then suddenly his fingers slid out of her and he pressed in hard and deep with a cock that felt thicker, more blunt, than it had last time. He always did that. She didn't ask him to change his face, or his body, so he altered his cock. She'd had it long, slim, curved, straight, thick, blunt... She actually hadn't thought penises could come in such great variation until she had been exposed to Trey's remarkably imaginative shapeshifting ability.

It was short suddenly, short and thick. She pressed her calves against his ass, urging him closer, deeper. He thrust hard, and as he did so, his cock changed shape, lengthening with each stroke, until it was lodged deep and firm inside her, filling her completely. He pressed into her a few times that way, so big she could barely contain him. The deep, intense friction drove her near to the heights again, enflaming her, until finally she keened out her pleasure, digging her fingers hard into his shoulders as he fucked her.

He changed then, the bulk of his shaft slimming until he slid easily in and out of her, still filling her, but not overwhelming her body. She moved with him, working herself on him, her inner tissues sensitized now from the too-bulky shaft that had just invaded her. The combination drove the sensation to a nearly unimaginable peak, higher and higher — then he reached between them, and touched her...

His finger brushed over her clit and she fell apart, shuddering and crying out, her body caught in a long, slow pulsation of ecstasy. As her body arched, he slid an arm under her, supporting her, his mouth finding hers, taking in the sounds of her climax. She was lost, open beneath him and falling to pieces, but he held her together, cradling her in her vulnerability.

She let out a long, slow breath, shivering. He kissed her one last time, then slid deep into her. She felt him pulse inside her, felt his body coil and then relax slowly, as he, too finished.

"I love you," he whispered, touching her face as the last of his climax was wrung from his body.

She smiled. "I love you, too." Looking down, she touched him gently, tracing his flagging erection with her finger. "Again?"

He grinned. "Yes?"

"Yes."

"Preferences?"

"Surprise me."

The expression on his face was more than worth it. He loved using his skills to please her, loved showing what he could do. She couldn't help returning his enthusiasm with smugness, though, because what she'd asked him to do would benefit her more than it would him.

Trey leaned back in the bed, resting his head against the pillow and closing his eyes. Piper rolled onto his chest and kissed him, his nipples, the concavity between his pectoral muscles, down onto his belly, to the soft smatter of light brown hair there, down to his navel. Her fingers massaged his cock as she moved, feeling it soften, easing around the shaft as it lost turgidity and slowly deflated.

And changed.

It shrank back into his body, changed shape, widening, opening, the sensitive tissue reconfiguring into soft lips, an open channel, a hardening clit. Piper kissed him, low on his abdomen, at the crease where belly became groin, right above the brown triangle of hair.

She'd done this before, and more than once, but she still always found it hard to begin. He changed so much when he shifted, not just the shapes of his body, the transformation of his sex from male to female, but the texture, the smell—everything was different. Turning her head, she nuzzled the rough hair against her cheek, closing her eyes, taking in all the different sensations. Her lips brushed Trey's skin as it softened, feminized. When she looked up, she saw a different body, breasts bulging up from a narrower chest, and Trey looked down at her with the face of a woman she recognized.

He'd chosen an actress again, someone Piper had seen on TV recently, and had commented the woman was attractive and not overly thin, like so many actresses and models. Piper liked a fuller-bodied woman—and that was something it had never ever occurred to her to think about, at least in sexual terms, until she'd met Trey.

His—her—hand came down to caress Piper's hair, and Piper obligingly dipped her head, pressing Trey's now-female legs open to slip her tongue between the warm, salty labia.

Even his voice had changed, gasping in a thoroughly female range as Piper explored the newly formed, perfectly textured cunt with her mouth and tongue, sliding her fingers along the smooth, hot skin, pushing two inside to feel the depths of a channel that grew and widened as she penetrated it, both from arousal and from Trey's purposeful transformation.

Licking and thrusting, Piper worked Trey's newly transformed body, feeling thighs, belly and cunt shiver under her ministrations, absorbing the by now familiar scent of his female arousal. But she'd learned how to work him, and while it had never occurred to her before she'd tried it that she might enjoy pleasuring another woman's body, she enjoyed this immensely. Of course, the fact she knew the body beneath her was Trey helped, but didn't change the fact that she was going down on a woman.

He trembled under her and suddenly she felt his body shake and pulse as his orgasm wrenched through him, and he let out a long, low, shuddering breath. Piper licked the hard, slick clit until Trey pushed her away, then, chuckling, lifted herself along Trey's transformed body to mouth his breasts, suckling at the thick nipples, laughing as he closed his woman's eyes and smiled in contentment.

"Should I change back?" he asked, his woman's voice soft and husky.

Piper considered, then set back to work laving the soft, round breasts. It was comforting, warm.

"Not yet."

He smiled, and closed his eyes.

* * * * *

He brought her breakfast later, a tray with poached eggs and toast, segmented oranges, a bowl of grapes. She could smell the coffee brewing in the other room, the rich odor filling the bedroom. Closing her eyes, she drew in the scent.

He approached the bed with the food. He was Trey again, broad-shouldered and masculine. "It'll be ready in a few minutes. I knew you'd want it."

"I always want coffee."

She adjusted the tray as he set it in her lap. He slid back into the bed beside her, smiling, then took a handful of grapes out of the bowl.

"Two years," he said. "It doesn't feel like that long."

"But it feels like forever, too, in a way."

He nodded. "I can barely remember what it was like not to have you with me."

Tears prickled her eyes, and she found herself at a loss for words. She could remember what it had been like before. She had been broken, still mourning Billy's death, even blaming herself for it. Then Trey had come into her life, wearing Billy's face, and changed everything.

She picked up a piece of orange and nibbled at it, blinking back her tears. She wasn't sure why she was crying. Maybe just because she was happy, but something mournful seemed to have come to life in the middle of her chest. Something empty.

Trey bent toward her, studying her face. "Are you all right?"

"I'm fine. Just...*post coitum triste*, maybe."

He smiled a little, running a hand over her hair. "I see."

She bit into the piece of orange and the juice ran down her chin. Laughing, Trey bent forward, just as she lifted a hand to intercept the drips. He won the race, his mouth covering her chin seconds before her hand made it there. His tongue laved her, cleaning her face, and she couldn't help returning his soft laughter.

"I love you," she said, pushing back the small, sad thought that had risen in the back of her mind.

"I love you, too," he said, and kissed her gently.

Chapter Two

The next day was Sunday morning, and Piper took advantage of the fact by staying in bed, blissfully tucked under a warm blanket. Trey had gotten out of bed an hour or so earlier, and she could hear him puttering in the other room.

Alone in the bed, she closed her eyes and let herself think. Allowed herself to dive down, into that emptiness in her chest, to discover what it was. Although she already knew. She had just hidden it, forced herself not to acknowledge it.

She wanted a child. A baby with Trey's blue eyes, his humor, his smile. But those things weren't really Trey's. He didn't own them—they had invented them together. And even if that were not the case, he was incapable of giving her a child.

She had known this, of course. He'd explained it to her before they had gotten married. He could not father a child with a human woman—only with another shapeshifter. She knew this and had told him it was all right, but it some ways it wasn't, and now it had begun to weigh on her.

Stupid, she thought. With everything they had—the love, the beauty they shared in bed and out, the small moments when they were so deeply connected it could feel like sex even when it wasn't—with all that, why was she pining for a baby? Especially when she knew full well she couldn't have one. Not by him, in any case.

It would pass. Eventually, her heart, mind and body would all catch up to each other, and she would be able to put the longing aside. It was a natural thing, hormones maybe, affecting her emotions. It would pass.

In the living room, the phone rang. Twice, three times, then she heard Trey answer it. She took a long, deep breath and sat up. She should get up and get dressed.

She was pulling on her sweater when Trey came into the bedroom, quiet, an oddly sober expression on his face.

"What is it?" Her first thought was that someone had died. She couldn't imagine who—they didn't know that many people. Unless it was someone in the shapeshifter community...

She forced the thought away as Trey bent in to kiss her softly. "Just something we need to talk about." He smiled a little. "Come on into the kitchen. I'll make you breakfast."

* * * * *

Trey placed a pancake on Piper's plate, then handed her the butter tray. She was waiting, patiently, he knew, for him to talk to her, but he wanted to wait until she was at least settled over her breakfast. Maybe it wasn't the best idea. Maybe he should have told her straight out, without delaying it.

He'd known this day would come the moment he'd realized how thoroughly in love with her he had fallen. It had been inevitable. More so when he'd been made the leader of the shapeshifter community, because an even greater onus had been placed upon him when he had shouldered that responsibility. But it couldn't be helped. And Piper knew—he hadn't hidden the facts from her.

But the look on her face right now worried him. She was quiet, a little withdrawn, and he saw sadness in her eyes. He wondered what she'd been thinking about before he'd come into the bedroom.

"Is everything all right?" she asked, her voice soft, as she spread butter over the pancakes. It melted, golden, into the smooth surface, dripped down onto the plate.

"Yeah. It's all right. I just have to talk to you about something."

She looked up, frowned, then blinked. "The phone call?"

"Yes."

Her fingers curled around her fork and she lifted it, staring at it. "It was one of them, wasn't it? They need you."

"Yes. There's been a request."

"Do you have to honor it?"

"The woman is of high rank, and has been through an approval process that takes a considerable amount of time. I can't deny her, not given the rank I have now."

Piper smiled sadly. "It's okay. I understand."

He frowned, saying nothing. She didn't understand—there really was no way she could. He hadn't faced this situation before, himself. So even he didn't quite understand.

"We knew it was coming," Piper went on. She seemed to be trying to reassure him. Ironic, he thought. It seemed he should be taking that role with her. This was his world, after all, impinging on the peacefulness they had built here together.

"Yes, we did. We knew it would happen eventually."

"It'll be all right," he said. "I'll be sure you're all right."

She quirked an eyebrow at him. "I appreciate the sentiment, but I'm not sure how you can guarantee that."

"I can't. I'll do my best."

Reaching across the table, she laid a hand on his. "I can't ask for anything more."

* * * * *

The Binghams' house was small, but in a nice neighborhood. Red brick, with white doors, and a small but very green lawn. It seemed homey to Piper, and that made her glad.

She forced that thought back. She didn't want to feel glad, or at home, or anything of the sort. She just wanted to get through the next couple of hours without falling apart.

Trey knocked on the door. Piper slipped her hand into his as they waited, then wished she hadn't. Somehow touching him made her misgivings even harder to bear. He squeezed her hand, undoubtedly trying to reassure her. It didn't help.

The woman answered the door. She was shorter than Piper, with hair a rich, burnished gold. Her face was round, her blue eyes uptilted, elfin. Piper wanted to be able to say she could sense something about her, something that told her she wasn't human, but it wasn't true. She'd lived with a shapeshifter for two years now; she should be able to discern these things. But she couldn't. Nothing about the woman indicated she was anything other than human. In her meticulously realistic construction of her appearance, she had even manufactured smile lines.

"Trey," she said. Her voice was light, with a little bit of smoke to it. "Piper. Thank you for seeing us." She held her hand out to Piper. "I'm Nadia Bingham."

Piper took the small hand, though reluctantly. "Nice to meet you."

Nadia smiled a little, then turned to Trey. She seemed more hesitant to shake his hand, but still held hers out. Trey took it.

God, could this be any more awkward? Piper wondered.

Of course it could.

"Come in and meet Brice," said Nadia, and Trey nodded.

Piper followed the others into the house. Small but homey inside, just like the outside. The smell of cinnamon filled the front room. Potpourri, she thought. It smelled too natural to be air freshener.

Brice emerged from the kitchen with a tray of hors d'oeuvres and a smile. He was about Trey's height, but slim, leaner, with knife-edge cheekbones and startlingly blue eyes. His dark hair curled against the collar of his casual chambray shirt.

"Hi," he said. "I'm Brice. Nice to meet you."

He shook Trey's hand, then Piper's. Piper made herself smile at him. She couldn't help but wonder how he felt about the situation.

"I'm really glad you came," he went on, and he sounded genuinely enthusiastic. "We've been waiting for a long time."

Trey nodded. "I know. Three years."

"Why did it take so long?"

With a wry smile, Trey reached for a mini-bagel. "I have to blame the previous administration."

Nadia gave a sober nod. "Not a good situation, that."

"No."

Piper nodded. The situation had been very bad, in fact, and had nearly cost Trey his life. But, in the end, it had brought them together.

And it had brought them here. Piper took a slow, careful breath, trying to collect herself.

Nadia seemed to sense her mood. "Why don't you two have a seat? Can I get you something to drink?"

"Iced tea?" Piper felt ridiculous. She wished they would just get to the point. They could pussyfoot around it all night, and it wouldn't change anything.

Nadia nodded. She took a step toward the kitchen, then turned back. "I know this is difficult. It's been difficult for us, too. We'll work it out, I promise."

Piper smiled a little, watching Nadia go to the kitchen. She seemed nice enough. Piper hoped she was right.

Brice put the tray of food down on the coffee table and took a seat in a recliner opposite Piper. "I know this probably all seems very sudden to you."

"I knew it would happen, at some point. Probably more than once."

Brice nodded. "The approval procedure is extensive and time-consuming. We were beginning to wonder if it would ever go through, especially after the…changes."

Piper had never thought to wonder how the events of two years ago might have affected anyone other than herself and Trey. Of course there had been the gathering of the shapeshifter community, and she'd realized there were others who would be affected, but not on this kind of personal level. To have waited so long for an approval to have a baby, then to have something change so drastically in the hierarchy...

"It must have come as a horrible shock," she offered.

"Yes. We were optimistic, even though we knew things were deteriorating, but we were very much afraid we might have to start over."

Piper looked at Trey, remembering numerous phone calls, trips to Australia, in the earlier days of their marriage.

"That didn't seem fair to me," he said. "Though it was suggested on more than one occasion, that everyone in pending approval be backed up, and the whole process started over. There was some concern that Mesharet might have skewed the process."

Brice frowned. "He didn't, did he?"

"Not that I could tell."

Piper wondered what criteria Mesharet might have used. His ideas of racial superiority had led to most of the troubles, so she imagined that particular train of thought had entered into considerations of procreation, as well. Then she couldn't help but wonder what criteria Trey might have used. This was the first time a woman had been approved to have a child since Trey had come into his leadership position. Why her? Had he made judgments, himself? Picked her because she appealed to him?

She pushed that thought back. They were shapeshifters. Physical attractiveness meant nothing—they could take on any form they chose. Still, a shapeshifter mated to a human was more likely, as she understood it, to adopt a semi-permanent form, much as Trey had. Maybe this Nadia face had sparked a spark—

Nadia returned from the kitchen, carrying a tray of iced teas. She set the tray on the table next to the hors d'oeuvres, then picked up a glass and handed it to Piper. Piper took it.

"Thank you."

"You're welcome." Nadia took a seat in the chair next to her husband. "So. This is incredibly awkward."

Piper laughed, surprising herself. "Yes, it is."

"Maybe we should just cut to the chase, then," said Brice. "Trey, sir, I'd like you to do me the honor of sleeping with my wife."

There was a moment of silence, then suddenly Piper laughed. The surge of relief surprised her. If they all had a sense of humor, maybe this would go more smoothly than she'd thought.

Brice turned toward her, his mouth twitching nearly into a smile. "With your express and carefully worded permission, of course."

"Of course," said Piper. "Wouldn't have it any other way."

Quietly, Nadia cleared her throat. "Actually, there was one other thing we wanted to mention."

The silence fell again, taut and uncomfortable. Piper carefully set her iced tea back down on the table. "What's that?"

"Well..." Nadia began, stopped, then began again. "We know that you're in a similar situation, Piper. I mean, in that you can't have a child with Trey. We thought...we thought perhaps we might offer to help with that."

Piper's eyes widened. The thought had never occurred to her. Of course, she'd thought often about the fact she couldn't have Trey's children. She'd also thought about the inevitability of his being called essentially to do stud service to another shapeshifter. But this... This hadn't even crossed her mind.

"You mean—" She broke off, at a loss as to how to voice the thought.

"That's right," said Nadia, smiling. "I'm offering you Brice's sperm."

Piper looked at Trey. Trey seemed surprised, as well.

"We hadn't discussed this as a possibility," he said.

"I thought you might not have." Nadia set her own glass back down and rubbed her small hands together as if to warm them. "It seemed fair, though, to us."

Before she realized what she was doing, Piper brushed her fingers over her stomach. "I...I don't know. I'll have to think about it." She glanced at Brice. He was an attractive man. But maybe they had something else in mind...

"There are options," Brice put in, almost as if he'd read her mind. "Artificial insemination—I know Nadia and Trey can't go that route, because of what they are, but we certainly could. I don't want you to think—" He broke off.

Just when I thought things couldn't get any more awkward, Piper thought. She managed to smile at Brice. "I'll definitely have to think about it. I'd gotten used to the idea that we would never have children. I was thinking about adoption, or some other options..." She trailed off. It seemed overly difficult to finish a sentence in this room, for some reason.

Trey was regarding her soberly. "Yes, we'll definitely have to give it some thought." He looked at Nadia. "It's a very generous offer, and we appreciate it."

There was a strange edge to his voice, and Piper wondered what he was thinking. Surely he wasn't upset by Brice's offer. She'd lived for two years with the knowledge that he would have to, at some point, sleep with another woman to fulfill his duty as leader of the shapeshifter community. Likely this would happen more than once. Surely he wasn't upset at the thought she might do the same thing, for basically the same reasons.

Although, to be honest, she had to admit it was all quite odd.

"Certainly we didn't expect an answer right away," said Nadia. She seemed more comfortable with the situation than any of the rest of them. "It's a big decision, having a child."

"Yes, it is." Piper looked again at Trey. Small talk, she decided. A little small talk would fix everything. "So... Nadia, what do you do for a living?"

* * * * *

Piper was quiet and contemplative on the drive home. There were far too many things to mull over. But her mind remained mostly blank. She almost didn't want to think about any of it.

Trey remained quiet, as well, but he kept looking in her direction, as if waiting for her to speak. He didn't push, though, for which she was grateful.

When they arrived back home, Piper took off her coat and headed to the bedroom, to remove her makeup. She stood in front of the bathroom mirror for a time, just looking at her own face, scrubbed clean of makeup and pretense. Her eyes were dark, she noticed, the irises a deeper gray than usual. She looked tired.

A small sound behind her caught her attention and she turned to see Trey in the doorway behind her. He looked thoughtful, serious.

"Are you okay?" he asked.

She nodded. "Yeah, I think so." One last look in the mirror to see the small frown lines between her brows, then she turned back to face him. "A lot to think about."

"Do you want a baby?"

It seemed a straightforward enough question, but she found herself stuttering over the answer, mentally as well as verbally. "I...I hadn't really thought about it."

"Of course you have."

She shook her head and walked past him, out of the bathroom into the bedroom. "No, I really haven't. I've thought about the fact that I can't have a baby, not with you, and about the fact that I love you and wish sometimes that things were different—" She broke off. "That's not the same as thinking seriously about whether I want to have a baby."

"I do."

The statement was blunt, but gentle. Piper looked at him, surprised. He was sober, a weight of sadness in his eyes.

"Do you?"

"Yes. A child for us to raise together—even a child not of my blood—it's more than I ever dared to hope for."

Piper swallowed, her throat suddenly thick. She'd had no idea Trey felt this way. They hadn't talked about it; she'd assumed the point was moot.

"I think I do," she said. "When I think about you and I not being able to—it makes me sad."

He nodded. "It's not for me to decide, certainly."

She nodded and settled down onto the bed. "If we decide to do this, though…"

"I know." He came to sit next to her on the bed. Gently, he stroked her hair. "We can think about it. We don't have to decide now."

Piper nodded. They had told Nadia they would get back to her in a few days. She hadn't seemed to mind their putting her off for a bit; she'd waited three years, she could wait a few more days. But Piper knew full well Trey would have to answer her, if only to fulfill his personal obligation to her.

Trey's fingers gently tucked her hair behind her ear. "I have to sleep with her. You understand that. You understand why. But you don't have to sleep with him."

She looked at him sidelong. "Are you telling me you don't want me to?"

He shrugged. "Actually, I think it might be better if you did. I just don't want you to think you have to."

Piper's eyes widened. "Really? You think I *should*?"

"Artificial insemination is a complicated and expensive procedure. Invasive, but impersonal. If you don't want to have to go through that, you shouldn't have to."

"I think the expensive part was the key, there." She gave him a wry grin to let him know she was kidding, and his return smile held more than a little relief.

"No, not really."

"It might be more likely to take, the natural way," she offered.

"Maybe, maybe not. I would think it would depend on how nervous you were about it."

"That's a good point."

His fingers touched the back of her neck, gently rubbing. The contact relaxed her.

"I just want you to know I'm behind whatever decision you make. If you want to have a baby, this is an opportunity that might not come again. But there are other ways. Artificial insemination from an anonymous donor, or another donor…we could adopt…"

"On the other hand," she said, breaking through his voice as he trailed off, "you get to sleep with her, so what's good for the goose…"

"I *have* to sleep with her. Artificial insemination doesn't work with shapeshifters."

"Why is that?"

"Shapeshifter sperm dies very quickly. It can't be stored outside the body. There's been a lot of experimentation, and you just can't keep the stuff alive."

"Interesting. What about the eggs?"

"The eggs are much hardier, but still more delicate than human eggs. Human sperm is delicate, too, you know—just not as much as shapeshifter sperm."

"It sounds like a crock to me. Some kind of conspiracy so shapeshifter men can sleep around."

He smiled at her teasing tone. "I could show you the documentation. It's all very official and scientific."

"No, that's all right." She leaned toward him, resting her head on his shoulder. "I don't want you to. I really don't."

"You knew this would happen."

"I know. I just needed to get that out of the way. I figure it's probably better to be honest about how I feel than to keep it bottled up."

He nodded. "Fair enough. Honestly, I don't want you to sleep with him, either. But if you want to have a baby, I think that would be the easiest solution, in a lot of ways."

"Not the emotional ways, though, maybe."

"Maybe not." He sighed. "This has never been an easy thing for those of us who have chosen to be with humans. I've seen relationships fall apart over it, and I don't want that to happen to us."

She nodded. That thought had occurred to her, as well. "We need to keep talking to each other. We need to share."

"Yeah." Gently, he kissed her forehead. "We need to share."

* * * * *

Piper sat up that night, in the living room with a book she wasn't reading. Trey had gone to bed a few hours earlier; he had to see a client in the morning, and needed his sleep. Piper needed hers, too, but it was elusive tonight.

She kept thinking about Brice. He was an attractive man, certainly, but not her usual type. She liked her men more substantial, wide, solid, and Brice was lean and slim. What would a child of his look like? Would he have the clear blue eyes? She had green eyes—so there was every possibility the genes might align properly for a blue-eyed child.

She shook the thought off. Maybe they should go with one of the other available options—artificial insemination by an anonymous donor, or adoption. It would be easier, in some ways.

But they would still have to deal with Trey's need to sleep with Nadia. She thought about the small, blonde woman for a time, remembering the details of her delicate face, her golden hair. Would Trey want her to maintain that form when they made love? Or would he want her to change?

To her surprise, she felt tears prick her eyes, but at the same time, a wave of arousal passed through her body. In her mind's eye, she saw herself watching him as he touched Nadia's small body, caressing her, as she writhed beneath his expert fingers. Even thought about reaching in, herself, her own hands cupping Nadia's breasts... Was it possible she could do such a thing? Lean in over Trey's reaching hand and take a taut, pouting nipple into her mouth...

She had made love to Trey more than once with him in the form of a woman. She'd even made love to him while he wore her own face. Making love to herself — it had been a unique experience. But all the time she'd known it was Trey. Another man's face, a variety of men's faces, a variety of bodies — yet all Trey — this she had become somewhat accustomed to, in spite of her preference for stability, for the blondish, blue-eyed Trey she considered his "true" form. But another person, another man, Brice or Nadia or both...

Again, arousal slid through her. All four of them in bed together... Trey with Nadia, she with Brice — Brice and Trey with her at the same time —

She stood quickly, feeling her body go weak, wetness rising between her legs. The possibilities... Forbidden lusts she'd thought never to indulge. A fantasy come to life, illicit yet allowed. It was a bit too much to think about all at once, right now, when everything about the situation remained so uncertain.

She put her book down and headed into the bedroom, quietly, so as not to wake Trey. She gathered her nightclothes and went into the bathroom to change.

In the bathroom, she slid into her soft pink flannel pajamas. They were functional but feminine, with a row of delicate lace at the throat and sleeves. The thread holding the top button in place was frayed, the button hanging on by the last shred of pale pink cotton. She eased it carefully into the buttonhole, thinking once again that she should repair it.

Looking up, she found herself looking into her own reflection. She normally didn't linger over mirrors, usually looking at herself only when necessary, to put on makeup or adjust her hair. But, for some reason, her reflection drew her tonight.

She looked into her own eyes—gray-green, tired, a darker ring of near-brown surrounding the pupil. Her black hair fell straight around her face. She pulled it back, holding it tightly in a ponytail behind her head. Her face looked more severe that way, with her hairline rendered stark and firm.

With a sigh, she released her hair and brushed her teeth. Then, quietly, she slipped back into the bedroom, and into the bed.

Trey lay warm on the opposite side of the bed, his breathing deep and slow. Piper slid in next to him, careful not to disturb the blankets too much. She settled into place on the mattress, tucking the quilt under her chin and letting her head relax into the pillow. Her back barely brushed Trey's, and she could feel his warmth radiating into her. It felt good, to have him close. It would have been nice if he'd been awake, but just this was a blessing of soft warmth and companionship. She closed her eyes, feeling his warmth, drawing in his smell.

"Piper?"

She jumped a little, eyes opening wide. She'd been drifting into the beginning edges of sleep, and the sound of his voice, even as soft as it was, had startled her.

"Sorry," he said. He must have felt her reaction. "I didn't mean to scare you."

Piper rolled over. "I thought you were asleep. Then you started talking. It was a little disconcerting."

He smiled, the flash of teeth barely visible in the darkness. "Sorry."

She reached out to trace her hand down the side of his face. "It's all right."

"I just wanted to talk to you about something."

"What?"

He shifted, sitting up in the bed. She moved with him, holding the blankets against her chest as she moved.

"This isn't the first time something like this has happened."

She quirked an eyebrow, not at all certain what he was getting at. "You mean to you?"

"No." He chuckled. "It's never happened to me. But it's happened to other couples. It's happened enough over the centuries that there's actually a ceremony."

"A ceremony?" That was intriguing. As secretive as the shapeshifter community tended to be, Piper was surprised there would be enough shifter/human pairings to make a ceremony necessary.

"Yes. Not everyone opts to use it, but I've heard it's particularly effective for those who do."

"Effective?"

Trey frowned. "That's not the right word. Moving. Meaningful. But also that it seems the successful pregnancy rate is higher when it's used."

"I don't know how they could determine that. The sample size must be tremendously small."

"That's true. So there's no way to know for sure."

"So what kind of ceremony is it? A bonding thing? Sort of a marriage pact among all involved parties or something?"

"No." Trey reached over and took her hand, almost as if to comfort her. His thumb traced rhythmically over the back of her hand. "It has to do with the sex itself—how we relate to one another. There's incense, I believe, of a certain type, to reduce inhibitions…" He trailed off. "It's actually a religious ceremony, though it doesn't sound like it."

"No, I get that." She shifted a little, squeezing his hand. "Sanctifying the act."

"Yes, exactly."

The unbidden thoughts she'd had earlier drifted through her brain again. Four male hands on her body, two cocks prodding into her…

"It might make it easier," she said. "Following a tradition, something that's worked for other people."

"More than that, though. It makes it sacred, as you said. I personally think it creates a level of protection, for the mothers, for the children. I think that's why the pregnancies tend to be more successful."

She smiled, unable to resist teasing him a little. "You think it's magic?"

He regarded her soberly. "I can change my face at will. Everything seems like magic to me."

Her smile faded. "I would almost think it would be the other way around, when something so incredible is such a part of everyday life."

He shook his head. "I can't explain it. I guess I look at things differently—I consider that nothing may be quite what it seems on the surface."

"So…the ceremony. How does it work?"

"I'd have to look up all the details. But I know it involves all four parties participating at once."

Piper looked at him. "For the ceremony only, or for the sexual acts?"

"For everything. Four in a bed and the little one said…" He stopped.

"Lame joke, Trey," Piper said blandly. "This is all very odd."

"Yes, I'm sure it seems that way to you."

"I think it would seem that way to anyone. Anyone not a shapeshifter, anyway."

"Even some who are shifters, I think. Anyone who hasn't had to face this situation before."

Piper nodded. "I'll have to think about it, you know. As much, if not more, than I would have had to have thought about it, anyway."

"I know. I understand."

She smiled softly at him. "Thank you."

He put his arms around her, and she settled against him and slowly drifted into sleep.

Chapter Three

Trey woke first in the morning. For a while, he lay watching Piper sleep, taking in the peacefulness of her face. Hesitantly, he brushed a finger down her cheek, afraid of waking her but unable to resist the need to touch her. She shifted a little at the contact, but didn't wake up.

He rolled carefully out of bed and got dressed, then went out to the kitchen to grab a quick breakfast before he headed out to work. Piper would be heading out a bit later; Trey's client had wanted to meet at eight a.m., and she didn't have to be at work until nine.

With a cup of coffee in a travel mug and a nicely portable bagel and egg sandwich, Trey headed out to the subway. The routine had finally started to feel familiar to him, after two years. He couldn't say he enjoyed it, but it was necessary.

Until he'd married Piper, Trey hadn't had any particular need to hold down a job. He'd gone from place to place, picking up odd jobs here and there, enough for food and lodging, looking for people he could help. Broken people, who needed to put to rest the last shreds of a relationship. He'd been a hundred different men, a hundred different women, helping them move on. He hadn't always slept with them—more often than not it hadn't been necessary. But when it had seemed necessary, he had done it. It was this that had brought him into Piper's bed.

Piper had informed him, shortly after they were married, that his methods were questionable. He knew that, but he hadn't spent a great deal of time thinking about it. It had seemed, to him, that he'd done some good. He'd even gone back to visit some of the people he'd helped, and, based on that experience, felt the results had been positive.

It really hadn't proved to be a transferable skill, though. He didn't have any educational background to pursue a career in counseling, and professional shapeshifting wasn't really an option. So he'd taken a few courses at the local community college, and, after putting some time and effort into building a client base, he made a fairly nice salary doing web page and graphics design for several small businesses—and a few larger ones—in the area. He enjoyed the work, and although they could have lived fairly comfortably on Piper's salary alone, he liked the fact that he could contribute.

He spent an hour with this latest client, discussing the basic setup the young woman was after. She seemed well-organized and motivated, and he found himself enthused along with her, and hoped her small jewelry business would take off nicely with the help of his website. She'd already built a nice customer base, which presented a definite advantage.

Finally, he shook her hand, took her check, and left with notes, a game plan and a deadline. Heading back to his car, he called Piper.

"Hey," he said when she answered the phone. "How's it going?"

"Okay so far." She sounded happy, or at least not overly stressed. "Not a bad day, overall."

"Good to hear. Hey, I thought I might invite the Binghams over for dinner."

Piper hesitated. "Um, okay."

"Is there a problem?"

"No, not at all. I just... I'll have to come home early to get things ready."

"No, don't worry about that. I'll be home all day working. I'll take care of it."

"Oh, okay. Do you need me to pick anything up on the way home?"

"I'll let you know."

"Okay." She sounded like she was about to say something else, but instead she cleared her throat, then said suddenly, "Oh, sorry, gotta get back to work."

She hung up the phone before he could say goodbye, leaving him to assume her boss had just meandered past her cubicle, as he had a habit of doing.

He called Brice Bingham to confirm, then stopped by the grocery store on the way home, picking up the makings of a nice, laidback Italian dinner. After a few hours of work at home, he took a break, then called Nadia Bingham at work.

"Oh, hello, Trey," she said, sounding not displeased to hear from him. "Brice told me we're having dinner with you tonight."

"Yes, that's the plan."

"So you and Piper have made your decision?"

"Not entirely." Trey wandered through the quiet apartment, straightening knickknacks. He really should dust before the Binghams came over. "I suggested the ritual last night. To Piper."

There was a moment of silence on the other end of the line. "Really? What did she say?"

"She said she'd think about it. She seemed in favor, though."

He heard Nadia let out a slow breath. "I was hoping someone would bring that up. I didn't really want to, though."

"It would make you feel better, then?"

"Yes. The sanctification—it just would seem better with a ritual, I think." She paused. "I was conceived in a four-way ritual. I'm sure you didn't know that."

"No, I didn't. Ironic then, I suppose."

"Not really. I grew up with a human father—it seemed natural to take a human husband, and I knew what I might be getting into by taking that route."

"We all do. We all know it could come down to sharing, if we take a human partner. But for them—it's so much more difficult."

Nadia was silent again for a moment, then said gently, "Is there a problem with Piper?"

Trey shook his head reflexively. "No. I don't think so. There doesn't seem to be." He picked up a porcelain dragon from a shelf and dusted it with his shirt sleeve, holding the phone between chin and shoulder. "Thank you for the offer. I don't think she'd really considered the possibility of having a naturally conceived child."

"Does she seem interested in the idea?"

"Yeah, she does."

"Good. I was hoping she might." She laughed a little. "Not that I'm crazy about the idea of Brice sleeping with someone else, but it seemed fair."

Trey smiled. "I know what you mean. I feel the same way." His smile faded. "It's broken marriages to pieces. I had a friend who lost her husband over this."

"I know. My first husband left me when I told him I wanted a baby."

"I didn't know that." It hadn't been in her paperwork, but then it hadn't been relevant to the current reproduction request.

"Yeah. It was tough. I don't want that to happen again. I think—" She stopped, laughed again. The sound was strained this time. "For some reason it seems like the ritual might make it safer. Less likely to go awry."

"I know. It feels that way to me, too." He gave a decisive nod. "Well. We'll see how it goes. All we can do is the best we can do."

"That's right." Her voice trembled a little, though, and he pressed his lips together, sympathizing perhaps a little too strongly with her distress. He had the same worries, himself.

"I'll see you tonight, then. We can talk more, with all of us together."

"Yes. Yes, I'll see you tonight."

* * * * *

Piper set out silverware, checking each piece to be sure it wasn't water-spotted or tarnished. She'd never given much thought to her silverware. She and Trey didn't have company very often, much less company like this. Carefully, she arranged cloth napkins and set the plates in the exact center of the placemats.

Trey didn't seem nearly as concerned. He had prepared a casual dinner of pasta and salad, with store-bought tiramisu for dessert. He'd picked up a wine which she recognized as a nice one, but not terribly expensive.

"I spoke to Nadia today," he told her as she came back into the kitchen.

She opened a cabinet and took out a set of salad plates. "To invite them over. I know."

"No, I called Brice to invite them over. I talked to Nadia later."

Piper eyed him, surprised at the stab of jealousy that passed through her chest. "Oh. What about?"

"I mentioned the ritual to her."

"Oh." Piper took the plates in to the kitchen and carefully arranged them on the table. "What did she say?"

"She's very much in favor. I thought she might be. We've both seen relationships fall apart over this exact situation. The ritual is a good way to get around that."

Piper adjusted a salad plate, trying to make sure it was perfectly positioned. "Why would the ritual make any difference?"

"Because it sanctifies the act. Places it within certain boundaries that make it acceptable. There's less awkwardness, fewer doubts, fewer questions."

"Like, 'Does he really feel obligated to do this, or does he just want to fuck a pretty little blonde?'" The words came out much more sharply than Piper had intended.

Trey looked at her, eyebrows raised in surprised. "I *am* obligated to do this," he said, his voice quiet.

"Do you really think the ritual would help?" Piper asked. She had her doubts. A few words spoken over their bed wouldn't change the fact they were sharing themselves with other people.

"Yes, I do." He said it with such sincerity Piper couldn't help but believe him.

"It would mean something to you, to do it that way?"

"Yes, it would." His voice and expression remained sober. "It would mean a great deal to me, in fact, to go back to the traditional ways. I think we've gotten too far away from many of them."

Quietly, Piper sat down in a chair at the table, letting out a slow breath. "I'd venture a guess, that one of the traditional ways involved not marrying humans at all."

Trey nodded. "You'd be right."

"So…not one of the traditional ways you're in favor of?"

"I just don't think it's realistic. You can't put limits on love. It happens when it happens, and with whom. But when it comes to dealing with the ramifications of that…yes, I think the traditional ways have a lot to offer."

Piper studied his face. He was being as honest as she'd ever seen him; she could tell from his expression, from the heavy sincerity in his eyes.

"Well, then—" she started, but just then the doorbell rang, cutting her words off. She smiled a little, frustrated, then went to answer the door.

Brice and Nadia stood outside on the doorstep. Nadia held a wicker basket full of brightly colored packages of gourmet cookies. She smiled brightly at Piper, her green eyes shining.

"Hi!" she said. "I brought dessert."

Piper normally found that kind of perkiness disconcerting at best, annoying at worst. But there was something about Nadia that she found alluring. Maybe because her attitude didn't seem affected. She seemed very real. Which was ironic, considering she was a shapeshifter.

She took the basket from Nadia with a smile. "It looks wonderful. Come on in." She gave Brice a smile, then looked away as he returned it, suddenly uncomfortable. Shy, even. She hadn't felt genuinely shy in years. But Brice looked at her with such open friendliness that it made her uncomfortable. It wouldn't have if the circumstances were different. He seemed like a genuinely nice man.

He moved into the kitchen, his gait almost puppylike in its enthusiasm. "I smell pasta," he said.

Trey looked up. "Yeah. I made pasta. Nothing fancy."

"Good." Brice rubbed his hands together. "I was really afraid there would be four forks and two different bowls and five courses or something. That stuff really makes me nervous."

Piper smiled. "Me, too, but I was headed that way."

"Thank God I was here to bring you back to earth." Trey smiled at her warmly.

Brice looked over the immaculately set table. "It's nice. It really is." He hesitantly touched Piper's arm.

"Thank you." He seemed like a decent guy. Genuine. She liked that. She allowed herself to smile at him without worrying about connotations or unintended signals, and was rewarded by a genuine twinkle in his sapphire eyes. "Well, then," Piper said, "Let's sit down and eat."

* * * * *

After dinner, Trey shifted the proceedings to the living room, providing everyone with tiramisu, Nadia's cookies, and coffee. Piper, deciding to go with the informal setup rather than try to fight it, sat on the floor next to the coffee table, leaning against the couch, where Trey had sat down.

The dinner had gone well. If nothing else, the four of them seemed to be conversationally compatible. They'd found plenty to talk about. Brice was an appealing man, prone to bursting out into unabashed, genuine laughter. Nadia was equally genuine, as far as Piper could tell. She included Piper in the conversation as often as she did Trey, for which Piper was grateful.

"This is lovely tiramisu," Nadia commented. "Did you make it, Piper?"

"Yes, she did," said Trey.

Piper slapped his knee playfully. "I didn't. Trey picked it up at the store."

Nadia smiled. "That's what I would have done."

"I can't imagine trying to make tiramisu. Chocolate chip cookies are about my limit."

"I have trouble with chocolate chip cookies, myself," Nadia admitted. "I can't seem to actually get the dough into the oven. I'm too busy eating it out of the bowl."

Piper laughed. She liked this woman—she couldn't help it. And she liked Brice, and when it came down to it she couldn't think of any reason why she shouldn't accept the offer they had so generously put forth for her and Trey. She glanced at Brice, who was smiling at his wife, and their eyes met briefly. Quickly, Piper looked away.

"I'd like to try something," she said suddenly.

Trey looked at her, an eyebrow quirked, obviously curious as to what had made her speak out so abruptly. "What's that?"

Piper cleared her throat, self-conscious now that she'd made herself the center of attention. "Um..." She looked at Trey, who smiled a little and nodded, encouraging her. "I've been thinking. About the offer. About having a baby."

The atmosphere in the room changed abruptly. Tension, Piper thought, and she certainly hadn't intended to cause that. She looked uncomfortably at her hands.

"What did you decide?" Trey asked gently.

She looked up at him, grateful for his soft tone. "I want to have a baby."

"You don't mind that it would be mine?" There was an edge of humor in Brice's voice, and Piper was grateful for that, as well. She smiled at him.

"Actually, I think it would be nice that it was yours." She looked quickly at Nadia, afraid of her reaction, but the other woman, though she had lifted an eyebrow, was also smiling.

"I was hoping you'd feel that way," Nadia said. "It really seemed like the most fair thing to do."

Piper nodded. "It actually makes me feel better, too, that there's a ritual. It makes it seem less... Well, less like I'm alone. Does that make sense?" She felt her face going hot.

"It does," said Brice. "People have done this before, and have found it powerful, and have given it a sense of grace, with a ritual."

His words surprised Piper. "A sense of grace. Yes, that expresses it very well, I think." She smiled gently at him, grateful she wasn't alone in her attempts to work through the situation.

"You said you wanted to do something," Trey said. "What is it?"

Piper gathered herself. In spite of the rapport the four of them seemed to have developed, and in spite of the openness that was coming into play, she was nervous about speaking out.

"I want—" She broke off. "Just promise you won't say it's silly."

"Of course not," said Trey. "If it helps you feel better, then it's important, and I want to hear it."

"I just…" She took a deep breath. "I want you and Nadia and Brice to all go into another room, and when you come out, I want you to all be Brice. I want to know I can tell. I need to be sure I can know it's you, Trey."

Trey smiled a little. "I understand that. But we've tested this before."

She nodded. He was right, of course. He had appeared to her more than once as a stranger, without warning, and she had always been certain it was him, without being told. She wasn't sure how she did it—it was a feeling, nebulous and nothing she could explain. But this was different, and in this situation she felt an overwhelming need to know for certain she would be able to know who she was with, in the intimate situation they would be entering into.

"I know, and it might seem trivial, but I need to be sure."

Brice was studying her, his expression serious. "Yes. I think that might be something I would need to know, too." He looked at his wife, who grinned at him.

"You need to know you can tell it's Trey?" Her smile was teasing, but the look in her eyes told Piper she wasn't mocking him. She understood.

"No." He touched her face. "I need to know it's you." His soft quirk of a smile touched Piper; it told her that he knew she understood.

It occurred to her that she didn't think she'd be able to live with herself if anything she did broke this couple apart. They seemed so well-suited, so perfect for each other. She wondered if she and Trey gave that impression.

"That's an easy enough request," Trey said. He pushed to his feet and looked at the other two, obviously ready to get started.

Nadia looked at Brice and shrugged. "Okay. Let's go, then."

Trey led the way into the bedroom. Piper watched them depart, wondering how long they would be. She still had some tiramisu left; she busied herself finishing it, taking miniscule bites, sipping her coffee. Her hands were shaking. She wondered why.

As it turned out, it didn't take very long. She was just scraping the last of the tiramisu from her plate when Brice emerged from the bedroom. Behind him was Brice, and then Brice again.

Carefully, Piper set her coffee cup down on its saucer. She'd seen Trey shift many times, but this was strange, unlike anything she'd seen before. Three identical men, identical faces, identical walks, emerging from the bedroom. They had even changed clothes, each wearing generic jeans and plain black T-shirts undoubtedly swiped from Trey's closet.

Piper rose slowly to her feet, wiping suddenly clammy hands on her pants. She was unaccountably nervous. She felt like there would be consequences if she failed. The three men regarded her with different expressions—contemplative, wondering, curious—but nothing that would give away individual identity.

They were exactly alike in every detail. The dark, combed-back hair, the sapphire eyes, the prominent cheekbones. The shape of the mouth, the chin that didn't quite balance the rest of the face. The lean, slim body. Everything.

Piper stepped closer, drawing in a careful breath, trying to catch their scent. It seemed worth a try, though she wasn't sure she could tell them apart that way.

The Brice standing to her left smiled a small, quirking smile. The one in the middle gave him a chastising look, and the one to her right just stood regarding her quietly. Absolutely identical. It was mind-boggling, really. Every pore, every small variation in skin pigmentation. The small tracery of blue veins on the temples. Everything identical.

She looked more closely, studying each face. Identical sapphire eyes tracked her small movements. Even the small, dark blue blotch in the iris had been duplicated. Absolute artistry. Or was it instinct? It didn't matter—theory wouldn't help her figure out which one of these men was Trey.

All she could do was guess, at this point, then work through process of elimination.

She decided to start in the middle. Taking a step toward that Brice—identical to the other two—she lifted a hand and touched his face. His skin was warm and soft, a slight scruff of stubble rasping against her fingers. It told her nothing.

She looked into her eyes. His expression was neutral. Piper leaned in. Brice—or Trey, or Nadia—didn't move.

It was like an odd game of chicken, and neither of them gave way. Piper moved closer, slowly, studying his face, but there was no hint, no hesitation. She kissed him.

His mouth was soft, willing, and tasted of coffee. Piper explored it hesitantly, then more firmly. His tongue touched hers, gentle. She drew back.

Frowning a little, she studied his face again. His lips quirked a little, into a smile—almost a smirk. She smiled back at him and shook her head in mock disgust, then turned to his twin.

"Do I get a kiss, too?" he asked.

"Yes," she said, and hooked an arm behind his neck, bringing him down to kiss him thoroughly.

She didn't even care if it was Trey or not anymore. It was a game suddenly, nothing serious, nothing life or death. She just kissed this man who may or may not be Brice, who may or may not be Trey, and enjoyed the hell out of it.

He tasted a bit more of tiramisu than Brice number one had, the coffee flavor still strong. He kissed her less hesitantly, his tongue pressing in almost before she opened to him.

She drew the kiss into herself, savoring the sensations, the flavor, the way his mouth fit against hers. Then let him go, and moved to the third.

He was less aggressive, seemingly less ready, but kissed her softly, sweetly. She drew back with a soft smile for his tenderness, then looked at them all, one at a time.

One Brice looked at another, lips slightly pursed in amusement, then looked back at Piper.

"Verdict?" said Brice number three.

Piper considered. She gave serious thought to kissing all of them again, just for the hell of it. In the end, though, she just pointed at Brice number one.

"You're Trey."

He stepped a bit away from the others.

"Furthermore," Piper went on, "You're Nadia." She pointed to the Brice who had kissed her most aggressively. "And that means you're Brice."

She didn't need confirmation—she was certain. At least she told herself that, but there was a small tremor of doubt in the few seconds before the three Brices finally looked at each other, then one shifted and melted and became Trey, while the other became Nadia.

Piper had been right. She smiled, trying to hide the sudden relief. She had been certain—but in a way she hadn't.

Unless—

"You're not shifting on me, the two of you? Pretending to be each other?"

Trey laughed. "Don't be so paranoid." He moved to her and embraced her. "You've always had a talent for picking me out. Remember?"

"I know." She rested her head against his chest. "But…stressful circumstances, you know?"

"I'm sorry if it's stressful," said Nadia. She seemed a little uncomfortable.

Piper turned around to face her. "And you. What was with the major tongue-kissing?"

Somewhat to Piper's chagrin, Nadia's face went bright pink. Brice put an arm around her shoulders, grinning.

"I thought it was hot."

Piper laughed. Trey laughed. Nadia snorted and shook her head.

Brice kissed the top of his wife's head. "I want more dessert. Anybody else?"

* * * * *

After dinner, Trey took Nadia back to his office to discuss the finer points of Photoshop. Piper found it interesting that shapeshifters seemed to gravitate toward artistic pursuits—Trey was much more skilled at the graphic design aspects of his chosen profession than the technical side. Maybe it was related to their ability to recreate a human face in such intricate detail. Or maybe she was completely off the mark—after all, she'd only met a few shapeshifters, and, to be fair, really only knew Trey. But it was an interesting theory.

Brice, who had been putting away the dishes, came back out carrying a cup of coffee. He glanced toward the door that Trey had just opened for Nadia and smiled.

"She loves passing on tips on blending and smudge tools and whatever." Settling into a chair across from Piper, he shrugged. "I don't understand a damn word she says about it half the time."

"Maybe she'll teach him something," Piper said. She'd wanted to tag along, but it hadn't seemed right.

Brice nodded. "They wanted a little alone time, I think."

"Yeah."

Sipping his coffee, Brice studied Piper's face. "Does that bother you?"

"Of course it bothers me. Doesn't it bother you?" Quickly, Piper collected herself, embarrassed at the near-outburst. She'd been fairly calm the entire evening, taking things in stride—why was she hitting the end of her rope now, when things were actually calmer than they'd been most of the day?

"Yeah." Brice's voice was calm, unruffled, but he looked at Piper and she saw a hint of uncertainty in his eyes. "But I think you and I could use a little alone time, too."

Surprised, Piper looked up at him. His expression was open, searching her at the same time.

"I suppose we could," Piper conceded. She let her gaze fall from his, her attention going instead to his hands. They were good hands, square, with nicely tapered fingers. She thought about what they might feel like touching her, kneading her breasts, working her cunt. She fought the urge to close her eyes, to lose herself in the thought.

A smile curled the corner of Brice's mouth, as if perhaps he realized what she was thinking, and she felt her own face go hot at the thought. He leaned back in his chair and picked up his coffee cup.

"How..." she ventured, but paused, gathering courage before she went on. "How does Nadia feel about...this?"

"She very much wants to have a child. She has for a long time." Brice's voice was low and serious. "I want a family, too, and if this is the only way, then..." He trailed off, then looked up at her, meeting her gaze squarely. "I love her. I knew what I was getting into when I married her. I knew this would happen, and we had talked about it. We came very close about three years ago, then Mesharet pulled the rug out from under us—" He shook his head. "I can't see her go through that again. She wants this more than anything."

Piper nodded soberly. "I understand that."

"What about you? Do you want a baby?"

"I do." She answered immediately, without thinking. And it was true—she did. "I do. I just...hadn't pictured it happening this way."

"Did you ever picture yourself meeting and marrying anyone like Trey?"

"No. Of course not." She smiled a little, his point taken.

"Neither did I. Neither did Nadia, and I'm sure Trey didn't plan any of this, either." The words could have been taken as criticism, but his tone was gentle. He shrugged, picking up his coffee cup again. "We just have to make the best of it."

Piper eyed him, until her scrutiny seemed to make him uncomfortable. Finally she said, quietly, "Do you love her?"

"Of course I do. Why else would I do this?"

Smiling, Piper nodded. "I think I like you," she said. "Maybe that'll make things easier."

"I hope so." He looked away, his expression a little embarrassed, and rubbed his hands on his jeans. "Because honestly, Piper, I'm nervous as hell."

To her own surprise, Piper laughed. "Yeah. So am I." Suddenly daring, she reached over and laid a hand on his knee. "That honestly makes me feel a lot better. Thank you."

Brice laid his hand on top of hers. The contact warmed her, and suddenly she thought of herself not as having sex with him, but as mothering his child, nurturing a part of him inside her. She smiled.

"It'll be okay."

* * * * *

Brice and Nadia bid them farewell a few hours later. Alone in her bathroom, Piper changed into her pajamas and regarded herself in the mirror. Nothing had changed since the last time she had looked at herself. She wondered if she would look different after she became a mother.

In the bedroom, Trey had already settled into bed. Piper crawled in next to him and slid against him, cradling her head against his chest. Surprised, Trey lifted his arm and put it around her shoulders. "What's wrong?"

"Nothing. I just wanted to cuddle a little."

He nodded and kissed her hair. "I can live with that."

Closing her eyes, she nuzzled into him, breathing in his smell, smiling. She fit against him as if she was meant to be there. Sometimes she wondered if he had arranged himself that way, made his body a certain shape, just so she could lie here like this, pillowed against his heartbeat.

"Kiss me," she said, and he obligingly bent down to press his lips to hers. She leaned into the kiss, savoring his taste, the subtle flavors that had made her certain which man had been him.

After a time, he drew back. "How did you know?"

She smiled up at him. "That. What you just did. The way you kiss me. The way you taste."

"I didn't try very hard."

"I know. That was part of it, too."

He stroked her hair, his fingers gentle, soft. "I like knowing you can do that."

"Me, too."

"I can't believe you kissed Nadia, though. Man—she was all over you."

Piper chuckled, settling back against Trey's body. "Yeah, she surprised me, too."

"I knew it was her. That made it hotter."

"Well, play your cards right, maybe I'll kiss her again while she looks like a woman."

He bent his head back to look into her eyes. "Don't tease me like that."

"What makes you think I'm teasing? I've kissed you when you were a woman. Made love to you, even."

His expression sobered. "Yes, you have."

"All right, then. So you know I can be flexible."

"I know you can be flexible with me."

She shrugged. "I don't know what might happen. It's not exactly the kind of situation I'm familiar with."

"But you're willing to accept it." His fingers traced her face. "That means a great deal to me."

"I want a baby." Her tone was firm, stubborn. She was surprised by its intractability.

"It's more than that, though," said Trey, and he caressed her forehead, slipped the tips of his fingers into her hair.

She nodded. "I know. Please don't ask me to explain."

"I won't."

"Because I don't think I can."

"I won't ask. I promise."

His heartbeat was firm and steady beneath her ear. The rhythm had picked up a bit as they had spoken. It seemed quick and eager now, a slightly accelerated pitter-patter to match his quickened breath.

"I love you," she said, and turned her head, and kissed his bare chest.

Chapter Four

Trey had to acquire supplies, before they could pursue the ritual in earnest. Some were easily obtained at the local health food store — herbs, a certain kind of scented candle, essential oils — but others were more difficult to find. A particular kind of wine, for instance, produced by a shapeshifter colony in North Africa. He ended up on the phone again with Nadia, who agreed to meet with him for lunch, so they could discuss the situation.

"I know where we can get the wine for half that price," she told him, daintily eating the French fries that had come with her veggie melt. She'd only eaten a couple of bites of the sandwich.

"Is it authentic? I think that's important."

"Yeah, it's authentic." She trailed a fry through the puddle of ketchup and mayonnaise she'd made in her plate. "I'm wondering if we should do this."

Trey eyed her quizzically. "Really? You've been waiting a long time. Is Brice…is he having difficulty with the situation?"

"Of course he is. He'd never admit it, though."

She picked at her sandwich finally, opening it up and taking out the circles of black olives, eating them one by one.

"What about you?" Trey asked. He knew this would be difficult for all of them, but he was surprised Nadia was actually considering backing out, as long as she'd waited.

Still not looking at Trey, Nadia took a long breath. "It's not an easy thing. But nothing about what we are is ever easy."

"That's true."

They sat in silence for a time while Nadia finally gave her sandwich the attention it deserved. Trey pulled out his cell phone and called the number Nadia supplied to acquire the wine. A short conversation, interspersed with "passwords" only another shapeshifter would use as everyday vocabulary, assured Trey the supplier was genuine.

Finally finished with lunch, and with all the necessary preparations either done or in progress, Trey walked Nadia back to her car.

"I'll call you in a couple of days, then," he told her. "As soon as everything's ready, we can decide on a date and time."

"Undoubtedly based on mutual fertility cycles, temperature, and the phase of the moon." She gave a wry smile. "Romantic. Another issue, I guess."

Trey looked at her, noting her strained expression. "I think it'll be all right. It'll be fine in the long run."

She nodded. "I'm sure it will be. It's just…getting through the short run that's giving me some issues."

He cupped her face gently and smiled. "Don't worry. Worry will make it worse."

"I know." She smiled back at him, looking a little more relieved than nervous, finally. He watched her get into the car and closed the door behind her, then headed for his own car, and home.

* * * * *

"How was lunch?" Piper asked him when he came home.

"It was fine." He laid his bags of purchases on the table and she walked over to take a look. She unloaded the bags, examining each item as she took it out.

"Interesting shopping you've done here," she commented.

"It's for the ritual."

She set down a small bag of loose, dried sage. "I see."

Trey turned at her tone. "Are you all right?"

Piper shrugged. "I don't know. I think I will be." She gave him a direct look. "This isn't going to be easy. For any of us."

He stepped up to her and put his hands on her shoulders, gently. "I know. But we'll do what we can. We'll keep it together." He kissed her forehead. "We'll keep it holy."

She looked up at him, then suddenly reached up to grab the back of his neck. Pulling him down, she kissed him, hard and needy.

The suddenness of it, the urgency, surprised him. He put an arm around her, holding her close, as she harshly plundered his mouth. Her teeth scraped his tongue almost painfully, her fingers digging into his shoulders.

He drew back as gently as he could, considering her intensity. "Piper, what's wrong?"

"I need you." Her voice was soft, a little broken. "I just... I need you."

He nodded, understanding on a level that didn't allow words. Her fingers clenched into his shoulders again, and she dragged him backwards, until she was against the kitchen cabinet.

He kissed her as hard as she seemed to need him to, holding her with one arm wrapped around her waist, the other braced against the cabinet. She moved in his embrace, jumping up onto the cabinet, wrapping her legs around him.

"You're mine," she said against his face. "Mine. You know that. I own you. Because of what you did—"

He silenced her with his mouth, his tongue pressing against hers. His hands moved down her body, cupping her breasts, her hips, soothing and quieting her. When she seemed less frantic, he moved back a little.

"Yes. You own me. Now and always. Nothing will ever change that."

She fell against him, letting him support her. The action both flattered and disturbed him. She trusted him to save her from falling—hopefully in more ways than one.

He sensed what she needed, the emotion shivering over the surface of her consciousness, just there where he could read it.

Following her need, he jerked at her shirt, tearing it off over her head and throwing it across the room. He jerked her bra open, roughly, threw it, as well. He thought he heard it hit one of the kitchen chairs, but he wasn't sure.

She gasped as he bent forward and took her breast in his mouth, his teeth scraping her nipple until she cried out. He could feel her urgency, her need. She needed to be...branded, she was thinking. Marked. The thought made his own desire rise, hot and intense, filling him. He wanted her, wanted to own her before he had to let her go, even that little bit, for that short time it would take to do what they needed to do.

Releasing her breast from his mouth, he cupped it with his hand, mounding the firm, round flesh against her body. She pressed her face against his hair, breathing hard. "I need you inside me," she managed. "Hard. Fast. Now."

He knew this, of course. But decided it might not be prudent to point out there would be a slight delay, since she still had on her jeans. Instead he jerked the button open and yanked the zipper down, shoving his hand between jeans and panties. The soft cotton was damp under his fingers and she opened her thighs convulsively as he touched her there. He could feel the soft, springy cushion of hair, the heat, the outline of her labia, the protrusion of her clit between hot, swollen lips.

She jerked under his touch, fingers digging into his shoulders. The tip of his finger grazed lightly over the pebbled nub, teasing. Feathery contact, barely a touch at all, just enough to stimulate, arouse, ignite her.

The warmth of her desire moved over him like water. He kissed her throat, licking her skin, sucking at her pulse, while his fingers traced the shape of her sex beneath her panties. The heat pooled there, greatest above her opening. He pushed in a little, taking the cotton with him, feeling the wetness soak through and drench his fingers as he did so.

He could smell her, the rich, musky odor of her desire floating to him. His cock strained against his zipper, shifting in its own, instinctive way, growing larger, changing shape so that when he entered her it would fill her completely. The shape of the inside of her body had imprinted on him; his cock filled her exactly every time, unless he made a conscious effort to shorten, lengthen, thicken, or narrow. After two years he still hadn't explored all the combinations, still hadn't found all the ways he could love her.

He lifted her against him, raising her hips off the counter so he could push off her jeans and panties. She grabbed at them, too, shoving them over the curve of her ass, out of the way, then kicked them off her feet. They hit the floor in a soft shush of collapsing fabric. He settled her back on the cabinet, and she lifted her knees, draping one over each of his shoulders.

Trey looked down. She was open, thighs spread, so he could look into the wide, damp folds of her sex, the dark, curling hair, the open channel of her vagina. He went to his knees in front of the cabinet and buried his face between her legs.

She gasped, arching back. He shoved his tongue inside her, tasting the thick, sweet salt of her arousal. Sucked hard at the slick, tender flesh of her labia until she dug her fingers into his scalp and cried out.

"Too much?" he asked, lips moving right against her heat.

"No. No. No."

Her grasp on his head wasn't urging him away, but it wasn't moving him forward, either. He eased back a little, licking softly, feeling her clit harden and rise under his ministrations. She was pushing into him a little, encouraging him, and he could feel the shivery tension growing in her thighs. He stroked her there, fingers slipping softly over the velvety skin.

So close. He could sense it, knew she was nearly there, ready to topple over the precipice into orgasm. He didn't want her to. Not yet. Backing away, he traced his tongue along the insides of her thighs.

"God," she breathed. "Don't stop."

He chuckled. "I'm not stopping. Just taking a break."

"You don't need to take a break."

"You were about to come."

"I know!"

Her obvious annoyance amused him. "It was too soon."

"Not for me."

"Yes, it was." He sobered, straightening. He pressed his chest to hers. "That's not what you need."

She looked into his face, her own expression softening. Tears pooled in her eyes and he touched her face.

"What do I need?" she asked him.

"This."

He shifted, his hips moving her thigh apart, he shoved inside her, hard, all the way to the root in a single stroke. She gasped and grabbed his hair, her fingers twisting in the strands until he felt some separate from his scalp. Her head tipped back and her eyes went dark, almost vacant, empty of anything but lust.

"Who am I?" he demanded. He shoved into her again, impaling her, taking her hard, so she could feel it deep inside her, as deep inside her as he could go.

"Trey," she said, automatically, he thought. Her eyes met his briefly and he heard her swallow. Her fingers dug into his shoulders, fingernails nearly breaking his skin.

"You're mine," he said, his voice rough as he speared her. "Mine. Always."

"Yes..."

He reached between them and touched her clit, gently, in contrast to the rough violence of his penetration. Her body lurched, then shuddered at the contact, then suddenly she let out a low, keening moan and he felt her come apart around him, her body pulsing on his cock. His own breath hitched and his body, too, let go, his release tearing through him as he emptied deep inside her.

A fingernail broke through his skin. The sharp, momentary stab of pain barely registered. Looking into Piper's face, he saw she was crying. He cradled her against his chest.

"Mine," he whispered.

"Yes," she whispered back, and kissed him softly.

Chapter Five

They made arrangements to see Brice and Nadia that weekend. The Binghams owned a cabin in the Poconos, and Piper and Trey would meet them there some time Friday afternoon. It was a long drive, so they'd decided to take the day off. Piper had arranged to take a day off on Monday, as well.

Trey had decided he wanted to drive. He didn't get much opportunity—living in the city as they did, they both usually ended up walking or taking the subway. But Piper had had a car most of her adult life in spite of not really needing one, just because she liked the freedom it implied. She could take off any time she wanted, without having to rely on anyone else for transportation. Not that she did very often, but it was nice to know the option existed.

It took him a few minutes to reacclimatize himself to the car, during which time he accidentally turned on the blinkers twice, the windshield wipers once, and flicked on the high beams trying to squirt wiper fluid onto the windshield.

Piper couldn't help laughing at him. "I guess you should drive more."

He took her ribbing in stride. "You'd probably have the same problem. Neither one of us drives on a regular basis, after all."

"This is true." She settled back into the seat, watching the city slowly disappear as they headed for the untamed wilds of Pennsylvania. She chuckled a little at the thought.

"What?" he asked.

She shook her head, still amused. "Nothing. Have you been to the Poconos before?"

"Yeah, but I went to one of the touristy places. Where they have the tubs shaped like champagne glasses."

Piper wrinkled her nose, then grinned. "Someday I want you to take me to one of those places. I always thought those tubs looked fun."

He shrugged. "They're okay." Casting her a sly look, he added, "It depends on who you're with."

"Then they'd be fun with you."

She was feeling surprisingly maudlin and romantic, she thought, considering they were going to the secluded cabin in the Poconos so they could sleep with other people. But she found herself not thinking about that quite so much. She was thinking instead of a baby, cuddled against her breast, of the way Trey would look at it, the way they would all be together. A family.

There was a big difference between a couple and a family, she thought, and thinking about that made her warm inside. They would be a family, the three of them, and maybe they could get a puppy.

She laughed again. Trey smiled.

"Okay, this time you have to tell me," he said.

"I was just thinking we should get a puppy."

"Why?"

"So we could have a baby and a puppy."

He shook his head. "We can't have a puppy in our apartment."

"Oh, fine. Be all logical and annoying. I don't care." She looked out the window, content. "A baby will be nice."

"Yes. I think it will be."

She sobered a little, thinking of Brice and Nadia. "How long have they been waiting?"

"Several years. Mesharet kept delaying their petition. He wasn't in favor of human/shapeshifter pairings."

"He was an odd duck, wasn't he?"

"That's one way of putting it."

Piper struggled for different words. Mesharet had nearly killed both of them, and her assessment had seemed to trivialize that. "I mean, because in one way he wanted to turn away from the old ways, but in other ways he seemed to cling to them."

"We're all like that, in one way or another."

"I suppose that's true." She thought about class structure as it still existed even among humans, who weren't a species fighting for their very existence, as the shapeshifters were. Even there, class and race played far too large a part in everyday existence, in how people judged each other. When there were so few remaining, perhaps things such as who married whom seemed that much more important.

"It's been a long time for them, then." She was thinking aloud, more or less, and realized she wasn't making a great deal of sense.

Trey looked at her, a curious look on his face. "Yes. A long time." He reached over, laying a hand on her knee. "They want this child a great deal. They'll take good care of it."

"I had no question of that." But she had, she realized suddenly. She had in a way been concerned that Brice might not see the child as his, that Trey's child, given to the Binghams, might not receive the love it deserved. The kind of love she would have given it.

She shook her head. He was still looking at her, concern on his face. "Are you all right?"

"I'm fine. It's all just...very strange. But you knew that already."

He smiled. "I did."

She veered away from the topic after that, chatting instead about things that had happened at work, asking him about his latest clients. Everyday conversation. Normal things. Not, "What do you think it'll be like to have a foursome in the Poconos?"

It had been a good shift to make, she thought a few hours later, when Trey turned the car onto a narrow dirt road—more of a path, really—leading deeper into the forest.

"It's nice out this way," Piper said. "Quiet. Woodsy." She grinned at her own inability to express herself.

Trey smiled. "Yeah. Woodsy. Deer, squirrels—back to nature kind of thing."

"Did Nadia say if the cabin has electricity?"

"It does. And indoor plumbing. So we won't be completely roughing it."

"That's a relief. I don't have the fortitude for that kind of thing."

"Sure you do. You have the fortitude for just about anything."

His tone caught her attention and she sobered, looking at him. There was a smolder in his eyes that made her go weak and warm.

"Only because you helped me find it." His hand lay on her knee; she closed hers over it, holding it tight. "Without you I'd still be crying in that bar."

"No. You're a strong woman. You always will be. I love you for it."

"Just for that?"

"Amongst other things. A lot of other things."

He leaned toward her to kiss her, but just then the car hit a large rut and bounced violently. Laughing, Trey pulled it back under control.

Laughing, as well, but with her heart still in her throat, Piper looked out the window. "Look. Mailbox. We must be getting close."

The mailbox, painted a medium pine-green and decorated with hummingbirds, was shiny and looked as if it had rarely been used, but it said BINGHAM on the side. Piper wondered if they really spent enough time here to justify a mailbox, or if it was more for decoration. Not that it mattered. She peered ahead through the trees, trying to get a glimpse of the cabin.

It came into view after a few more seconds, and she smiled. The little wooden structure couldn't have been much more than a thousand square feet. A small, blue car sat in front, and smoke was coming out of the chimney.

"They're here already," she said.

"Nadia said they probably would be." Trey maneuvered the car up beside the Binghams'. "They started out pretty early this morning. She wanted to be sure the fire was going, so the place would be warm."

Piper watched him shut off the car, nerves taking her over again. "She probably cooked."

Trey gave a tentative smile. "Yeah, I would imagine so."

They got out of the car, retrieved their bags from the trunk, and walked together to the front door. Trey knocked.

They waited. Piper looked around, at the soft afternoon sun slanting down through the branches of the trees, the curl of smoke rising from the little cabin to meet a small square of blue sky visible above. The smell of the wood smoke tickled her nostrils, warm and homey.

"They're good people," Piper said, as if reminding herself.

"They are."

He started to say something else, but just then the door opened. Nadia stood on the other side, smiling. She had flour on her hands.

"Sorry. I was making cookies." She stepped back, holding the door open. "Thought you guys might like some. I even managed to cook most of the dough."

Piper walked into the front room, setting her bags down just inside the door. The sweet smell filling the cabin made her smile. "Chocolate chip. Nice."

"My favorite," Trey added.

"Mine, too." Brice emerged from the kitchen, wiping his hands on a dishtowel. "I was just cleaning up," he explained.

Piper smiled at Nadia. "It's nice he's domestic."

She grinned back. "Yes. I've trained him well."

Piper looked at Brice and her smile faded again. He was giving her a friendly look, but it felt odd, as if his gaze were palpable on her skin.

In a few hours, she would make love to this man.

The thought made her tingle, but it felt so strange. Uncomfortable. Ritual or no ritual, she wasn't sure how she was going to make it through.

Looking over her shoulder, she found Trey, her rock, her guide. He would be there to help her. Then she looked at Nadia. Nadia would be there, too…

Piper shook off the thought. No point borrowing trouble. They'd get through this the way they'd gotten through everything, even the weirdest things that had plagued them in their decidedly odd relationship. One step at a time.

Brice took a seat on the couch in the living room. "So how was the drive?"

Staunchly, Piper went to take a seat, as well, on a chair next to the couch. "It was nice. This is a pretty area. Lots of trees."

"Yes, there are a lot of trees," Nadia agreed, and Piper suddenly got the impression Nadia was as nervous as she was. This was the first time it had seemed that way to her, and the realization relieved her. So she wasn't the only one at a loss. She glanced at Brice. He was still rubbing at his hands, which she was certain were already clean. Not exactly at ease, then, either. Apparently they were all in the same boat.

Nadia, still standing near the front door, finally turned and walked back toward the kitchen. "The cookies will be done in a few minutes. Does everybody want milk?"

A few minutes later, they were cozily ensconced in living room chairs, eating cookies and milk. Trey had finished an account of his and Piper's trip from New York, and Piper kept looking at Brice, sometimes finding him looking back at her. She liked the way he regarded her, with a certain gentleness in his eyes that she thought might be sympathy. Not pity—just a kind of understanding that comforted her.

She glanced at Trey and smiled. He, too, had a soft, comforting expression on his face. It eased her, to think they both might be particularly concerned with caring for her.

It'll be all right. She'd told herself this a hundred times during the drive, but she wasn't sure she believed it. Until now. Now she felt like it might be true.

* * * * *

Evening came softly, almost unexpectedly. Piper was involved with the game of rummy they'd started about an hour before, and barely noticed the fall of darkness until she looked up and found her own reflection looking back at her from the front window, rather than a view of the tree-filled yard.

Trey looked up, as well, following her gaze. He looked surprised, as well, and looked at his watch. "Goodness. Getting late."

Nadia looked at the clock on the wall. "Yes, it is."

She looked at Brice. Brice looked back, then looked at Piper, who looked at Trey and then at Nadia. A sense of unease drifted over the room.

"Four nines," said Trey, and laid the cards down on the table. "If I haven't won yet, I will within ten minutes. Mark my words."

Piper smiled at him. He seemed to be deliberately hanging on to normality, bringing it constantly back into the circle, whether to ease himself or to ease her, she wasn't sure. It didn't matter. It helped.

"I concede to you, then," Nadia said, and laid down her cards. She glanced toward the kitchen; Piper wasn't sure why. "So...time for bed?"

Brice nodded. He put down his cards and walked into the kitchen.

"Tonight?" Piper whispered to Trey.

Trey shrugged. "We should."

Piper nodded. "Is the ritual long?"

"It can be. It depends…" He placed a hand on her shoulder. "If you need more time—"

"No, I get it. It's okay."

Brice emerged from the kitchen with a bottle of wine and a paper bag. Piper recognized the bottle of wine as the one they'd brought with them, the special vintage from South Africa, made by shapeshifters. A soft hint of the sharp odor of eucalyptus leaves drifted toward her. Herbs in the bag, then. Perhaps the candles. She looked at Trey, and he smiled reassuringly.

Nadia rose from her chair and held a hand out to Piper. "Come on," she said, smiling.

Piper took her hand and let her lead the way into the bedroom. Brice was ahead of them, Trey trailing behind. Brice set the bottle of wine on the chest of drawers and opened the paper bag, taking out candles one at a time, setting them on the chest. Trey joined him, drawing additional candles and small bags of herbs from the bag.

Nadia squeezed Piper's hand, and Piper was surprised to realize she was still holding it. The other woman's hand was small and warm in hers, and she enjoyed the way it felt. Another surprise.

Brice was putting together the pieces of a potpourri burner; when he was done he lit the votive candle on the bottom and opened the bottle of wine, pouring it into the bowl. Trey sorted through the small bags of herbs, picking out four. He took a bit out of each bag and dropped the dried leaves and stems into the bowl of wine. Then he took four small glasses from the bag and poured wine into them, passing them around.

Piper took her glass and looked into the dark, purple depths. It was a rich wine, and the fruity smell drifted up to her as she held it, waiting. She wondered what might be in it besides alcohol and the remains of crushed grapes. And plums. Trey had said it had plums.

When they all had their glasses, Trey lifted his. Piper half expected some sort of toast, but she had no idea what might be appropriate in this situation.

He spoke, but not in English. The language was unfamiliar, softly susurrant, strange. Piper felt almost like she should have been able to make some sense of it, but it was only sounds. She thought perhaps she might have heard something like it in the caves in Australia, when the other shapeshifters had accepted Trey's promotion to leader of the community.

He spoke for a few seconds, then smiled at Piper, at Nadia, at Brice, and sipped from his glass. The others followed suit.

The wine had a dark, rich flavor, fruity but more, and again she wondered what might be in it. It moved warmly down through her, the alcohol hitting her quickly. The taste was indescribable. It tasted like lust, somehow, like desire and need and the throbbing of enflamed blood.

Fragrances from the potpourri burner had started to fill the room, as well. Piper had recognized the individual herbs, but mingled with the warmed wine, the smell was something entirely new. Again, it was thick, heady, lusty. She swallowed. Arousal tremored over her skin. She needed — something. Someone.

Trey drank all of the contents of his glass, and Piper did the same, assuming it was the right thing to do. Nadia and Brice drained their glasses, as well. Carefully, feeling a little woozy, Piper set her empty glass on the dresser.

Trey looked at her and smiled warmly. "You and I, then," he said.

She regarded him, unsure what he meant. "You and I?"

Nadia gave Trey an accusatory look. "You didn't explain the details of the ritual?"

"I asked him not to," Piper broke in, before Nadia could jump to further conclusions. "I was stressing enough, I thought, without knowing all the...specifics."

Nadia nodded. Her smile, while understanding, was somehow also sad.

"It'll be all right," she said softly. "We're doing everything we can to be sure of that."

"I know. And the more people tell me that, the more nervous I get about it, so —" She broke off with a wry smile, hoping she wasn't coming off like a bitch.

Apparently she wasn't, because Brice laughed. "Piper, I know exactly what you mean. I know it'll work out, but it's all damn freaky-weird right now. And is it just me, or is that wine like triple octane or something?"

"It's the herbs, and the wine...it's the whole effect," Trey offered. He held his hand out to Piper. "So. You and me."

It finally struck her exactly what he meant by that. She and Trey, together. Making love. While the other two watched.

She put her hand in Trey's and let him lead her to the bed. "Why?"

Trey sat on the bed and bent to untie his shoes, then hers. "To learn. Through observation, they learn us. Then they go, and we learn each other. Then — all of us together, and the seeds are planted."

The formal sound of the words made her think he was quoting something. Probably he was — quoting the relevant sections of the ritual. She wondered how old it was, how many times it had been used. If it worked.

She leaned back a bit as Trey pulled her socks off, his fingers tracing up the soles of her feet. She shivered; she was ticklish there and he knew it, and he laughed a little at her reaction.

The herbs and the wine were obviously working. Piper felt loose and languid, relaxed. Almost like she actually could fuck her husband in front of another couple and not be particularly concerned by the action. She felt a little high, a little drunk, and a lot happy.

Trey straightened, and she reached toward him, unbuttoning his shirt. She had no idea where Brice and Nadia were right now, and had no desire to look to find out. She assumed they were nearby, standing near the door perhaps, watching, quiet. It didn't matter. Her head was swimming, and the only thing she was really aware of was Trey.

Which was as it should be, she thought, at least for now. The rest would work itself out later.

She unfastened his shirt, a button at a time, slipping her fingers under the fabric to touch his skin. The smell and taste of the wine—lust, desire, uncontrollable need—had filled her mind, her body, seemed to move under her skin, into her nerves. She wanted him so badly right now she didn't care where she was, didn't care that they weren't alone. That was the idea, probably. That was why the wine and the herbs were part of the ritual. To release the inhibitions, to make it easier.

She pushed Trey's shirt open, letting her hands move over the familiar shapes and textures. The springy hair on his chest, the soft nubs of his nipples, which rose and hardened as she touched them. His hand rose to cup the back of her neck, holding her. She just watched his chest, watched his nipples rise, watched the steady rise and fall of his breathing as it began to quicken. Her fingers explored, touching the small moles, the places where she could see the blue tracery of veins through his skin.

He was beautiful. There was no question of that. And the fact that he could change this beauty at any time, become anyone else, someone just as beautiful, more beautiful, become a woman if he chose, didn't change the fact that this body, that they had chosen together, was beautiful and perfect and lit desire in her in a way no other man ever had. Not even Billy, though it had taken her a long time to understand that. Trey was Trey, and Trey was the other half of her heart.

He leaned down toward her and she moved to meet him halfway, her lips touching his. His lips tasted of the thick, lusty wine, and she drank the flavor, devouring his mouth, need pounding through her body. Whether induced by the liquor or not, she had never wanted him this badly.

She kissed him hard, devouring him, her hands pulling at his shirt, seeking his skin. Her breath was coming fast and shallow, rapid with need. She smoothed her hands over the firm planes of his body, the familiar bumps and textures seeming amplified under her fingers. Reading the Braille of his body, the small ridges here, the bumps here, the textures of his hair. Smooth here, rough here, places she rarely touched, places she had memorized.

His big hands cupped her shoulders, moved down to unbutton her blouse, peeled it back, palmed her breasts. Piper bent her head back, arching her body into him—

And saw Brice.

He stood on the other side of the room, leaning against the wall next to the dresser. His eyelids drooped sleepily, obscuring the cool sapphire, but he was watching. As Piper looked at him, his attention seemed to focus, to sharpen. His eyes opened a little and she caught a vague flash of the bright blue.

She smiled at him. *Learn. Watch, learn how to touch me.* His mouth curled up on one corner, a smug little grin. To her own surprise, desire curled through her. She'd thought she couldn't contain any more need, but there it was, a slow, easy frisson of warmth. Just for him.

Trey jerked her harshly closer, his teeth scraping along her neck, and she moaned at the sensation, at his sudden, rough possessiveness. One hand pushed down the back of her trousers, fingers digging into her, pulling her close and hard. His mouth plundered hers, exploring every corner, every crevice. His free hand found her jeans button, the zipper, and he loosened them, pushed the clothing out of the way.

Brice was watching. Piper could feel it now, the imagined caress of his attention like fire on her skin. Her eyes were closed, her attention focused totally on Trey, but now that she had met Brice's eyes, acknowledged his presence, it was as if he were there, next to her. Touching her.

The herbs, perhaps, or something in the wine. She knew Trey had a superficial telepathic ability, that he could sense her emotions to some extent, that he knew the levels of her desire and what nurtured them. If she would let him, he would change, shift to suit her mood. She rarely wanted this, but when she did—the results were sensational, intense. Worth the wait. Worth making them rare.

Maybe one of the effects of the wine was to give her that ability. And if it gave her that ability, was it having the same effect on Brice? She opened her eyes to look at him again, but there was no way to tell.

Nadia was there now. Where had she been before? Close by, certainly, but Piper hadn't seen her. She was leaning against Brice, and Brice had put his hand down the front of her pants.

But he was still looking at Piper.

Trey was intensely aware of Piper's focus on Brice. This was good—it was part of what the ritual was supposed to do, to make the process easier on everyone. But he couldn't help a pang of jealousy. Ridiculous, he knew. He focused on it, let himself feel it, while he molded his hands to Piper's body.

She felt so good. He had wondered once, a long time ago when he was still too young and stupid to know any better, why any shapeshifter would want to commit to a human for life. Humans stayed the same all the time. Humans were boring. Why would anyone want the same woman or man every day for a lifetime when they could have a mate who could change faces at a moment's whim? It seemed wrong. Perverted, almost, from his perspective at the time.

He'd been an idiot. Not surprising—most men in their teens were, human or not. In spite of her "handicap" of possessing

Elizabeth Jewell

static features, Piper was perfect. His perfect mate. He couldn't imagine ever leaving her.

His hands slid over her breasts, the firm pebbles of her nipples pressing against the centers of his palms. She arched into him, rubbing her nipples across his hands. Her body was taut, and her hands rose to close on his shoulders, her fingers digging into him hard. He smiled. The smell of the herbs, simmering in the wine in the potpourri burner on the dresser, had gone to his head, as well, stoking his need, lowering whatever inhibitions he might have had. He had a few, though not many.

He could sense the emotions swirling in the room, the sensations augmented by the herbs. The currents of need, the flow of desire. Brice wanted Piper. Piper wanted Brice. Nadia wanted Trey. Nadia wanted Brice. Brice wanted Nadia…

Trey wanted Piper. More than he'd ever wanted her before, his need increased exponentially by the simmering herbs. He pushed her down into the bed suddenly, pulling at her shirt, ripping it back and off her. He heard a sharp intake of breath behind him—Brice. Trey looked up, directly at him, then yanked at Piper's jeans, tearing them down, shoving them out of his way.

Without taking his eyes away from Brice, he cupped Piper's face in his hand. She had softened under him, her body loose and waiting, her breath coming hard and fast. He lowered his other hand between her legs, touched her gently, rolled her clit until he felt her cunt begin to tighten, then pushed hard into her, all the while looking straight into the deep sapphire of Brice's eyes.

Piper gasped as he entered her, hot and hard, startled by the roughness. She grabbed tight to his shoulders, anchoring herself as he pounded her into the bed.

He wasn't looking at her. She looked up and saw his throat, his head turned away, and realized he was looking at the others, at Brice and Nadia, and he was pummeling her, spearing her, taking her harder than he'd ever taken her before. His cock had

258

grown inside her, widening until she could barely accommodate it. It was almost more than she could take.

She leaned up, put her mouth against his shoulder, and bit him.

His head jerked back, and he looked at her, finally, his eyes dark with desire and a deep, primal, possessive lust. She met his gaze and held it, wrapping her legs tight around his waist.

"Look at me," she said. "Look at me."

Trey finally focused completely on her. And gentled, but only a little. He thrust into her, again, again, and she felt his body tighten, ready...

She pushed him back, hard. He blinked, staring down at her. "What?"

"Give it to her..." The words seemed to come out of someone other than herself. She felt disconnected, high in a way. But she knew this was the right thing to do, the proper way to play it.

Trey looked up, across the small room at Nadia. Piper, looked, too, and saw the need burning in the small woman's eyes.

"Do it," she said.

Nadia took a sudden, staggering step forward, and Piper realized Brice had nudged her. Not hard, but obviously enough to catch her off-guard. Nadia looked back toward him, uncertain, but Brice nodded.

She stepped forward. Piper continued to hold Trey back, her hand in the middle of his chest. She looked at Nadia, then Brice, then down at Trey's cock, still erect and slick with her own juices. Pushing him farther away, she moved out from under him.

Trey rose from the bed, watching Nadia. She was unbuttoning her shirt as she walked the few steps across the room, and let it drop to the floor when she met him there next to the bed. Trey closed his hand around the waistband of her jeans and yanked her close, unbuttoned her, unzipped. She pushed the jeans down. Trey grabbed the side of her thong panties and ripped the fragile silk. The rent garment fell to the floor.

Piper watched, unabashedly, with longing. She took in the sight of Nadia—her small, slim body, her large, round breasts. The soft down of hair between her legs. She wondered what she would taste like, if her pussy held the same salt-bitter, musky flavor as her own.

Trey's big, square hands closed on either side of Nadia's hips, and he pulled her against him, then turned her around. She was facing Piper now, and she looked down, at Piper's open thighs, her open cunt. Piper shuddered at the sensation of being watched, at Nadia's intense regard.

Nadia jumped then, her body lurching tautly, and Trey made a sharp grunting sound. Piper's eyes widened. Trey had taken Nadia, hard, from behind. Piper fought the urge to look down, afraid to look, afraid to see Trey's cock inside Nadia.

Nadia's body jumped a few times as Trey drove into her. Then Trey leaned in and whispered in her ear, "Do it."

Nadia nodded. Piper shivered suddenly at the look in the other woman's eyes. And Nadia looked down.

Piper tried not to follow her gaze, but she couldn't stop herself. Her attention jerked down, past the soft curve of her stomach, to the soft, curling, blonde hair.

Out of which a cock had begun to erupt. Piper watched in fascination as what had been the small, pink nub of Nadia's clitoris rose, grew, expanded. Her hips jerked as Trey continued to push into her from behind, but she seemed almost disconnected from the act as she reached down to wrap her fingers around the growing appendage sprouting from her body.

"How big do you want it?" Nadia asked.

Piper's eyes jerked up to look at her, disbelieving. She hadn't expected this. She'd thought of a lot of things that could happen during this encounter—this had not been one of them.

"I...I don't know."

"Make it slim." Brice came up behind them, and Piper looked at him in surprise. He gave her a reassuring smile.

She realized then that he was naked, that he had come not just to join them, but to join in. He had a determined expression on his face and he was erect, ready.

Piper glanced down at his tumescent cock. It was blunt and heavy, thicker than she'd expected, given his lean build. Then she looked back up at his face, and he kissed her.

It startled her. Perhaps the effects of the wine and the herbs were wearing off, or perhaps she simply wasn't as prepared for this as she'd thought she was, but the sudden press of his lips against hers caught her off-guard. She pushed her hands against his shoulders, starting to push him away.

"Do it," Trey murmured.

Piper started to look back over her shoulder, but Brice cupped her face in his hand and turned her toward him. He kissed her again, his hands going to her breasts. It felt good—his square hands kneading her, manipulating her. Fire moved quickly through her, filling her, skating along her skin, pooling between her legs.

He caressed her confidently, stroking down her ribs, over her belly, her back, and then she felt Nadia touching her, as well, her smaller, softer hands tracing down Piper's spine, over her hips. Then slipping between the tops of her thighs, and small, female fingers dipped into her sex, trailing her creamy, wet arousal back along her skin.

Nadia's small fingers touched her anus, and Piper flinched a little, then relaxed. Made herself melt, settle, as Nadia's fingers invaded her, pressing in gently. She understood, now, what was coming.

Nadia worked her gently for a few seconds. Trey must have stopped, waiting, because Piper had no sense anymore that he was thrusting. But Brice's hands were gentle on her body, easing her, and he kissed her face as his wife gently invaded her from behind.

Piper kissed him back, brushing her lips over his carved cheekbones, the jut of his nose, his forehead, his chin, absorbing his taste, his smell. This would be the father of her child. She let that thought float up, like a bubble, let herself accept it, then let it disappear.

Nadia's fingers pressed deeper, and Piper felt her body relaxing, responding, begging for more. She was surprised at how good it felt. Intense, burning, but deep, satisfying. When she slid her fingers back out—Piper was fairly sure there had been three inside her, at the last—the sensation came slick and sweet.

Then Piper felt the head of a cock—Nadia's specially grown, female Shapeshifter cock—press against her. She pushed back, facilitating, bringing it in. She felt the shape change a little, narrowing to accommodate the tighter girth and the taut muscles of the opening. Piper let out a deep, keening sigh.

Finally, Nadia was all the way in, and thrust softly, a few times, heightening the intense sensation, the burning pleasure. Piper looked up at Brice.

He was watching over her shoulder and jerked his attention back to her. Piper reached down and palmed his cock.

He closed his eyes and gasped as she worked him, then touched her wrist, stopping her. At her questioning look, he sat on the bed and drew her close to him.

Piper moved carefully over him, straddling his cock as he lay back on the bed. She bent forward as she moved, to allow Nadia better access. Somehow Nadia stayed inside her, pressing deep. She was shapeshifting, Piper thought, to accommodate Piper's change in position. Brice's thick, blunt cock pushed high into her and Piper moaned. She was so full, Brice filling her vagina, Nadia filling her ass. She felt as if she might burst open. Her head had started swimming again, dizzy from arousal, from the herbs.

She straddled him and he thrust from beneath as Nadia thrust from behind, and Trey began to work, as well, embedded in Nadia from behind. Piper had little sense of what he was doing, or how Nadia and Trey had shifted to make it all possible, but she could feel Nadia's body jerking, off-rhythm a little from her own thrusting into Piper. Only a little, though, and only a few times, as the superficial empathy the shapeshifters enjoyed brought them into more exact synchronization with each other.

Arousal, physical stimulation, chemical stimulation, had all combined to force all rational thought from Piper's head. She didn't have the thought or the energy to focus on the fact she was being fucked by two cocks, one of which was attached to a woman, the other of which was not attached to her husband. Or that her husband was fucking the woman who was fucking her... There was no point. There was only the wave of intense sensation, the burning penetration of Nadia's cock in her ass, the intense invasion of Brice in her pussy. Trey's familiar, breathy moans behind her as he took Nadia.

Then, suddenly, his sudden gasp as he came.

Nadia tensed behind her, and Piper felt the pulsing of her cock, deep inside, as she, too, came, and a moment later Brice came, hard, pounding one last, hard stroke into Piper's body, and then Piper let out a choking keen as she hit the precipice. The orgasm spiraled through her, harder and harder, shaking her apart. She dug her fingers into Brice's shoulders, anchoring herself as best she could, riding the high, unbelievably intense wave of deep, deep fire.

They all clutched at each other, hanging on, making that final connection as the chain reaction of orgasm bound them together. Piper could hardly breathe, and her eyes were overflowing with tears.

Slowly, gradually, they slid apart. Nadia moved back first, slipping free from Piper's body. Then Brice's erection flagged, and he, too, broke the connection. Piper looked up into his face and saw his formerly sapphire eyes gray with spent desire.

Brice rolled back on the bed, taking a place on the far side. He looked up at Piper and smiled, a little awkwardly, as if finding it difficult to acknowledge what they had just done. Piper felt much the same way. It had all been surreal, strange. She moved as Nadia brushed past her, noting as the small blonde woman snuggled against her husband that she had returned her body to fully female constitution.

Piper turned to Trey. He stood gloriously naked, his flagging cock wet with Nadia's juices. He took a step toward her and put his arms around her, kissing her forehead, then led her toward the bed.

Piper said nothing as he lay down, as she lay down next to him. He spread the blankets over her and took her in his arms. His warm lips against the back of her neck were the last thing she felt before she drifted into sleep.

Chapter Six

When she woke, she no longer lay in Trey's embrace, instead curled up against his warm back. She opened her eyes, looking at him, cataloguing the familiar lines, shapes, the patterns of moles and color variations. How did he maintain every miniscule detail in his sleep? She had often wondered. Once she'd asked him, and he'd shrugged, and said that it required no thought, no focus. It was automatic, like breathing.

She reached out, touching his skin. He stirred a little at the contact.

"Trey?" she whispered, flattening her hand against his shoulder blade.

He rolled over and looked at her through bleary, blue-gray eyes. After a moment, he smiled and pulled her against him.

His arms around her felt good, right. She closed her eyes and let her face settle against the rough curls on his chest, drawing in his scent, his warmth.

"Are you all right?" he murmured.

She nodded. The memory of what had happened last night was clear, but not clear, as if it had been a very vivid dream rather than an actual occurrence. But she could still feel the aftermath on her body—as if Nadia and Brice both were still inside her.

"It was strange," she whispered, and he smiled a little, the expression not so much amused as understanding.

"Yeah. For me, too, believe it or not."

He stroked a hand over her hair, smoothing it, combing through the length of it. His fingers touched her lips, tracing the line of her mouth as she smiled. "I love you," he said. "Always."

"I love you. Always."

Barely aware of where she was, that Brice and Nadia still lay sleeping only inches away, on the other side of the big bed, Piper leaned against him and kissed him gently, then more thoroughly, exploring the familiar landscape of his mouth. He kissed her back, his mouth opening hers, tongue exploring carefully.

She let her hands move over his body, the lines of his shoulders and arms and ribs, reminding herself of his shape, his smell, all his lines and textures. Reminding herself of him, reacquainting herself. Brice had been fine, satisfying, and that encounter would likely give her a child. But Trey was home.

She rolled into him, pressing him back into the pillow, kissing him, stroking his body. Strong, wide shoulders, solid chest, the tight, springy hair, firm, erect nipples thrusting against her fingers. Smooth abdomen, the textures and firm shapes of the well-formed muscles twitching a little under her touch, as if she might be tickling him.

His arms went around her, hands sliding down her back, cupping her ass, pulling her close. She spread out on top of him, letting her body cover his, feeling every inch of his skin against hers. His cock rose, hardening against her stomach, until it lay thick and hard between them.

His fingers dug into her ass, tilting her hips so she rubbed against his hard shaft. Looking down into his face, she let him maneuver her, grinding herself into him. His cock rubbed into her, the shaft pressing between wet, open labia, the head dragging over her clit.

She breathed out her arousal, softly, trying to keep the sound under control, aware of Nadia and Brice next to them. What did it matter though, really, if they woke up? They'd all been fucking each other last night—so what if they woke to find Piper and Trey in flagrante delicto?

Trey pulled her head down, kissed her hard, his tongue stabbing into her mouth, his fingers taut on the back of her neck.

Her legs opened further over his abdomen, and he tilted his hips. The head of his cock slid inside her and she reached down to grasp his hips, adjusting him, bringing him in deeper.

He shifted, pushing inside her, pressing hard, thrusting while she held herself steady on top of him, clenching him tight with her inner muscles. He was a hard brand deep inside her, thrusting, releasing, claiming her.

This felt right. Brice had felt good, but this felt right. This was where she belonged. Trey shoved up hard into her and she pressed down to meet him, enveloping him, molding to him.

"I love you," she whispered, and he smiled.

Movement in the bed next to them distracted her momentarily. She glanced over to see Brice watching. Nadia still had her eyes closed, but Brice had reached over to touch her breasts, fondle her rising, brown-pink nipples. If she was asleep, Piper doubted she would be for long.

Piper smiled at him. And tightened herself on Trey, drew him in deep, and looked back down into his eyes as he came.

Trey slipped his fingers between them, nudging her clit, rolling it, and Piper rose and burned and slid over the edge herself, her body clenching and tightening on Trey's cock as the waves of ecstasy flowed through her.

Brice drew in a sudden breath. Piper looked over to see him on his back, hands splayed over the bed, while Nadia sucked his cock into her mouth, laving it with her tongue. She looked up to meet Piper's gaze, and smiled.

Still holding Trey inside her as best she could, Piper leaned over and laid her hand on Brice's. He looked at her, startled, then smiled.

Piper looked back down at Trey. Trey, too, smiled. Piper felt his cock shift and reconfigure inside her—a shapeshifter trick to sustain an erection, by effectively constructing a new one. His hips began to pulse again, and Piper held Brice's hand as an orgasm built inside her again, rising, the fire taut and intense...

She exploded, and her hand tightened on Brice's, and Trey bucked into her and came, and Brice let out a gasp and lifted his head, his back arching. Nadia's head shifted and she looked into his eyes, smiling a little. Piper saw her throat bob as she swallowed, Brice coming down her throat.

Nadia drew back after a moment, and Brice took hold of her waist and rolled over, positioning her above him. He pressed his face between her legs, his tongue separating the pink lips of her pussy. He shifted her a little so Piper could watch.

Piper couldn't tear her eyes away. She stared, unabashed, watching Brice's tongue dart and tease amidst the soft golden curls between Nadia's legs, toying with the pink, soft tissue of labia, flicking at her clit. Saw him lap up the white cream of her arousal, watched him push his tongue deep into her sex, until she arched her back and shivered through a long, sustained orgasm.

Piper turned to look at Trey, amazed, in a way, at what had just happened. He smiled and ran a hand down her arm. Piper looked back at the others. Nadia had settled down into Brice's embrace, and she smiled.

* * * * *

The rest of the weekend was quiet. They went hiking, fished a bit in the nearby river. Watched movies, ate popcorn, talked. They didn't discuss the sexual interlude, though no one seemed uncomfortable. It was as if it had been a normal, everyday thing, something expected, like a good morning kiss, or breakfast, that didn't need to be talked over afterward.

The comfortable atmosphere surprised Piper. It felt good, as if she were among friends, or family, which she supposed in a way they were, now. Provided all went well, in nine months they would all be bonded by blood, made into a family by the presence of children of shared parentage.

In the meantime, she was pleased to discover they were friends. She could sit and talk with Brice without embarrassment, could make off-color jokes with Nadia without worrying she might take it the wrong way. Trey seemed equally at ease.

The sex from their first night seemed real enough in her memory, but dreamlike in its way, and that helped. What seemed almost more real to her was the sensation in her belly, a sort of heaviness, that persisted throughout the weekend. Her body perhaps telling her the attempt at conception had been successful. It seemed unrealistic, though, to think that could be the case.

The drive home was quiet. Trey pointed out the window from time to time, bringing her attention to colorful leaves, or a deer at the roadside. She responded, smiled, looked at his quiet expression. There was no tension between them. She could feel his affection, soft and warm, and wondered if what she felt now was anything like what he felt all the time, the superficial reading of her emotions.

At home, he opened the car door for her, touched her back as she got out. He walked her to the apartment door, but stopped before he put the keys in the lock.

She looked at him questioningly as he took her by the shoulders and turned her around, looked into her eyes.

He smiled. "I love you, Piper," he said.

She smiled back, and folded her hands against his chest. "I love you, too."

Nine Months Later

"Almost there, love."

Trey squeezed Piper's hand, kissing her fingers. Piper barely felt it, concentrating on the intense, fiery pain between her legs. The baby's head crowning, the doctor had said. It was just another flavor of pain to her, at this point.

The contractions had started twelve hours ago. At first it hadn't seemed bad, but it had gotten gradually worse and worse, intensifying until she could hardly bear it. She'd refused drugs, somehow terrified of an epidural, of anything that might harm the baby.

Now, finally, she'd hit the home stretch. Wave after wave after wave of brutal pain, and now, finally, she could push, do something actively to bring the baby into the world.

"Push," said the doctor. She had been there for quite some time, supervising, her gentle voice and quiet manner keeping Piper from descending into panicked hysteria. Trey had been rock-steady as well, calm and quiet, holding her hand, holding her, doing whatever she asked.

Piper pushed. Pain flared, an intense burn, and she felt the small body rush out of her, the wetness of amniotic fluid flooding after.

"He's beautiful," Trey breathed, and Piper mustered a smile.

A few minutes later, she held her son, his face scrunched up in displeasure at having been dislodged from the womb so abruptly. With a little encouragement, the little boy took her nipple and began to nurse.

Trey watched, smiling, and touched the baby's head. "Matthew," he said.

Piper nodded. "Yes." She brushed the tiny cheek, then looked up at Trey. "It's not fair, you know."

"What's not fair?"

"Nadia had such an easy time of it."

"Yeah. It's a shapeshifter adaptation."

Nadia's body, able to transform its appearance, had also been able to shift and move in such a way as to allow the child to be born with minimal effort. The downside being that the little girl was a shapeshifter baby, with features blank and unformed, that would remain that way until she grew old enough to learn to control her transformations. The birth had taken place in a tiny facility, owned and staffed by shapeshifters, so the child would not be diagnosed as abnormal.

Piper wasn't sure who'd gotten the better deal. It would be hard for Nadia and Brice, sheltering their child for a year or more, until her instincts kicked in and she created a human face.

She looked up at Trey. "Is he here?"

"Yeah. He's in the waiting room."

"Bring him in."

Trey nodded. He stood and left the room.

Piper sat quietly, actually feeling a little nervous. She looked down at the baby's face. He seemed to have fallen asleep. His face was round and soft; she wondered if he would someday have Brice's razor-sharp cheekbones.

Trey returned a few minutes later, Brice right behind him. Brice looked tense, eager, and when he saw the baby a bright smile spread over his face.

Piper smiled back. "Come and see him."

Brice came to the bed and sat gingerly on the edge. Hesitant, he reached toward Matthew's face, then paused, looking at Piper for permission. She nodded.

She watched as he touched the baby's cheek, a look of reverent awe on his face. He'd followed the pregnancy throughout, as Trey had followed Nadia's. Now he had the look of a proud daddy, and it warmed her heart.

She looked at Trey, who was also smiling.

"Matthew?" Brice asked.

Piper nodded.

"He's beautiful."

"Yes, he is." She touched Brice's hand. "Thank you."

Brice nodded. "You know, if anything ever happens, if you ever need anything, or if he does, I'll be there."

Piper smiled. "I know. Same goes for you."

He turned his hand, curling his fingers around hers. Piper looked up into his face, then looked at Trey. It seemed incomplete somehow, without Nadia.

"You were right," she said to Trey, her voice quiet, not quite steady. "Everything's going to be all right."

About the author:

Elizabeth Jewell is new to the world of erotic romance, but has been writing paranormal and contemporary romance for several years. On the personal front, she is married with two children. She is a voracious reader who also watches far too much TV!

Elizabeth welcomes mail from readers. You can write to her c/o Ellora's Cave Publishing at 1056 Home Avenue, Akron OH 44310-3502.

Also by Elizabeth Jewell:

Enjoy this excerpt from
Crag
Knights of the Ruby Order
© Copyright Kate Hill 2003

Chapter 1

Lily's daughter sickened in winter.

Her husband had been dead for nearly a month, killed in the war with the kingdom of Zaltana.

Battles continued to destroy village after village, forcing many to surrender to the powerful, vicious Zaltanian army. Lily's home had been long destroyed, and she and her daughter had been living in the mountains with a small group of villagers who'd taken to hiding. They scratched out an existence under overhangs and in makeshift shelters. Even by the first snow, most of them were cold and hungry. Lily believed their poor living conditions caused her daughter's illness, but hiding had been her only course of action. The Zaltanians killed their enemies' children, all except the ones old enough to work in the mines. Women and men were raped and taken into slavery. Better for Lily and her daughter to die in the mountains than at the hands of some Zaltanian pig.

Still, part of her had believed she and Vina would survive. The belief was strangled at the onset of Vina's fever, at her sudden lack of appetite, and at her incessant crying for which there was no comfort.

"Twenty miles north is a village called Tanek which has managed to fend off the Zaltanian army," said Cormac, one of the only other survivors of Lily's village. "It's a long walk, but if the snow holds off, you should make it."

"What good can they do me?" she asked, tired from spending the past several nights tending Vina, and hungry since there hadn't been enough food for more than a meal a day for each adult in the settlement. At that moment, she wished the Zaltanians *had* killed her.

"They fought off Zaltana because they're backed by Knights of the Ruby Order."

Lily drew a deep breath, feeling the first glint of hope in months. Knights of the Ruby Order were known throughout the land as the finest warriors and healers, but they only fought for just causes, never for profit. If anyone could help Vina, it would be them.

Immediately, she packed her few belongings and set off on foot with Vina in her arms. She didn't relish such a long hike with a sickly infant, but it was her only choice.

The day remained sunny and warm as she waded through calf-high snow. Ice melted from the trees and rocks, and the sound of running water might have been musical had she been in the frame of mind to listen. She simply felt too tired and worried to care about the beauty of the countryside. Trees, some green, others skeletons decorated with glistening icicles, covered the mountains. She passed streams of rushing white water where she stopped for a drink and sat on a rock, attempting to feed Vina. The infant took some milk, but was promptly sick.

Lily rocked her, whispering to her, wondering if the baby sensed her mother's desolation.

It was dusk when Lily saw the welcoming fires of Tanek, and she could have cried from relief. Her feet ached, her arms felt sore, and her stomach hurt from hunger.

As she neared the settlement, some of her hope waned. Though its people had chased off the Zaltanians, Tanek had suffered. Most of the houses lay in ruins, and people and animals huddled under lean-tos scarcely stronger than the ones in her own mountain hideaway.

She noticed some rebuilding had taken place, but it was not an easy task in the middle of winter. Several men dressed in black tunics, a red circle of thorns embroidered around a ruby over their hearts, trudged through the wreckage. She closed her eyes and whispered a prayer of thanks as she recognized the uniforms of the Ruby Order. The Knights carried themselves with pride and determination, even the ones whose arms and legs were bandaged. They had obviously fought hard for Tanek, and she knew more of their troops still battled throughout the continent, attempting to force the hated Zaltanians into submission.

As she neared the settlement, a tall, bearded Knight with two muscular, tawny dogs at his side, approached.

"Please help me," Lily said. "My village was destroyed months ago. I've walked twenty miles to find you. My daughter's sick, and we have nowhere to go."

The Knight glanced down at Vina. He offered to carry Lily's pack of belongings and bid her to follow him to one of the long, wooden buildings still standing amidst the rubble.

"We have survivors from most of the villages in the north," he told her. "Tanek has other settlements similar to this one. I'm afraid our resources are spread rather thin. Most of the settlements have one or two healers to look after everyone, but you're welcome to stay."

He opened the door of the longhouse, and Lily nearly gagged. Stuffy from smoke, the place reeked of herbs, blood, sickness, and death. Water from melting ice dripped through holes in the ceiling, and men, women, and children covered the dirt floor, some leaning against walls, others sprawled in the center of the single large room. She saw movement in the dim loft and knew there were even more people pressed, back to back, above them.

She gazed down at Vina's flushed face and felt a lump form in her throat. This place was scarcely better than where they'd come from. Still, the Knights were here. The Ruby Order possessed the finest healers in the world.

"Right this way, missy," said the Knight who'd escorted her in. They edged around people, stepping over some and nudging others aside, to the more open space in the center of the room.

Lily glanced at the hearth and saw two women turning a deer over a spit. At least they had food. The sounds of coughing and sneezing mingled with moans, soft conversation, and the snapping of flames from the fires and torches throughout the building.

The bearded Knight paused behind a man draped in a gray tunic stained with dirt and blood. Dark brown hair was tied with a piece of rope at the man's nape. Lily noticed his neck was rather thick and his shoulders broad in spite of his slimness. He applied a bandage to the stump where his patient's hand had once been. The patient was an older man with grayish hair and a battle-scarred face. Eyes closed, he gritted his teeth against the pain.

The healer finished with the bandage, and the bearded Knight said, "Crag will take good care of you, missy."

The healer's head jerked over his shoulder, and Lily stared at him. His cheekbones were high and wide, a rich brown beard covered his face beneath. A full lower lip peeked out from beneath the wiry hair. The tip of his straight nose was gently rounded, a streak of dried blood running down its tip. Blue eyes glanced from beneath thick, dark brows. Lily noted those eyes didn't look at all welcoming.

"Crag, this woman's walked twenty miles with a sick baby to get here. Where would you like her?"

Crag looked at Lily hard, his expression saying he'd like her to go anywhere but here. He stood, his shadow falling across Vina's face. He was very tall, very lean, and Lily noted his face looked nearly as gray as his robe. He appeared more like a nightmare than a healer. Surely he wasn't a Knight? Yet a circle of red thorns was embroidered over his heart, the symbol of his Order.

"Space is limited, Sir Rain," Crag said, his voice a low timbre. The sound of it might have been comforting had his expression not been colder than the snow outside. "But we'll find a place."

"Of course you will." Sir Rain placed a hand on Lily's shoulder, then turned to leave.

"Sir," Crag followed Rain, "have the reinforcements arrived yet? We have close to two hundred people in our settlement now, and with just me and Sir

Wood—"

"Crag, I'm sure the Order is sending more men as quickly as they can. We'll just have to make do in the meantime. You're doing well." Rain nodded and left.

"Doing well," Crag muttered under his breath, his jaw working.

Vina wailed, and Lily did her best to quiet her. Hesitantly, she said, "Sir Crag, where can I get some water?"

"Just Crag," he said. "I'm not yet a Knight. I'm serving here as part of my training."

Lily didn't really care about his training. She only wanted some water, food, and a place to rest. He seemed to sense her thoughts as he pointed to the women by the spit. "Go ask them. They'll tell you where to find supplies. Come with me first. I'll get you a place to stay and examine your baby."

"Help! A healer! I need a healer!" shrieked a woman from across the room. "My husband's not breathing!"

"Just find an empty space somewhere," Crag called over his shoulder as he stepped over people and wooden supply trunks toward the woman crying for help. "I'll be with you as soon as I can."

Hoisting Vina over her shoulder and rubbing her small back, Lily muttered, "Some Knight he's going to make. The epitome of manhood and compassion."

She found a place beside an old woman who reeked of must and rotted teeth. Lily noted that her odor had to be especially foul if it was discernable above the general stench of the place. At least the hearth was nearby, and if she turned her back, the scent of smoke and burning wood overpowered the old woman's pungency. She dropped her pack and rested Vina against it before turning to one of the women by the spit.

"Is there anyplace I can get some water?"

"Surely." The woman smiled, and Lily wondered how she was able to remain cheerful in such horrific surroundings. "The well is outside. Here's a bucket." She edged the large wooden pail toward Lily with her foot. "We need more water in here anyway. I'll keep an eye on your baby while you fetch it."

Lily hesitated, glancing at Vina. She didn't know the woman. She didn't know anyone there, but she desperately required water since Vina not only needed to be changed, but was covered in drying vomit.

Sighing, she took the bucket and walked outside. The well was located in the center of the settlement, and she took several moments to inhale the cleansing winter air while she filled the bucket. When she entered the building again, the smell wasn't so intolerable, and eventually, she'd learn to ignore it.

As she approached her space, she noticed Crag kneeling beside her pack, examining Vina.

He glanced at Lily, an eyebrow raised. "I hope you plan on using some of that water to wash her."

She dropped the bucket beside him, some of the water splashing on his filthy tunic.

"You look like you could use some washing yourself," she snapped, tired and angry from the long, tedious walk, the worry she felt for Vina, the nagging hunger in her belly, and the memories of the life she'd once had.

"You try staying clean in this place." His blue eyes flashed anger. "We have two healers right now. Me and Sir Wood who's been ministering to the ones in the lean-tos all morning."

"Well you try keeping a vomiting baby clean over a twenty mile walk in the middle of winter!" She shook her head. He was, after all, the healer. She'd traveled all this way for him to help Vina, and if she didn't hold her temper, he might not bother with her at all. Lily murmured, "I'm sorry."

"Bathe her in cool water. I'm going to prepare a medicine which should help settle her stomach. The truth is, I've seen a lot of this illness since I've arrived here. The outlook isn't good. I'm sorry."

Her stomach clenched and her head throbbed. *The outlook isn't good. I'm sorry...* His blue eyes held hers, and she noted he actually did look sorry.

Lily cleared her throat and said, "The man whose wife just called you. Is he all right?"

Crag stood, wiping his hands on his rough gray robe. "No. He's dead."

He disappeared across the room, and she sat beside Vina and bathed her. Tears slipped from Lily's eyes, dripping off the tip of her nose as she thought, *I should have just stayed in the mountains...*

Why an electronic book?

We live in the Information Age—an exciting time in the history of human civilization in which technology rules supreme and continues to progress in leaps and bounds every minute of every hour of every day. For a multitude of reasons, more and more avid literary fans are opting to purchase e-books instead of paperbacks. The question to those not yet initiated to the world of electronic reading is simply: *why?*

1. *Price.* An electronic title at Ellora's Cave Publishing and Cerridwen Press runs anywhere from 40-75% less than the cover price of the <u>exact same title</u> in paperback format. Why? Cold mathematics. It is less expensive to publish an e-book than it is to publish a paperback, so the savings are passed along to the consumer.

2. *Space.* Running out of room to house your paperback books? That is one worry you will never have with electronic novels. For a low one-time cost, you can purchase a handheld computer designed specifically for e-reading purposes. Many e-readers are larger than the average handheld, giving you plenty of screen room. Better yet, hundreds of titles can be stored within your new library—a single microchip. (Please note that Ellora's Cave and Cerridwen Press does not endorse any specific brands. You can check our website at www.ellorascave.com or

www.cerridwenpress.com for customer recommendations we make available to new consumers.)

3. *Mobility.* Because your new library now consists of only a microchip, your entire cache of books can be taken with you wherever you go.

4. *Personal preferences are accounted for.* Are the words you are currently reading too small? Too large? Too…**ANNOYING**? Paperback books cannot be modified according to personal preferences, but e-books can.

5. *Instant gratification.* Is it the middle of the night and all the bookstores are closed? Are you tired of waiting days—sometimes weeks—for online and offline bookstores to ship the novels you bought? Ellora's Cave Publishing sells instantaneous downloads 24 hours a day, 7 days a week, 365 days a year. Our e-book delivery system is 100% automated, meaning your order is filled as soon as you pay for it.

Those are a few of the top reasons why electronic novels are displacing paperbacks for many an avid reader. As always, Ellora's Cave and Cerridwen Press welcomes your questions and comments. We invite you to email us at service@ellorascave.com, service@cerridwenpress.com or write to us directly at: 1056 Home Ave. Akron OH 44310-3502.

THE
ELLORA'S CAVE
LIBRARY

Stay up to date with Ellora's Cave Titles
in Print with our Quarterly Catalog.

TO RECIEVE A CATALOG,
SEND AN EMAIL WITH YOUR NAME
AND MAILING ADDRESS TO:

CATALOG@ELLORASCAVE.COM
OR SEND A LETTER OR POSTCARD
WITH YOUR MAILING ADDRESS TO:
CATALOG REQUEST
C/O ELLORA'S CAVE PUBLISHING, INC.
1337 COMMERCE DRIVE #13
STOW, OH 44224

COMING TO A BOOKSTORE NEAR YOU!

ELLORA'S CAVE
2005
BEST SELLING AUTHORS TOUR

Discover for yourself why readers can't get enough of the multiple award-winning publisher Ellora's Cave. Whether you prefer e-books or paperbacks, be sure to visit EC on the web at www.ellorascave.com for an erotic reading experience that will leave you breathless.

www.ellorascave.com

Printed in the United States
31173LVS00002B/52-195